I0771419

Something About Nobility

Jonni Jordyn

Jordyn
@ Large

Copyright © 2024 by Jonni Jordyn

All rights reserved.

No part of this publication may be reproduced, distributed, or transmitted in any form or by any means, including photocopying, recording, or other electronic or mechanical methods, without the prior written permission of the publisher, except as permitted by U.S. copyright law. For permission requests, contact jonnijordyn@gmail.com.

The characters, places and events in this book are either fictitious or used fictitiously. No events or actions should be inferred as actually occurring by any historical persons (living or deceased.)

Book Cover by Deena Rae at eBookBuilders

Illustrations by Deena Rae at eBookBuilders

<u>**Other books by Jonni Jordyn**</u>

The Lost Art of Magic Series
The Lost Art of Magic
The Untold Prophecy
The Old Child
The Orb of Destiny

The Mother of All Viruses Series
The Mother of All Viruses
The Queen of All Viruses

The Valley of Hope Series
The Calling of the Grull
The Hammer and the Chain

The Beat of a Different Drummer

The Diva of Mud Flats

Something About Nobility

Dedicated to my bird Tweety who sat patiently on my shoulder and watched me write over a dozen novels. She is gone now, but I sometimes still feel her upon my shoulder when I write.

Something About Nobility

Jonni Jordyn

Chapter One

The ever-tightening noose around my neck, which was about to choke out all the hopes and dreams I had imagined for my future, still lingers in my memory, figuratively of course, but that day had not yet happened. I recall the days of my youth when I would wonder at what sort of man I would become and what memories I would create in the days to come. Never had I considered the disaster that would befall me from one misspent action, or how it would entangle me with kings and queens and hostile soldiers. It was then, while still in the cradle of my manhood, the prime of my youth, that I learned how many flavors of nobility truly exist. That was also the point in my existence where I had set upon the path that would forever tell the grand tale of my life. Whether it would be a tragedy or a comedy, I was yet to learn.

Please, allow me to introduce myself. My name is Hector Reynaldo Castillo de la Roca. From my earliest recollections, I had been in the service of the Leatherby family, as were my mother and father. What, you may ask, makes a servant like me such an expert on nobility? I shall explain, for not only do great deeds not define a man, but, fortunately for me, the opposite may also be said. My finest moment, my most defining of noble enterprises, did not come from such an altruistic action, but from a series of scandalous deceptions played upon the most generous and honest gentleman I have ever known. I should warn you now, that this tale may not be suitable for the purest of heart, and if that is you, you may wish to step away while you still can.

You've probably heard fair-minded people suggest that a man is best judged by his deeds. While on the surface, this may seem like sound advice, please allow me to set you straight. A noble deed says no more about a man's character than does a so-called noble birth. If it were so, then I expect all the scoundrels of the world would merely perform a few noble actions to balance the scales against their less admirable pursuits. An act of attrition may get you absolution in the confessional, but it does nothing to define your true character. A noble deed from such a miscreant would be more like a disguise worn by an actor; it only fools the audience because they want to be fooled.

The trouble all started in my nineteenth year. I had, as I said, worked for the Leatherby family, doing odd jobs since I was big enough to draw a rake. I was not forced into labor; Master Leatherby would never do that. He was as kind and just a master as ever this Earth has seen, and he treated me like his own family. It was my father that had set me to work, and toiling alongside him was a privilege that I had requested myself.

Lord Leatherby not only treated me as family, but he

helped raise me alongside his own daughter, the Lady Elizabeth, who was actually one year older than me. We even shared the same tutors, which was not the common rule amongst other noble families and their help. Her nanny watched over both of us. I suspect that she was sometimes grateful that Elizabeth had someone so near her own age with which she could play, leaving the nanny more time to read. Elizabeth and I became quite inseparable and confided in each other always.

As I had said, it was in my nineteenth year when the events that were to shape my future began. I was walking the path from my family's cottage to the duck pond found on the far edge of the estate when I heard, "Pssst. Hector, come here."

I clearly heard her voice, even though she kept it at barely more than a whisper. I stopped in the middle of the stone path to hunt down the source which beckoned me. "Elizabeth?" I only half whispered back, "Why, in Percival's name, do you hide in that bush? I certainly hope you do not expect me to join you in there."

"No. I guess we would look rather silly speaking in the bushes."

The manor was surrounded by several gardens, two spectacular fountains, a bathing pool, a grove of fruit trees, and a meandering stream which spilled into a shallow pond. Beyond the walls were many acres of farmland with small homes and tenants to tend the crops. Within the walls, there were a variety of paths surrounded by a bounty of gardens and beauty which we could walk without ever leaving the property. She emerged from her hiding place and we headed off, side by side, towards the apple orchards. "So, tell me now, why were you hiding in the bushes?"

"I didn't want anyone to see me."

"I gathered that, but why?"

She spoke in a hushed tone. "It's about Walter."

"You need not hide from Master Walter here, and if he has done something to make you fearful of him, I shall take umbrage and be forced to defend your honor."

"Must you continue to call him Master Walter? You've known him since the cradle."

"I think I must, and you are evading my question. Why were you hiding in the bushes?"

"I was not hiding from Walter."

When she offered no further answer, I stepped in front of her and examined her more closely. "Has he done something to you already? I see no bruises."

"What? You think Walter has done something to me? You know he would never harm me."

"Who then? From whom are you in hiding?"

"You sound like my father. Walter would never harm me. He loves me."

I continued looking for marks, but she pulled away and continued down the stone walkway. She wore her disappointment like a blush upon her face.

"Your father then?" I asked, "Has he finally found out about you and Master Walter?"

"No, he hasn't, and I would appreciate it if you would

lower your voice and not announce my personal affairs to the entire estate!"

Her gait quickened. She clearly had something to say, but was reluctant to say it.

"You still haven't told me why you were hiding in the bushes."

Elizabeth looked all around us to be sure we were alone, then swung her hand out in front of my face. It was a hand I knew almost as well as my own, only it was newly adorned with a rather shiny betrothal ring. I think my heart may have stopped beating momentarily, and I am quite certain that the world had started spinning around me, not from any romantic notions within me, but rather from sheer unadulterated panic.

I sucked in my breath, fearful that I may have lost my voice. "Put that away. Hide it! Have you taken leave of your senses? How dare he even ask you, let alone you agree to him?"

Elizabeth was crushed by my retort. "I thought you, of all people, would be happy for me. You have known all along about Walter and me, and never once had you ever uttered a single syllable against us. And now, at what should be the happiest moment of my life, you have turned into my father!"

"Your father? Do you think your father would be so reserved? I am not your father, and you had better be glad of it. I have no malice against Walter or his family. I think you and Walter are a good match, but you haven't even found the nerve to tell your father about him."

"You know I can't."

"I know you must! Especially now that you make plans to crush the poor man's heart!"

Elizabeth turned her back towards me and plucked a low apple from a tree. She turned it around in her hand as if studying its shape and texture. "You know my father would never allow it."

"Nonsense, your father is a reasonable man, and a modern man. How fortunate you are that he does not believe in purchasing a marriage contract for you."

Elizabeth swooned backwards, with the back of her hand placed against her forehead, and said ever so dramatically, "Oh! Let me count my very great fortune that my father has not chosen to sell me into slavery."

"I wonder if your Walter knows the sharpness of the blade you wag in your mouth."

"What difference, when my father would forbid such a union?"

"You haven't even tried to tell your father. How can you condemn him without ever giving him a chance?"

She threw the half-eaten apple to the ground and squarely faced me. "What chance would you have me give him? You know the feud between the Leatherbys and the Chamberlains. Given a chance, he would rather kill Walter and anyone else in his family who glanced my way."

"Your father would not take the life of his own godchild, no matter how bitter he has become towards his father."

"You have no idea how much my father blames Lord Chamberlain for my mother's death. He will not see reason in this matter."

Her face told me that she believed her fears completely,

but I didn't share her opinion of Lord Leatherby. "I didn't say it would be easy, but your father cares for you deeply. You must make his love for you and his desire for your happiness even more important to him than his feud with the Chamberlains."

"Maybe you don't really know my father as well as you think you do."

"Your father is near as much my father as my own. He includes me at Christmas. He always remembers my birthday. He ..."

"Yes, yes, yes. My father is a very generous man, and your family has been with us forever."

I tried getting her to look me in the eye, but she insisted on staring at the ground as she pouted. "He is more than just generous with me. Why, he even takes me fishing and hunting with him."

"And he makes you clean the fish, does he not?"

"He still takes me."

"Do you not see the grand mansion that I live in? Are you blind to the humble cottage where you were raised?"

"I know my place," I said firmly. "The question is do you know yours?"

My question brought a fire to her face, and moistness to her eyes. She shook her fists, as if she were about to scream then calmed herself and said, "I'm sorry, Hector, but there are things about my father you just don't know."

"Tell me then. Enlighten me to the secret nature of Lord Walter Leatherby the third."

"When I was but twelve years old, he came to me and we had 'the talk'. He lectured me about how I was getting older, and how you were getting older too. He told me to always remember my station and never forget that boys were not to be trusted. He told me you could still be my friend, but to be careful when outside these walls that we don't show our affection in public. He also said that I should never let you take advantage of me, because that is what boys do."

The truth of the matter was that there were times when I wished I were noble born so I could see her differently, but these were poisonous thoughts that could only vex me when I was with her, so I cast them from my mind.

A warmth rose in my cheeks as my pulse beat upon my temples. I had thought that I had fully understood my father's instructions regarding such matters, but it wasn't until I was faced with her dilemma and saw the implications on her face that I truly felt their meaning in my heart. "Good," I said, putting propriety before my most selfish of feelings. "I am glad he had this talk with you. It only proves that he loves you. My father had the same talk with me. I told him not to worry, you were too much like a sister and I could never see you otherwise."

"Don't you see? On the outside, he treats you like the son he never had, but on the inside, you are still naught more than a servant boy."

"I know what I am, and I am happy in my role. None of this changes the fact that you should have told your father about Walter long ago."

"Arrrghh! Men!" She stormed off muttering a stream of words under her breath, which, thankfully, I could neither hear nor attest to, but in my wildest most vivid imagination, her words were laced with expletives that I could not possibly repeat.

Chapter Two

After watching Elizabeth storm back to her home, I returned to my own, which she had so kindly reminded me was naught but a humble cottage. Though modest, it was a good home, adorned with more character and love than glittery trappings of wealth. It certainly was not an eyesore, surrounded as it was with fanciful vines and flowers of every hue. It was a charming home, and far enough from the stables to enjoy the sweet fragrances of the many beautifully-colored flora, and not just the local weeds, but exotic flowers from around the world.

My father was an accomplished gardener and was well respected for the grounds he kept on the Leatherby Estate, and his home was certainly no exception.

"Hector!"

I heard my mother's voice calling from behind. "Yes, Mama?"

"I just saw Elizabeth run into the house. She was quite upset about something. Perhaps you should go see what is troubling her?"

"I doubt that she would want to see me again so soon."

"Ehh? You have just seen her and now she is crying? What have you said to upset her? You must go apologize at once."

"No!" I barked at her. "Why must you assume it is something that *I* did or said?"

She wasn't accustomed to me raising my voice, but she merely tilted her head to hear more.

"I apologize, Mother, but I have said nothing that requires an apology to her; she is merely feeling extraordinarily emotional today."

"So, you already know what is troubling her? Perhaps we should go inside so you can tell me. If she truly is, as you say, just being emotional, perhaps she will require a woman's touch."

"No mother. It is a personal matter, and though a woman's touch may be just what she requires, I am bound by honor to keep this matter private."

I could see from her face that her mind was filling in the blanks with all the wrong assumptions, but I could not break my word to Elizabeth by divulging her relationship with Master Walter. "Fear not, mother. I have done nothing to bring shame or disgrace upon our family. I know my place, and I am not creating scandals with my betters."

Insult registered immediately upon my mother's face. "The Leatherbys are our good and dear friends. They have wealth and provide us with an honest income, and for that, we shall be forever grateful," she lowered her voice slightly and continued, "but that does not make them better than us, just more fortunate."

I was mildly shocked by my mother's riposte; I had never

before seen or heard this side of her. I simply nodded and said, "Perhaps you are correct. I think maybe I should go speak with Miss Elizabeth."

My poor mother must have grown exhausted from all the contortions that I put upon her face. She continued down the path to the cottage while I spun around and headed for the manor.

I entered the manor through the servants' entrance, as I often do, and worked my way through the kitchen. The cook was preparing some dough for the evening meal. Normally, I would have thought nothing of it, but this time my mind flashed back to my mother's expression.

I stood at the cook's side and watched her sprinkle flour onto the ball of dough and work it in. She glanced my way and said, "Good day Hector, did you need something?"

"No, no, not really, but I was wondering something. Are you happy here?"

She brutally slammed the dough ball onto the counter and slammed her fist into the center of it.

"Oh," I said after watching her abuse of the dough, "I guess not."

"Nonsense. 'Course I'm happy. I'm always happy in the kitchen. Life would be quite a chore for me if I didn't like kitchen work, now wouldn't it?"

"That's not what I meant. Are you happy being the Leatherbys' servant?"

"Oh, Lord yes! I've had me share of worse masters, let me tell you."

"That's not what I meant either. Are you happy being a servant? Working your fingers to the bone for your masters?"

"Oh, I see," she said as she stifled a wry smile. "I'm happy enough."

"Do you believe the Leatherbys are your betters?"

"The Leatherbys are fine people," she said, "and I won't speak ill of them, but that's not to say all of me past masters were any better than anyone of us. Where's this coming from, young Hector? Has someone been putting you down a peg?"

"No, I was just wondering how some people come to be so fortunate while others don't. I think I would like to make my fortune someday, but I wouldn't ever want to look down on my friends."

A smile spread across her face, and I swear her eyes smiled too. "I don't think you has to worry about that, love, you're a fine boy with as good a heart as any of them. You go make your fortune, and I'd be honored to make your bread." She lifted up the ball of dough and flipped it over, letting it fall into a large bowl which she set up on a warm shelf to rise. She flicked her fingers at me, shooing me out of the kitchen.

I think, were I ten years younger, she would have swatted me on the backside.

Remembering my true objective, I zipped up the back stairs

to the private wing. I stepped softly down the hall hoping to hear if she was crying before I intruded upon her when Mrs. Brindle, a matronly house maid, exited the master's bedroom carrying a pile of linen just ahead of me. She smiled at me, but her friendly greeting was abruptly aborted when she saw I was sneaking in the hall. She was used enough to seeing me about the manor and said nothing, but slowed her pace; making perfectly clear that her eye was upon me. There was nothing I could do, save push onward.

I slinked up to Elizabeth's room and peered inside the open door. I heard no crying from within and was about to announce myself when I was stung upon the back of my head. Elizabeth's voice rang out loud and clear, "Why on Earth are you prancing around like a thief in the night?"

I could hear Mrs. Brindle's guffaw as she trudged her load down the stairs to the laundry.

"I trust you did that for Mrs. Brindle's benefit, and I forgive you."

Her riding crop met this time with the side of my arm, with considerable more force than was used on my head. "I neither ask for nor accept any forgiveness from you, especially when none is warranted."

"I see you are to go riding. Good for you. My mother was concerned for you."

Elizabeth entered her room and fetched a small package. "Your mother was concerned for me?"

"She saw that you were upset and thought I may have said something disagreeable."

Alarm registered in her eyes. "And what did you tell her?"

"I told her it was a personal matter, and I was honor bound not to discuss it." I swore to myself that I would never understand women, for her face did not show any hint of relief, but instead twisted into a face on the verge of anger.

"I see," she said, "honor enough to keep my troubles private, but not enough honor to tell your mother the truth that you did indeed upset me?"

"That's not fair. If you are old enough to marry, then you are old enough to tell your father who the fortunate object of your affection would be."

"He won't allow it. He'll say that he is not good enough for me!"

"Then you must show him that Walter is indeed good enough for you. Build him up. Make him look like the best possible match for you."

She was quiet for a moment and just stared at me. "Do you not hear yourself? You must be jesting if you think we could convince father that Walter is the best match for me."

"But he is a fine match for you."

"He is a Chamberlain, and father will never see it that way. He'd sooner marry me to the smithy's son."

"Then we must show him what prospects you really have. If we bombard him with enough unsuitable suitors, Walter may not seem like such a bad match any longer."

Her eyes lit up, and she threw her arms around me. "I knew you would figure a way."

"Not so fast. We must find the right man for you. He must be unattached, of course, without wealth, and absolutely no station. He probably should be an attractive chap, maybe even an intelligent man who would have been a fine match for you if not for the unfortunate circumstances of his birth."

A smile beamed across her face and spread throughout her whole expression as she listened to my description.

"And he must be willing to put up with this charade or all's for naught."

Again, she wrung her arms around my neck, squealing, "Thank you, thank you, thank you!"

"Perhaps we should find the right man for you before you start celebrating."

"I already have!"

Lord Leatherby entered the hallway and saw her clinging to my neck. "What is going on here?"

Elizabeth bounded down the hall and proudly displayed the betrothal ring to her father. "Hector has asked me to marry him! Oh, I'm sorry; perhaps I should let him ask you for my hand first."

My jaw fell slack while Leatherby examined the ring on her finger; then he glanced over at my trembling form. He stepped down the hall towards me. His gait was stiff and measured, but still deadly silent upon the carpet. He grabbed my right hand in his and clapped me on the shoulders, "Well done, lad! I think I always knew this day would come! Splendid! This calls for a celebration. Where's your father? We must toast together." He breezed back down the main stairs, leaving Elizabeth and I staring blankly at each other, our jaws each fallen open and our spirits crashing down upon our hearts.

"No, Lord Leatherby," I pleaded, "please allow me..."

Leatherby held up his hand to stop me from talking. "How long have we known each other, Hector?"

"Since..."

Leatherby again held his hand to stop me again. "Since you were a baby? I'll have no more of this Lord Leatherby nonsense from you. We're practically family now. You may address me as Walter, at least in private, as we are now."

"But Your Lordship..."

"What did I just tell you? By God, I'd have you call me father if your own father weren't still with us. Speaking of your father, let us go find him now."

"You can't! I mean, of course you can, but I'd like to be the one to tell him."

Leatherby pursed his lips. "Of course. I quite understand, but do not dawdle. I wish to toast your good health with your father."

The world spun around in my head as I bowed my head and said, "As is your right."

"As is my right."

"Fear not, I shall speak with him posthaste."

"Do that," Leatherby replied, "And bring him straight on to me."

I bowed my head again and headed for the exit.

I had barely left the doorstep of the manor when Elizabeth pounced upon me. "What did you say to him?"

"I told him..."

"You told him?" she interrupted me. Are you crazy? He wouldn't believe you! Over me? He didn't believe you, did he?"

I waited for her to take a breath and said, "I told him that I wished to tell my father myself before he starts planning a big feast."

"A big feast?" she gasped.

"Or perhaps just a toast."

"A toast?"

"To our nuptials," I added as I gestured for her to walk with me.

"Has he gone mad?"

"Perhaps," I replied with a wry smile. "He may have gone quite mad, and you are so like him."

"I am what? Did you just call me mad?"

"I should say so. Did you not just tell your father, the Earl of Leatherby, that we were engaged to be married? You will be Countess of Leatherby someday, and I am but the lowly son of a gardener. Have you taken total leave of your senses?"

"It was a ploy." She sat upon a marble bench and smoothed the wrinkles from her skirt. "And it was your idea! He should have been furious."

"Well, he wasn't," I said as I sat next to her. "In fact, I'd say he was quite overjoyed with the prospect. It may be that your father is even more fair-minded than I ever gave him credit for being."

She shook her head slowly. "Something is amiss. This makes no sense."

"Something is most definitely amiss," I scolded her. "Why would you tell him such a bold lie? Did you not think of the trouble it could mean for me?"

"For you?" she quipped. "Being engaged to me can only improve your station. At least your father should be thrilled with the prospect."

"MY FATHER!" I yelped as I jumped up from the bench. "I must tell him and escort him back to your father so they can celebrate!"

"Celebrate?" she gasped. "So, we are to go through with this?"

"It was you that wove this web of deceit. We shall remain caught in it until I can figure a way for us to wriggle out."

I stood for a moment and watched Elizabeth return to the manor. There was something in her gait that told me she would not wait for me to find a solution. I couldn't believe my own thoughts. Even to myself, I tried to believe the best was possible, but she excels at creating trouble for everyone around her. I had no doubt that she intended to further this plot and would likely get me even deeper in trouble, but currently, I had bigger fish to fry.

My father was tending the south garden. He was always working, not only because it was his job, but I truly believe that he actually enjoyed his work. "Father?"

"Hector! Come give me a hand pulling up the bulbs to store for next spring."

I had a much more important discussion in store for him, but I fell to my knees alongside him, anyway.

"I saw you with young Lady Leatherby. What kind of trouble are the two of you cooking up now?"

"You do not want to know," I said as I shook my head slowly. "But you must know."

"I'm listening."

"Elizabeth found a ring and assumed it was from me."

"A ring? Why would she think it from you?"

I took a deep breath before explaining the nature of the ring. "It was a betrothal ring."

My father stopped pulling up bulbs and rocked back on his feet. "I know the two of you were raised together and have been friends forever, but have I not told you that you cannot become intimate with her?"

"You have," I replied, "but have you told her?"

"She is to be countess one day. It is not a gardener's place to tell her how to behave with the help."

"And yet, when her father saw the ring, she told him it was from me."

"Oh."

"And so, you see my predicament. I will fix this, but I need time. For now, however, Lord Leatherby would like to see us."

"He does, does he?"

I watched my father get up and brush the dirt off of his clothing. He seemed angry, but not at me. I had the distinct feeling that his ire was aimed at Lord Leatherby. "Don't let this worry you son, he will not sack us over this."

"I don't think he means to sack us," I said as we started walking towards the manor. "In fact, I'm frighteningly certain that he wants to toast us and bless the union."

"Oh, he does, does he?"

My father turned from the manor and headed towards our cottage at an even quicker pace, which left me even more bewildered.

This was not the first time that I struggled to understand my father. The look in his eye said he wasn't just going to meet with Lord Leatherby in the spirit with which he was summoned, but that he was going to confront him, and he planned to do so immediately. In fact, if I did not know better, I thought my father ready to strike Lord Leatherby and I'm not entirely certain that I did know better. Yet, as angry as he appeared, he had insisted on returning home to change, which is rather odd as Lord Leatherby has seen him many times covered in dirt and muck. I needed time to think anyway, and I could not do so with any sort of clarity while so much anger continued to pour off of him like smoke from a blaze.

At least the weather was good. If pacing was what I needed

to clear my thoughts, I could do so without muddy boots. The grounds outside our cottage home were as good as any on the estate, with a clean stone path that led up to a larger path that circled the estate. This was as good a place as any to meet my father as I know he would have to come this way when he was ready, at least, it *would* have been a good spot for me to wait if it weren't for Isabel coming this way right now.

I didn't have time for her, but she had already spotted me, leaving me no time to hide. She was Elizabeth's personal maid servant and often proclaimed herself to be quite smitten with me. In truth, I was somewhat fond of her as well, but I could not return the kind of affection she desired, and I had too much on my plate without having to hear her pledge her love to me again. Maybe she only meant to cross my path to another part of the estate.

"Hector!"

No, she was actually coming for me. I had not realized that I had been holding my breath until she called my name, and I heard the sigh escape my lungs. "Isabel! You look lovely this morning."

"I am on an errand, but I wanted to see you before I left."

"An errand? Has her ladyship sent you to market?"

"No," she said softly as she looked around to be sure we were alone. "She has sent me with a note for someone of whom I know you are aware."

I closed my eyes, hoping it would not be what I feared. "You mean the young Master Walter?"

"Shhh! Let us not speak his name!"

"Let me see that."

I took the message and opened it. At least she had the sense not to clasp it with the official seal. There were two pages to the note:

Walter, my darling. It has become painfully clear that our parents will never give us their blessing to wed. We must show them that you are the best match for me, but I fear that to do that, they must first learn of the less attractive suitors that I might favor. Soon, our parents shall see how you are a much better prospect for me than any other, and they may learn to regret their ways.

The second page was short and sweet:

The date has yet to be determined, but I am to wed Hector, the gardener's son. I trust that you will accept this news with all honor and humility.

Yours truly, Elizabeth Mariana Leatherby

I folded the communique and asked her, "Have you read this?"

"No."

"Good. For your own sake, you must remain ignorant of its contents. Be off now."

So, as I suspected, Elizabeth planned to further her lies without affording me the time to rectify this mess.

Isabel disappeared down the path towards the Chamberlain estate, and along came my father, but I didn't recognize what he was wearing. Isabel's interruption and my father's swiftness had left me no time to think of a way out of this pickle.

"Father," I said, pointing to his clothing, which looked more like a uniform than anything else I had ever seen him wear before. "What are you wearing?"

He breezed past me without saying a word.

"Father? What do you intend to do?"

He said nothing.

"I told you I can fix this, and I will. Have you not said, on many occasions, how clever I am?"

"No," he finally spoke, "I will handle this."

This will not end well for me. My father was a man of action, and when it came to trimming the roses or planting the irises, he was most reliable, but he was no statesman.

I had always thought him to be a fair and gentle man, but for the moment, he was someone else as he stormed into the manor and bellowed out, "Walter!"

I gasped at both the demanding tone of his voice and the familiar usage of Lord Leatherby's first name.

"Walter?"

Lord Leatherby was on the stairs, heading down, when he addressed my father. "Fernando, my old friend. Is this not a wonderful day?"

"It is not. I have taught my son the importance of recognizing his station. What is it that you have been teaching Elizabeth?"

Leatherby's expression changed as he reached the last step. I swear that it was at that same moment when he saw my father's attire and paused to digest the meaning, for although I knew not the message behind the uniform, I did not doubt that there was one. He shrugged his shoulders and asked,

"Fernando? What is this? Are you not pleased that your son can improve his station?"

My father stood very tall and asked, "Is that what this is? Is it *my son's* station that is truly at stake here?"

Much of what I was witnessing was too far from belief to convey, but Lord Leatherby seemed to cower from my father's stare. "What else could it be?"

"Do you think that I want my son to live in the limelight only by the grace of a woman's title? I have raised him to be his own man and to see his worth in his accomplishments and not his heredity."

The arrogance that normally accompanies a noble speaking to a servant evaporated from Leatherby's face. "We both know that this is not about him improving his station."

"Do we? Do we really know that, Walter? Whose then? What is your game here? Is this to be about Elizabeth's station, then?"

"Really Fernando, is that truly what you think of me?"

"Have you not considered the consequences to him should word of this get out?"

Lord Leatherby adopted the voice of one making excuses to his betters, which made absolutely no sense to me. "I'm sure that the other nobles and the gentry will learn to accept him as one of theirs."

"Perhaps, but only among those who wish to curry favor from you."

"Fernando, my friend, what about Elizabeth and Hector? Would you stand in the way of true love?"

This took some of the starch out of my father's sails. "Can we at least refrain from announcing this just yet? Can we have time to test the winds about this arrangement before diving headlong into it?"

"Of course, Fernando. We can give it some time."

I don't know how long my mouth had been hanging open, but there it was, nearly to my chest as I watched my father storm out of the manor without being dismissed first.

Lord Leatherby turned to me and asked, "Will that be alright with you, Hector? Can the two of you keep your betrothal quiet for the time being?"

I nodded my head as I reeled in my jaw and thought how this must have been a dream. A hellish twisted nightmare that was sure to bring me to an untimely end.

I left the manor in a daze; completely oblivious to the path I was on. I reviewed all the conversations of the day in my mind but could identify no single event that would have resulted in such a great upheaval as this course of events. How could I even try to fix this mess without knowing where my life began to unravel? Repeated strolls through my memory all led to the same conclusion: that I had done something truly evil in a previous life.

A sharp, hot sting across my cheek brought me out of my reverie and into the searing eyes of Isabel. I swear to you, that recalling the memory today, as I record this, also renews the same feeling that her handprint left upon my burning cheek as if it were new.

"You are going to marry her? The Earl of Leatherby's

daughter?"

"Isabel, did you read the message?"

"Are you not the one who has always gone on about knowing your place and staying within your station?"

"That would be my father," I said, straining to remain calm. "Did you read the message?"

"You should have heard what Master Walter said when he read it, but you won't hear such language from my lips."

"Did you read the message?"

"I'm surprised he didn't storm in here ahead of me to kill you."

I fought hard to keep my temper from unraveling on the poor girl. "Did you read the message?"

"He'd be within his rights, you know."

"ISABEL!! Did you read the message?!?!?"

"You know that I cannot read, but I saw Master Walter read it, and he wasn't too happy."

I breathed a small sigh of understanding as I said, "Then you don't know what was really in the note?"

"I know enough and stop changing the subject! How could you marry her? How could you do that to me?"

I closed my eyes and shook my head. "Isabel, I have told you before, there is nothing between us."

"Yes, there is! I can feel it in my heart."

"But I have never felt it in mine."

She hooked her arm in mine and said, "You just don't know it yet, but I know you love me."

I sighed heavily and told her, "Go back to your mistress to tell her the job is done."

The sting may have left my cheek, but I was quite sure at the time that Isabel's handprint remained emblazoned upon my face for the remainder of the afternoon. This was such a mess already, and it was sure to get worse before it would ever get any better. I resolved that I should be the one to tell my mother. If anyone was to believe me, it would be her.

Halfway back to the cottage, I heard a now familiar hissing from a bush. "What is this?" I cried out in mocked, melodramatic fashion. "Is it a snake? Perhaps I should whack the bush to rid the garden of this vile creature."

Elizabeth popped up and squealed, "It is not a snake! It is me!"

"I see! Not a snake, but a spider weaving her web of lies. I told you to let me handle it, but you could not."

"I had to tell Walter. He would have learned of this, eventually."

"You had to tell Walter, and now Isabel knows."

She extricated herself from the bush and brushed the leaves from her skirt. "So?"

"So? Is that all you have to say? So?"

She just looked at me with wide eyes, as if no further explanation was required.

"So," I explained, "my father asked that we keep this quiet for now and your father agreed, but you have blabbed it to

Walter and soon it will have spread all over Chamberlain Hall!"

She set her jaw and folded her arms as if she was totally confident, but her voice began to lose some of its assuredness. "He won't tell them the plan."

"No, he won't. He will tell them of our engagement as if it were real."

"So," she said with an air of success, "our plan will succeed."

"Will it? Or will Lord Chamberlain use this as an excuse to lodge a complaint against your father for being an embarrassment to the House of Lords? And all this after I told your father we would keep it to ourselves."

She bit her lip as she asked, "You told him that?"

"It was more like he told me."

"What else did my father say?"

"It was less what he said than how it was said."

She leaned her head upon my shoulder and said softly, "He can be quite forceful with his requests."

"He can be, but he wasn't this time. My father was the forceful one, and it was Lord Leatherby who acquiesced."

She screwed her face up in utter bewilderment.

"There!" I said sharply while pointing my finger at her expression. "Now you may see how twisted this tale has become."

"What will you do?"

"I do not know yet. You should go find something innocent to occupy your time while I figure this out."

I did not know whether Elizabeth would heed my suggestion and find something harmless to do. For as long as I had known her, and that is basically forever, she had been a pathological trouble maker, a busybody of the highest order. My mother had often warned me not to get caught up in her schemes, or at least to not get caught.

MY MOTHER!

I still had to tell my mother. It was better that she believe me to be tangled up in one of Elizabeth's machinations than to believe that I actually would have proposed a union between our families. Do not get me wrong. We love the Leatherbys, my mother no less than any of us, but a marriage between a gardener's son and a noblewoman would be scandalous.

I hoped to find her before my father did. It would have been most convenient if she had been in the garden selecting herbs for our evening meal. As a servant family, we were quite fortunate that she did not have to work in the manor's kitchen. She merely needed to collect the spices from our private garden, which father tended, and manage the household. In truth, she was quite capable and could have managed the manor if it were pressed upon her. She was surprisingly well educated for a gardener's wife.

Alas, I did not see her in the garden. If she was not inside,

I would have to wait for her, as she could be anywhere.

Opening the door and stepping into the cool cottage confirmed my fears. She was not inside, but my father was, and he was still dressed in that official-looking uniform. "Father?"

"Son."

"You still have not told me why you are wearing that costume."

"Do not concern yourself with my attire when you have put this whole family in jeopardy,"

"No, no, no, no..." My frustration was ready to burst out in a fit of temper; a temper that my father had often said was a family trait. "Do not put this on me until you hear me out."

He glared at me and growled, "I think I have heard all that I need to hear."

"Is that so?" I ratcheted my voice up a notch. "So, you have no need to hear the truth?"

"I know my son quite well." His face bore a combination of mirth and pride as he continued, "well enough to know how clever he can be in spinning the truth. Now let me tell you the truth. You cannot see Elizabeth. You cannot be seen with her. If you value the lives of your mother and father, you must end this thing with her immediately."

"What was that?" my mother asked from the doorway. "What kind of trouble has our son gotten himself into now?"

"He..." my father paced the floor as he measured his words. "Your son and the young countess are engaged to be married."

My mother was elated. "That's wonderful! I think they

make such a cute couple.”

“What??” my father yelled. “This is a disaster! Such a scandal!”

I distinctly heard the thud as my mother’s excitement fell and landed on the floor. “Oh dear! Is she...with...” She waved her hands over her midsection when her voice failed her, indicating a plump belly.

“What?” I snapped back at her. “Mother! How could you think that?”

The anger in my father’s face drained to a ghastly pale pallor. “I had not considered that. Of course, son, you must do the honorable thing.”

“Father! You too? I have done nothing to disgrace this family!”

My father regained his composure and said, “The disgrace would not be all yours, son, but still, if she is not in that condition, then you cannot be with that girl. I will say no more. You just have to trust me on this.”

The world spun around me as I sprinted out of our home, wondering what form of death I would find more preferable. Would it be hanging? Beheading? Or will the townsfolk simply chase me with pitchforks and torches until I leapt from the top of the highest cliff? The hole which I dug for my grave kept getting deeper and deeper. Even my own mother found it too easy to believe that I would father a child out of wedlock and with Elizabeth, no less.

Even while my mind's eye continued to play the last several hours over and over, my feet knew the way to my special place where I can always find peace and never be disturbed, except by the birds and the squirrels that frequented the trees on the edge of the property.

"Hector!"

The sound of Lord Leatherby's voice snapped my mind back to the present. Now what? Haven't I enough problems with my own parents? Why must I deal with a new would-be parent built on a falsehood? This jarring return from my daydreams to reality seems to be happening much more of late.

"Hector! A moment, please!"

"Lord Leatherby!" I forced my most polite and most irritation free voice from my throat. "I don't believe I have ever seen you this far out on the property before."

"My spirits are so light today that I feel like I am young again! It is not like I am walking, even. I am floating on the air and can freely transit around the grounds."

My eyebrows snuck upwards on my forehead, quite against my conscious desires. "But truly, you are so young!"

"Nonsense," he said. "The news of your betrothal has taken me back to the days when your father and I first met."

Uh oh. I felt a story coming on. "Is that so?"

"Yes indeed. I was traveling through Spain when I first came upon your mother."

"My mother?" Why did I ask that? Now the story was certain to be even longer.

"Yes, your mother. I was in the Spanish court when I first came upon her."

In the court? My mother was in the court? I tried hiding my surprise, but I could feel the wind slip between my lips as my mouth fell agape.

"She was as beautiful a woman as I had ever seen. Surely you have heard the story?"

Fear of what might come next froze my voice and barely allowed me to turn my head left and right.

"I was not yet married, although I had been promised to the late Lady Leatherby. Had it not been for your father, I think I would have desired your mother for my own bride, despite my parents' match making. We were fast friends, your mother and I, but she had eyes only for your father."

I blinked my eyes to remind myself that I was still alive. I didn't know which was more shocking: that my mother would have chosen my father, the gardener, over Lord Leatherby or that Lord Leatherby would consider marriage to a commoner. No wonder he was not alarmed by our false betrothal.

"There was a time when I thought your father would have challenged me to a duel over your mother, but your mother confessed her loyalty to him and, in the end, your father and I became inseparable friends."

My father, the gardener, who has spent so many years instilling within me the propriety of station, was willing to duel Lord Leatherby?

"There were those, however, who did not appreciate the pairing of your mother and father."

Why would anyone care about my parents' personal affairs?

"I think they liked my closeness with your father even less, and they chose to accuse him of heresy."

I managed to nod my head slowly. I was aware of the inquisition.

"That was when I helped bring your parents here to my lands so they could be free to marry."

It was at that moment that I became newly aware of many details of my parents' life that they had never actually shared with me, and yet, I felt like I understood nothing of it.

"And now look where we are. You and my Elizabeth are free to marry, away from the intrigues of court."

Away from the intrigues of court? I must speak, but I cannot speak to Lord Leatherby of the scandal without giving away that the betrothal is a sham.

"I'm sorry Hector. I feel like I am fluttering around like a butterfly, but am I keeping you from something?"

"No, your lordship, I was just going to find a quiet place to meditate."

"I think you can call me Walter now."

"That may require some additional effort," I replied, "and perhaps some time."

The smile on his face couldn't have been any broader. "I shall leave you to your meditation. I think I shall sing a song."

Thank God and all the ancient Gods that used to rule these lands that Lord Leatherby finally left me alone to my meditation. It seemed appropriate, in my mind, to include the old Gods when I sat to view the old duck pond from my favorite spot below an old oak that stood guard, majestically, over the calm water.

A Mallard glided effortlessly across the formerly still water, with three young ducklings splashing about to keep up with her. Even their playful splashing is peaceful in this idyllic corner of the world, but the stomping I heard to my left was not.

"Hector?"

I rose to my feet and raised my hands defensively. "Walter? Is that you? How did you know to find me here?"

"It is I. Did you think I would forget how we came here as children to escape our parents?"

I heard his voice, still in the bushes, and stepped backwards so I might still defend myself. "You are clever. I should have remembered this about you."

"I need a word with you."

"Please know," I said as he broke through the brush and into the small clearing below the oak, "that nothing has happened between Elizabeth and me. I am truly in favor of your pairing."

"At ease Hector. Do you not think that I can recognize the hand of Elizabeth in this twisted plot?"

His face looked neither menacing nor angry. "What then," I asked, "would drive you to sneak onto Leatherby lands?"

"I know what the two of you are plotting, but my father does not. To say he is angry would be lessening the blow."

"What does he have to be angry about? He should be thrilled that the rumors about you and Elizabeth can finally be put to an end."

Walter motioned to the grass below the oak. "Let us sit

together as friends. Please."

I nodded my head and settled down alongside him as if no time has passed since we were ten years old. "Are things so bad that I must be seated to hear what news you bring?"

"My father intercepted a page from Elizabeth's note. The page he got did not lay out the details of her deception, but it did describe the plans for you to marry Elizabeth."

"So, he knows that we are sending you messages, but is he aware that we know that he intercepted it?"

"He is not aware, and he will be on his guard, looking for any more messages that might come our way."

I pursed my lips as I considered what this could mean. "We can use that."

"Will you tell Elizabeth for me? I do not think I should spend any more time on Leatherby lands than necessary."

"No. I think that I shall not tell her. She would only try to weave a more complicated web if she knew. How has your father taken the news so far?"

Walter rolled his eyes and shook his head. "He was furious, which was quite unexpected. His closest advisor tried consoling him and even suggested that this could be grounds to have Lord Leatherby removed from the House of Lords, but it was as if he could not hear them over his own ranting about how you were not good enough for Elizabeth."

"He is right. It is not good for Elizabeth to promise herself to a gardener's son, but why would Lord Chamberlain care so much?"

"He should not. I am his own son, yet he has never shown so much concern over my own prospects for marriage and he was never this angry on those occasions when he heard rumors that I might be connected with her."

I climbed to my feet and pointed towards Chamberlain Hall. "But he will be angrier still, if he ever learns that you have come to the Leatherby home. I tell you, I had no idea that he hated me this much."

"I never thought that he did. I thought his beef had always been with Lord Leatherby."

"As did I. All the same, you should go."

"Agreed," Walter said with a curt nod of his head, "but not before we grip hands and renew our bond of friendship. You must believe that I hold no animosity towards you over this."

It was all true. His eyes, his smile, and his grip told me that he was sincere. "It is good to know that we, the next generation, have not lost our minds. It is up to us to figure out why our parents have all gone mad, and yes, you can add my father to the list."

Judging by his expression, the news of my father's madness was enough to pique his curiosity, but I think he knew there would be another time for an explanation.

Alone again, I looked across the pond, but even the tranquility there was not enough to soothe my mind.

It was not the sun that exuded moisture from my pores, but the sweat of defeat as I made my way back to my home; still with no understanding of what could have riled Lord Chamberlain so. It was certainly nice to see Walter again and especially good to learn that he holds no grudge towards me. We were once inseparable, as were our families and estates, but somewhere along the way Lord Chamberlain came to resent Lord Leatherby and our friendship was no longer tolerated, at least not officially or in public.

The well-manicured path from the pond had been serene, but from the hedge surrounding our cottage, I could already hear a commotion coming from inside.

It is not often that I heard my mother raise her voice, especially towards my father, but she was clearly chastising him. "Don't give me that look."

"What is wrong with my look?"

"You know perfectly well that you are not the victim here. Why were you so harsh with your son?"

Still outside the cottage, I dared not breach the door just yet. In the split moments of silence, I could almost see my father searching for a way out of the argument. "I was not so..."

"Stop right there! I do not want to hear your denials. You practically forbade him from seeing Elizabeth." I knew not what point she was making, but my breast filled with pride as I heard her control the conversation.

"I did..."

"I know what you did. Why shouldn't they find love with each other?"

My father cleared his throat dramatically before continuing, "Because she is like a sister to him."

It is a marvel how swiftly she could shift her voice from accusing to dismissive. "Obviously, that is not how he feels."

"He does not know..."

"And why do you suppose he does not know? You are his father, but have you told him?"

"He does not need to know."

"He does not need to know?" She mocked his own words. "He makes plans to marry the contessa. Perhaps this is not so bad a time that you should tell him?"

An eerie quiet followed, and the sudden loss of yelling caught me off guard.

A surprisingly soft voice from my father explained, "You do not know what you speak of. You cannot."

I opened the door and entered into the fray. "What is it that I do not know?"

Silence.

"Father? What do I not know?"

"Nothing."

"It certainly did not sound like nothing."

He straightened his posture and stood as erect as he could. It was something that he liked to do when he was about to pronounce something that he thought was indisputable. "Then it is nothing that you need to know."

I was quite certain that I could slice tomatoes on the edge of my mother's voice as she simply said his name, "Fernando..."

"What?" he spat back at her. "Exactly what do you think he should know?"

My mother's soft siren like voice said, "Rodrigo?"

I knew things were going to change when she pulled out his middle name.

"Esme, dear. Before I start to bare long hidden state secrets to our son, perhaps you should just tell me what you think he needs to know. In fact, let us speak in private so you can tell me exactly what it is that you know."

I didn't know what was more mysterious; my father claiming to hold 'state secrets' or him wanting to know what she knew.

"You are correct. We should speak in private. Soon."

Chapter Three

A new day; the sun rose; birds sang; and I awoke to the uncomfortable reality that it had not been all a dream, despite my prayers. Doing nothing would have seen me married to Elizabeth and probably disowned by my father. I must take action.

Mrs. Brindle fetched Elizabeth for me while I waited in the small hall. It was rather early for me to come calling, but the sun had already been up for a while and I had plans.

"Hector!" Elizabeth exclaimed with a bit of a shocked voice as she entered the room. "Do you think it wise to come visiting so early?"

"Why?" I asked. "Does it make me unseemly in some way?" I winked at her, but I didn't feel like she grasped my intent. "I thought we might skip the morning meal and head to town for a bite to eat. It would be a good opportunity for us to be seen together. I thought a little gossip might sway your father's favor of our union."

She nodded her head as if she understood, but her eyes betrayed her with the vacant, clueless look they were prone to give. "You want to go to town with me? I haven't seen you mount a horse since we were children. Do you think you can still ride?" she asked, changing the subject, then added, somewhat haltingly, "darling?"

I smiled at her attempt at subterfuge and admitted, "Not well, but perhaps you can teach me to ride better."

"Very well. Allow me some time to change and I'll meet you at the stables."

In the name of truthfulness, I didn't learn the full details of what happened next until much later, but I like to think that it went pretty much as I had planned it.

Elizabeth wasted little time after I had invited her to ride to town with me, but before she changed for our ride, she returned to the desk in her room and crafted a new letter to Walter, as I knew she would. I vividly recall Isabel rushing out of the manor and leaving the estate practically before I had even started for the stables. I only learned of the true contents of the letter years later when Walter showed it to me himself. It was a testament to her cunning and an excellent example of how much trouble she could make.

Dear Walter,

By now, I'm sure that you have heard of my in-tention to marry Hector. There may have been a time when I entertained thoughts of you asking for my hand, but much time has passed and I cannot be a spinster. So there you have it. Hector and I are making our plans, and everything is progressing accordingly. Perhaps in the future, you should be less reticent if you wish a lady's favor.

I must admit that it was a marvelously crafted letter, given that Walter was in on our plot. Elizabeth did not always think things through when she concocted her schemes, but I could not have written a better letter myself. The crux of it was that things were going to plan.

She told me, after I confronted her about Isabel's hasty departure, that she had written a letter to Walter and had given it to Isabel for delivery. I learned later that Lord Chamberlain had set one of the gardeners to spy on her arrival and alert him before she reached their home.

Lord Chamberlain met her at the steps and told her that he would hand it to his son personally.

I found it unusual, especially in those days, that, as able-bod-ied as I was, I had been given no duties toward the upkeep of the manor. In fact, I swear that I don't believe my father was ever actually required to garden, except by his own love for making things grow. I had complete autonomy to go where I wanted and do what I wished. If any limitations were placed upon my actions, it was by my father who tried to instill within me the propriety of station. Well, those days were gone. I had a plot to hatch and seeds that needed planting.

I returned home to change into something more suitable for horseback. I was not fortunate enough to have truly proper riding attire, as I'm sure Elizabeth would have, but I did at least have something that looked neatly pressed. I was on one of the many paths from the cottage to the stables when Lord Leatherby hailed me. "Hector! You have the determined look of a man on a mission. What devilish plot are you up to?"

I was momentarily taken aback by his inquiry, especially the way he called out my devilish plot, but I put on a brave smile to hide my fiendish intentions. "Who? Me?"

"The jig is up," he chuckled. "Confess your schemes or... or..."

I was grateful for his pause and still somewhat unaccustomed to such familiarity from his lordship and feared that I might stutter my response, but it was a completely unnecessary worry. "On a glorious day like this? I thought I would accompany Elizabeth to town."

The joy on his face was unmistakable. "Getting into mischief, no doubt?"

"Not at all. I thought we would ride to town to sample some of the sweets in the market. You know, give the cooks the morning to themselves. Would you care to join us?"

"That's a splendid idea, but I fear that I would just be in your way. There is something that I wanted to discuss with you, however. You are going to be part of the family now, and as such, I think you should be given a monthly salary. We can't have you representing the family on a gardener's son's allowance, can we?"

I stammered, "I... uh..."

Leatherby held up his hand to interrupt me and added, "Don't worry. This is not charity. I will take you under my wing and teach you the management of the surrounding farms."

Now I was really getting deep into this mess. My plans had always been to travel and see the world on my own terms.

He pulled a coin purse from his belt and held it out for me, saying, "We'll just call this an advance."

I couldn't refuse it, seeing how much more joy his offer had brought to his already happy face. "I don't know what to say."

"Say nothing. Go enjoy yourselves. Do give Nelly at the tavern my regards."

"We will."

Lord Chamberlain stalked the halls searching for his son and finally found him at the stables, ready to mount a horse. "Where are you off to?"

Walter shrugged. "I thought I might head to town."

"Circumstances have changed. You should read this letter."

Walter had barely opened the letter when he asked, "Have you read this? It is addressed to me."

"I have. How else might I have known to give it to you?"

"You sound angry, father."

Lord Chamberlain scowled as he barked, "Read the letter."

After reading it, Walter said, "So, it would seem that your prayers have been answered. Why does this news irk you so?"

"Why does it irk me? Is that what you ask? He's a peasant boy! We can't have a gardener's son marry the contessa! It's scandalous."

"Truly, you seem more upset that she would consider marriage with Hector than you are that she would favor him over me. Would you have me pursue her after all?"

I must pause now in my reminiscing of the events as they were told to me by Walter himself. I tell you with all honesty that I wish I had been there to see it all firsthand.

By all of Walter's accounts, Lord Chamberlain looked as though he could shoot arrows from his eyes when he said, "She is no good for you."

"Why, father? What is this to you?"

"I need not explain my whims to you. I'm just telling you now that you cannot be with her!"

"Well, that's not good enough. If you wish to offer no explanation, then I will hear no more on it."

Chamberlain's rage boiled over. "Go to town then! Just get out of my sight!"

Elizabeth was in the stables, dressed for a ride and waiting for our mounts to be prepared.

"Good morning darling," I said, loud enough for all in the stable to hear.

She turned to face me, eyes wide with shock.

"Don't look so surprised," I whispered as I reached her side, "we are betrothed, thanks to you I might add, so we may as well try to sell it."

"But," she replied, "I thought you said we were to keep it a secret for a few days at least."

"We were, but that ship sailed away when you wrote your letter to Walter and Isabel learned of its contents. Now, perhaps you can act like you are happy to see me."

She nodded her head and parted her lips slightly, but said nothing intelligible.

I shook my head and said softly, "You will have to do better than this when we are seen together."

"Of course," she replied. "I've asked Winston to prepare a horse for you. Sandy is a fairly tame ride. You should be fine."

In truth, I wasn't at all comfortable in the saddle, but if I was to play the part of a young man who would marry into the Leatherby house, then I would have to at least appear to be able to ride.

"Winston?" she turned and called out loudly. "Are we ready to go?"

"Yes, ma'am," Winston replied, as he brought the two mares out into the sunlight. I swear that I caught him looking at me a bit sideways. He knew full well that I was the gardener's son, and I saw it in his expression.

I could not have planned a better opportunity to launch my plans. I took Elizabeth in my arms and pulled her close to me, then pressed our lips together and whispered, "I told you not to look so shocked."

"What woman wouldn't be shocked by such a public display of affection?"

I dared not glance over at Winston, but I could imagine the surprise registered on his face. "Perhaps you are right. That may have gone too far."

"Or, if word gets to my father, he may think you too roguish for me."

I snickered and said, "I can't imagine the fellow who would be too roguish for you, but let's hope I am too daring for your father."

She slapped my arm playfully. "I don't believe I liked that. Where shall we ride? I often follow the creek where it leaves the estate to the forest, where it pours into a charming stream."

"That sounds lovely," I said while slowly shaking my head, "but I thought we might go to town so we could be seen by more people. I think maybe some gossip might tarnish your father's notion of our union."

She grinned devilishly and said, "You are a clever one."

The weather was relatively good for a ride, I suppose, but I took no notice after mounting sweet docile Sandy, as I was too acutely aware of the relationship between my bum and the saddle. I found myself constantly tossed into the air, only to land back onto the leather with a hard thud. "Why are we in such a hurry? Can we not take a more gentle pace?"

Elizabeth did little to hide the mirth on her face as she asked, "Would you rather walk?"

I didn't answer immediately, as I considered the option.

"Hector, darling. This is a snail's pace."

"Are you certain then that dear Sandy here is a gentle nag? I feel like a caber being tossed into the air."

Now she laughed out loud. "You are not being tossed out of the saddle."

"Try explaining that to my backside."

"Grip her a little tighter."

I sighed and sunk my head. "My knuckles are already white from the death grip I use to hold the pommel."

"No, you must also grip her with your legs."

I nodded my head and dug my heels in. Sandy lurched forward, allowing me to slide off the back of the saddle. I hung on, bouncing off her haunches until she came to a stop. Only then did I see Elizabeth at her head, holding the reins and soothing Sandy, apologizing for being given such an ill-trained rider.

"You apologize to her? Am I not the one that was only moments from death, and you offer comfort to her?"

She spread her arms as if in a curtsy while remaining still in the saddle. "My apologies dear Sir. I should not make light of your misfortune. However, if you would like to try again, I do believe we can solve this together."

I slid off the back of Sandy and mounted her again.

"Honestly, Hector. Has it really been that long since we rode together as children?"

"As I recall," I reminded her, "those were but ponies, not yet fully grown. Perhaps this is one of them having her revenge upon me for being absent so long."

"Now," Elizabeth said, still on the verge of laughter, "when you grip the horse with your legs, use your thighs and not your heels. And please don't use the death-defying grip displayed by your knuckles. You will exhaust your energy before we ever reach town. Just hold on a bit, as I'm sure you did with your father when he would carry you around on his back."

I nodded my head and accepted her instruction, but I'm positive that I may have squeezed some breath from my father's lungs in her example.

Between her tutelage and some newly found familiarity with the saddle, the ride became bearable with the town just over the final hill.

Greenshire was barely a full-fledged town by London's standards, but it had sprung up when the earlier village of Sir Lledr had begun to service many of the smaller villages surrounding the area. The name was changed out of respect to the bond between the Leatherbys and the Chamberlains as it was located equidistant between the two and the Chamberlains had undertaken an equal share of expanding the previous village.

It served as a trading hub for the surrounding villages and had a relatively small local population, but it had a pub that was said to be as fine as any pub found in London, even if said compliments came mostly from the proprietors.

The streets were relatively empty as we first entered the confines of the town, but they filled rapidly when we turned the corner towards the market square.

"What do you think?" I asked as I dismounted Sandy. "Should we walk the market together or head straight to the pub?"

She glanced at the morning sun, which wasn't very high yet in the sky, and gave me a quizzical look. "Isn't it a little early for the pub? Or is that part of your plan to tarnish your image?"

I nodded my head. "It is indeed early. I think we will find more people browsing the market stalls than in the pub, but I have forced you to skip your morning meal for this jaunt."

She hooked her arm in mine, a bold move, but definitely in the spirit of our charade. "Being seen is all well and good," she said, "but do you think the people in the market will know you?"

"Of course they will. Maybe."

"Who?" she asked. "The errand boys who are here on command of their masters? Or maybe you were thinking of the cooks who have come to market to fill their stores? Is that your master plan? To create gossip amongst the service workers?"

I scowled a moment before replying, "That matters not. Any aristocrats in the square will know you and if they do not know me, they will certainly wonder whose arm it is that you have so securely attached yourself. They will ask who I am."

We scrolled the marketplace where I purchased some sweetbreads, but she was more inclined to examine every kind of scarf hung in every stall. I thought I had it planned out perfectly: we would stroll through the market in front of everybody until someone objected, but I was never confronted by anyone. Some eyes may have rolled, and I thought I might have detected some whispering behind us, but we were never actually looked down upon, which was a bit of a disappointment to me.

I waited outside a merchant stall that was filled with materials of every imaginable color while she browsed. She exited the stall and tossed a handsome brown scarf around my neck and rubbed it against my cheek. "Isn't that the softest material you have ever felt? They said it comes from a rabbit's fur and is spun into the finest cloths."

I felt somewhat awkward appreciating the softness, but could say nothing against it. "Perhaps it is time that we should head on to the pub. The sun is high enough that we might find a decent mid-day meal there."

She nodded her head and took her new place at my side.

The tavern had their regulars, some of whom were sleeping off their last round in dark dusty corners; a few more found that any time of day was a good time to play cards, but clearly, we weren't the only ones looking for a simple meal. I say simple, but in fact, the cook here had a reputation for trying exotic spices imported from just about every known location, plus a few we had never heard of. Greenshire proved to be an excellent place for the cook to discover and collect new spices from every corner of the world, although his mastery of them had yet to mature.

Some laughter caught my attention as it arose from one of the center tables. I pointed and asked, "Isn't that Agnes? One of your father's farmers?"

"Her father is."

"Perfect. Let us go pay our respects. The more we surround your father with rumors about us, the more he'll see how unsuitable I am."

Elizabeth arched her eyebrows and asked, "You don't think they would be proud of you for courting the Earl's daughter?"

"How could they? They know their station as well as mine and we clearly don't belong in your world. They may even prove to be jealous of my attempts to join you at your station."

She looked at me as if I hadn't a clue of what transpired

around me. "Have you met some of the noble sons and daughters of the realm? You, Hector, are nobler than clearly half of them."

"Well, then let me show them what a lout I can be."

The expression on her face looked unconvinced as I waved to Agnes's table and led Elizabeth by the hand. "Good day to you, Agnes. How are things?" I looked suspiciously around the room to see who might be listening before I asked, "Tell me, are you still seeing George over at the Chamberlain's?"

She giggled joyously as two of the other women at the table also giggled and tried to cover their faces, as if to hide their laughter.

Thomas, the sole man at the table, chuckled and said, "She's been doing a bit more than seeing ole George, if you be getting my meaning." The woman next to him hit his arm, which was enough to tell him he had said too much already.

Agnes bit her lip as she looked hesitantly at Elizabeth. Margaret leaned over and whispered, "Are you going to tell them?"

Agnes whispered back, "She's a Leatherby!"

"She is that," Margaret replied, "but look at the way she's hanging on to Hector's arm. There be something going on there."

"The truth is," Agnes said, "that George an' I have been married for a year now, but things being what they is between Lord Leatherby and Lord Chamberlain, we thought it might be best to keep mum until we saves up enough to move away to London."

"It's a shame," I said, "that the silly old feud should force the two of you to hide your marriage like that."

"That ain't all they is hiding," Thomas added, earning him a smack on the back of the head.

Agnes held back saying anything, but the glow on her face gave her away, to Elizabeth at least who blurted out, "A baby?"

Agnes nodded her head with a broad smile spreading across her face.

Elizabeth clapped her hands and seated herself at the table. "You must let us do something to help you."

I pulled the purse that had been gifted to me by Lord Leatherby and joined Elizabeth at the table. "Yes! Let us start a collection so the two of you may find a place in London!"

"No!" Agnes objected. "We can't take your money like that."

Elizabeth looked sideways at the purse of coins and gave me a suspicious glance before saying, "But you must let us help somehow."

"Yes!" I said enthusiastically. "Perhaps a blanket."

"Or a cradle," Elizabeth said.

Walter entered the tavern and caught Agnes' attention. She lowered her voice and looked directly at Elizabeth to ask,

"Didn't George tell me that you was with Lord Chamberlain's son?"

Elizabeth nodded. "I was, but you know how hard it was for you and George to see each other. Just imagine how difficult it was for Walter and me."

Agnes froze for a moment, except for her temple, that actively displayed her heartbeat. "Well," she said as she nodded towards Walter, "this might get a bit sticky too."

Walter came over and very deliberately ignored my presence as he said, "Good day, Elizabeth. Could I possibly have a word with you?" After a short pause, he added, "In private?"

Elizabeth put her hand over mine, which was still on the table holding the coin purse. "This is not a good time, Walter. I'm here with Hector."

Walter made a big show of looking surprised to see me there, and asked, "You're WITH Hector? The gardener's son?"

Agnes looked shocked and asked, "Haven't the two of you been friends since you was little?"

"We were, until my father impressed upon me the importance of station," Walter paused dramatically before adding, "that and the whole family feud and all."

What he didn't say was that since his mother died when he was still young, his father was all too glad to be rid of him. "All true," I said, "but I was hoping that I could still count you among my friends."

Walter sighed heavily and shook his head. "Under the current circumstances, I just don't know if that can be possible."

I nodded slowly and said, "I under-"

Walter didn't let me finish and blurted out, "Agnes, I

understand congratulations are in order."

Agnes froze. I swear that even her temple skipped a beat.

"Fear not," Walter said, "George told me. Don't tell me that George has never told you that we were confidants?"

"He may have said something to that nature," she squeaked out in a nervous voice, "but I thought that he may have been boasting and it would be better if I didn't make such an assumption, given the feud and all."

Walter put his hand over his heart and said, "You have nothing to worry about with me. Besides, the feud is between our fathers. And given our circumstance and the need for Elizabeth and I to hide our past familiarity from our fathers, I am shocked to find that my childhood friend would take advantage of the situation and stab me in the back like this."

I took Elizabeth's hand in mine and rose from my seat. "If you will excuse us, I shall refrain from any further backstabbing so we might do some shopping for the coming baby."

"What a splendid idea," Walter said. "I think I shall join you."

"Nonsense," I said, "you only just arrived. You must be parched from your journey."

"Truth be told," Elizabeth interjected, "we just arrived here ourselves. I thought we were to eat something."

"Yes!" Walter said. "Please stay. Let us eat as old friends and toast the coming baby. I'm sure that all the best gifts for the coming child will still be there waiting for us."

I cocked my head at Walter and asked, "But did you not just say that we could no longer be friends?"

"Let us be acquaintances, then. We shall always know each

other."

Elizabeth looked at me pleadingly and Walter snuck me a sly wink that only I could see.

"Very well," I relented. "I suppose that we could eat."

Walter sat at the table as if to eat, but he barely touched his food as his attention was squarely on Elizabeth and me. "This makes no sense," he said, idly motioning towards the two of us. "You, Elizabeth, well I guess I can understand how you...you've always been a free spirit, considering your willingness to be with me, at least for a time, but you, Hector? I've always known you to be very proper, with an impeccable sense of propriety. How could you bring so much shame upon Elizabeth? Have you even considered the scandal?"

"Walter..." I tried to explain.

"And what of Lord Leatherby?" He interrupted me. "After everything he has done for you? For your family?"

"Walter..."

"And what about your own family? Do you not see the dishonor you bring to your father? I swear he acts with as much nobility as half the House of Lords! More even! Where will your family go?"

"Walter..."

"It is not Lord Leatherby's wrath that they must fear, but the House of Lords will surely come down upon your family and force them into exile."

"Really now..."

"And they may even strip Lord Leatherby of his title and holdings! Where will he live? And what of Elizabeth? Would you then hold her to her promise of marriage when you are not only a gardener's son, but also a penniless pauper?"

I sat silent, waiting for him to finish.

"Well? Have you nothing to say?"

"Walter..."

"Well, I have plenty to say. I shall not give up my Elizabeth so easily. If it is a contest you would like, then so be it. While I would rather it be a contest of skill, perhaps swords, I would not take advantage of a servant's son that way and shall conduct a contest of wooing. I shall win Lady Elizabeth's hand back with my generous nature."

This time, it was Elizabeth to speak. "Walter! I am not a prize medallion to be awarded to the winner of your stupid contest!"

"Stupid?" he asked. "Do you really think it stupid that I should try to win back your hand?"

"My hand is *MY* hand," she said sharply, "and not an award for the best archer or whatever you are scheming."

"Your love then," he replied. "I shall woo you to win back your love."

She opened her mouth as if to reply, but her face softened, and she fell silent.

"You may find," I said calmly, "that winning back her love would not only be a contest against me, but also a contest against your past self that was, shall we say, often late to the starting line?"

"Fine!" he said. "I accept your challenge and will endeavor for absolution over my past conduct, all the while doing what I must to impress Lady Elizabeth with the sincerity of my love for her!"

As we left the tavern for the market, I told Walter, "You should be a thespian. I'm quite sure that Mr. Shakespeare would hire you on the spot."

Walter bowed deeply at the waist. "Thank you. Thank you. You are too kind. Are those flowers for me?"

I barely refrained from laughing so heartily that I would have been heard by both the Leatherby and the Chamberlain estate.

Elizabeth looked confused. "Do you mean that you were only pretending to act jealous of me?"

Walter smiled broadly and said, "If I thought for a moment that the two of you were serious, then I would be most sincerely jealous and would probably challenge my boyhood friend to a duel, but given that you are acting yourselves, I had no choice but to feign jealousy."

"And you should continue to do so," I said, "as we shop at the mall."

The first stall we checked had no cradles, but it had some very soft blankets. Elizabeth picked up a fine blue blanket and rubbed it against her cheek. "You must feel this." She rubbed it against my own cheek.

"That is a very fine color," Walter said as he crowded in to hold it to feel it for himself. "You have a very fine eye, Elizabeth."

I saw what he was doing and put my arm around the small of her back and guided her over to a stand of white and yellow blankets. "Look! This one has a bunny rabbit image sewn onto it."

Elizabeth cooed. "Isn't that adorable?"

"Sure," Walter said, "if the infant doesn't wake in the night to find a monstrous rabbit atop him."

Elizabeth frowned and shook her head. "Is that how you were as a child? Afraid of bunny rabbits?"

I snickered and said, "I shall get this blanket as protection, so the child should have no fear of Walter attacking it in its sleep."

"Well then," Walter said, "I shall get the matching pillow over here."

We exchanged our coin and moved onto the next stall.

I pointed further down the walkway and said, "I think the woodcrafters are on the far side of the mall. I think I shall head that way to find a cradle for the child."

"Then I shall join you," Walter said. "Before you find a cradle shaped like a bear's head."

We barely took five paces before turning to see Elizabeth left behind.

"Are you coming?" I asked.

"I don't know," she replied. "Am I invited?"

"Of course, darling."

"Darling?" Walter asked.

"Watch and learn," I said, "and I will show you how to woo a girl, should you ever get another opportunity."

Walter laughed as he waved me off. "I think I can do the wooing just fine."

There were three woodcrafters conveniently near each other. While I entered the first stall and started looking at their many wares, Walter skipped to the second one to look on his own. Elizabeth was more interested in the flowers and plants of a nearby stall.

I must admit that I have never spent much time looking at finely crafted wood. Our home was modestly furnished with hand-me-downs from Lord Leatherby. This craftsman must be very good. The chest of drawers near the entrance shone like a finely glazed porcelain vase. Beyond the drawers I found an array of kitchen items, but in the back corner I found a solitary cradle. I called out, "Elizabeth! I found one!"

I heard Walter call out, "I found one too!"

I lifted the cradle and carried it to the entrance, then held it aloft and yelled, "You must come see this, Elizabeth! The craftsmanship is extraordinary!"

"You should see this one!" Walter responded. "It's far too big and sturdy to hold aloft like that diminutive piece!"

Elizabeth emerged from the flower stall and rolled her eyes. "Will you two never grow up?"

"Never!" Walter replied. "Not if you forsake me for the gardener's son!"

She rolled her eyes again and said, "The small cradle will do for a child of such humble origins."

Walter would not quit after Elizabeth had selected the cradle which I found. He raised a small hobby horse and said, "This is perfect!"

Elizabeth laughed and said, "Don't you think that will be a bit large for a newborn?"

"He'll grow...eventually."

"What if he's a girl?"

Walter looked defeated and put the toy back.

I shrugged at him and said, "Better luck next time. It's getting late and we should head back home."

"Before you go," he said quietly, "I would like a chance to speak with you."

I judged from his voice that this was to be a private conversation, so I strolled out beyond the stalls, out of earshot.

"I went to our pond, hoping to run into you actually, but instead I found your father there. Did you know that he knew about our pond?"

"I did not, but then, he is the groundskeeper, and it would make sense that he would know every feature of the property. Besides, it's not really our pond, is it?"

"No," Walter continued, "but he was there, I guess, for much the same reasons we would go there. I found him talking to a turtle at the edge of the pond. The turtle seemed strangely attentive."

"That was Uncle Horatio," I said, "who had the great misfortune of crossing a witch many years ago."

"I'm being serious."

"Apologies," I said with a bow of my head. "Please continue."

"As I was saying, your father was talking to this turtle. He expressed his love for his wife and then he said the strangest thing. He said that he has always loved you as his own son, but that he feared he may be losing you to Lord Leatherby. Then, he argued back and forth with himself that you were his son, and it was unfair to ever consider you otherwise."

I didn't bother to hide my amusement. "My father is many things, but indecisive is not one of them. He has a powerful temper, a family trait that he has passed on to me. He is probably concerned that this whole betrothal may be losing me to Lord Leatherby. I should ease his concerns."

"You know him best. Do you think our antics today will bear the fruit you had hoped for?"

"We shall see." I gripped his arm and bade him farewell.

I worried at first that we may have overplayed our hands, but gossip soon spread of the two young dolts vying for the fair maiden's attention, and if nothing else comes from it, George and Agnes will have a new rocker for their baby.

The sun had not quite set by the time we had returned to the manor, but it was naught but an orange glow in the western sky. Winston took our horses, still giving me the evil eye as I offered Elizabeth my arm so I could escort her home. All in all, I think we played a successful campaign today. We established ourselves as a couple in town and we managed to show some conflict between myself and Walter. With Agnes and her friends there at the tavern, I have no doubt that word of our exploits will eventually reach both Lord Leatherby and Lord Chamberlain.

On the porch of the door, she asked, "Are you sure we

should be doing this? I feel as though we are playing with people's emotions."

"Are you not the one who started this whole mess when you told your father that the betrothal ring was from me? Do you now wish to toy with my emotions?"

She sighed and shook her head.

I had barely cracked the door open for her when I heard my father's voice from within. We both froze in place to listen.

"Why?" my father shouted, and when I say shouted, I mean with the force and authority of a man speaking to a servant. "After all this time, how do you now accept this union, and don't you try to deny it. I see it in your face that you approve. Do you not see how inappropriate this appears to others? Have you no consideration for the consequences? Have you no concern for our safety?"

Elizabeth and I looked at each other and shrugged. No matter how preposterous I thought our union might be, I had no idea how it could possibly put our safety in jeopardy.

"Those were tumultuous times, Fernando."

"Yes, Walter, they were."

Elizabeth and I both covered our mouths, lest our gasps alert everyone to our presence.

"But," Lord Leatherby continued, "they were so long ago. Has not enough time passed?"

"For you maybe, your head would not be on the chopping block."

"I would not let anything happen to you. We have been through too much together. You even stole Luisa from me, yet we still remain friends through it all."

"You were married! I didn't steal her from you. I rescued her from a lecherous satyr!"

Leatherby bellowed in laughter. "Truer words about my character, you have never said, but let me remind you that I was not yet married. I was only promised to a woman by my father."

"Have you told that lie so often now that you have begun to believe it yourself?"

I heard only silence from Lord Leatherby.

"If," my father continued, "as you have suggested, enough time has passed, then we must show that not only is this a good match, but that no better match exists in all of England."

Lord Leatherby grunted, something that usually indicated he was thinking. "What do you propose?"

"Invite more suitors for your daughter's hand. Let us see if she is serious about my son and let the rest of the realm see if he is the best match for her."

"Might we also let them know whose son he really is?"

"No!" my father snapped. "We will not broach that subject!"

I pushed the door open and said, rather loudly, "Thank you for a wonderful day, Elizabeth. I shall sleep tonight with dreams of seeing you again tomorrow."

Chapter Four

I woke up feeling quite accomplished after yesterday's escapades and had slept sounder than I could recall in quite some time. I thought I would ask Elizabeth to give me another riding lesson, perhaps to her favorite spot this time, but as I approached the manor, I saw something most unexpected.

Lord Leatherby stood before the manor, speaking with the very wood craftsman that had sold me the cradle. He should have delivered it directly to Agnes' home, but right now he was backing away with his hat in his hands and his head bowed.

I considered hailing him, but something in his demeanor suggested that this might not be the best time. A convenient copse proved an adequate hiding place as he quietly slipped away and back towards the stables where he had left his cart.

I didn't know what this meant, but I felt it in my bones that this was something that I should know about, yet I didn't feel like questioning Leatherby directly would yield the answers I desired.

I tried backing away from the manor, but it was too late. Lord Leatherby had already seen me and was hailing me. I could not deduce, from his expression, what might be on his mind.

"Hector, my dear boy, how are things?"

"Fine, sir. Thank you for asking. I was hoping to ride with Elizabeth again today."

"How was your day yesterday? Did you and Elizabeth do anything special?"

I fully expected rumors of our betrothal to circulate around the town, and I expected Walter's pledge to also hit the rumor mill, but Leatherby was fishing for something. "I suppose you must mean us running into Walter Chamberlain. It's a small town, and we were bound to run into him, eventually."

"I heard about that," he said, looking confused and somewhat unsatisfied with my answers. "I was thinking of something between you and Elizabeth."

Now it was my turn to look confused. "I have admitted to her that my riding prowess was greatly exaggerated, but she proved to be a patient teacher."

"You know you can tell me anything. I have a great deal

of respect for honesty and truth. In fact, you might say that I can't abide dishonesty, especially in personal matters. Such treachery always leaves a bad taste in my mouth. Are you sure there is nothing that you'd like to tell me?"

I hid my true feelings about his honesty, having recently learned about his deceit regarding his marriage while in Spain. He either knew or suspected something, but I wasn't about to start confessing everything I knew until I had an inkling about what he wanted to hear. I had to think fast. He must have learned the truth about our fake engagement, but I can't admit to such a scheme after his claim about respecting honesty. I had to craft a sincerely honest, yet crafty statement. "I am quite sure, Lord Leatherby, that there is nothing that I wish to tell you."

Disappointment clouded his face, and I thought that maybe I caught a hint of anger as he turned to return inside.

"I'll tell Elizabeth to meet you at the stables."

He closed the door behind him before I could answer.

According to Walter's somewhat colorful depiction, his father had spouted steam from his ears as he expressed his rage. He insisted that Lord Chamberlain's face was as red as an apple, and he had spittle dripping from his lips.

"Why," he shouted to Walter, "must I hear these stories from commoners? Why were they even allowed to witness you fawning over that... that... that Leatherby girl? Have I taught you nothing?"

"Her name is Elizabeth."

"Do not use that name in my household."

"I will use it. Elizabeth! Elizabeth! Elizabeth! You should try using it as well."

I have no doubt that Walter had exaggerated his part in the conversation with his father, especially how forcefully he stood up to his father, but I am also sure that the gist of it is how it happened.

"Have I not told you before how you cannot be with that girl?"

"No, Father. You have not told me HOW I cannot be with her. I love her and can't imagine HOW I could *not* be with her. Neither have you told me WHY I cannot be with her, and I can't think of a single reason."

As Walter described it to me, this was the part where smoke billowed up from his father's collar. "You have no choice. This match cannot be. I forbid it."

"You forbid it? Or WHAT?!?"

That was when Walter stormed out of the room, but he never left the manor.

Winston was reluctant to ready a horse for me without Elizabeth having ordered him to do so. I told him that she would be here shortly, but he still proceeded to move along at a sloth's pace. I don't know that I blamed his reticence, but I couldn't stand there and watch him. Nor could I pretend that I was the lord of the manor and bark out orders to him, so I chose to wait outside by the gate.

It wasn't long before Elizabeth came along. "Good morning," she said with a nervous edge to her voice, "at least I hope it is a good morning. Is Winston preparing the horses?"

"Barely," I replied, "but I'm sure he'll have them ready for us now that he has heard the voice of his mistress."

She looked suitably confused.

"Never mind that," I said. "I just had the strangest conversation with your father."

"You too? Did he ask you if you had something special you wanted to share with him?"

"Not in so many words, but he certainly was fishing for something."

Winston brought out her mount and offered her a hand to climb it.

"I shouldn't let it bother you," she said. "He never was very accomplished at small talk."

"It felt more like an interrogation."

She nodded her head and admitted, "As did he just now with me. I wonder what brought that on?"

"The woodcrafter who had sold us the cradle had been here speaking with him and was just leaving as I approached. I heard nothing of what was said between them, but it was immediately after his departure that your father spoke with me."

"So, he knows we were together, but he already knew that! Does he resent our buying a gift for Agnes?"

"I can't believe that. His interest was keen on the two of us, so I don't believe his anger was aimed at George and Agnes. It must be something else. Perhaps it was Walter's declaration of love that has set his pants on fire."

She just shrugged and nodded towards the other horse.

Our ride revealed nothing new for our situation, save that I was showing some slight improvement in my ability to remain in the saddle. We found little to talk about and rode silently out to a fork in the river that Elizabeth thought would have lifted our spirits some, but the odd conversations that we had each undergone with her father followed us around like a drizzling cloud.

We remained on our mounts as they gladly sipped the cool, refreshing water. Even the idyllic scene did nothing to lift the mood I now found myself entwined in.

Elizabeth sighed and said, "I'm sorry, Hector. I know I promised to give you more riding instructions, but I really don't think I feel like riding this morning."

"I understand. I can't stop thinking about what your father had asked me."

She nodded her agreement. "And I can't stop thinking about what the wood carver could have possibly said to set this off."

"Should we just head back?"

She pulled her horse around, needing to supply no further response. As we rode past my parents' cottage, we saw Lord Leatherby leaving with a marked scowl on his face.

Elizabeth's voice was faint and airy as she asked, "Father? Is something amiss?"

"How can you ask that?" he growled, then he pointed at me and continued, "You know better than any of us how stubborn your father can be. He is not taking this well and I suggest you tell him the truth sooner than later."

Elizabeth and I shared a confused glance.

Lord Leatherby balled his fists together and shook them at his side as he growled, "I hope you have enjoyed yourselves, because the fun and games may be over. We've agreed to move up your wedding to the soonest date possible."

My jaw fell open as Elizabeth asked, "You what?"

"You will have a small, intimate wedding. I had always imagined a large gathering with all the pomp I felt you deserved, but we mustn't waste time with invitations and such. We'll hold it here and have all the preparations ready by mid-month."

"What?" she ratcheted her voice up a bit. "Have we no say in this?"

He bounced his finger between the two of us and barked, "I think you've said and done just about all you could in this matter. We'll be handling things from here on."

Lord Leatherby stormed off towards the manor and Elizabeth turned to me and cried, "And what of you? Have you nothing to say?"

I shook my head slowly. I doubt there were many times in my life that I was so utterly speechless. I slid off my horse and said, "I have no idea what is going on here, but I'm going to speak to my father to see if I can get to the bottom of this."

"Shall I go in with you? I don't believe I wish any further conversations with my father."

"No," I said softly as I handed her the reins to my mount.

"I don't know what has transpired between our fathers, but I have a feeling that much yelling will be involved, and you don't need to be present for that."

"You think your father would raise his voice in my presence?"

"We've both heard how he has spoken to your father as of late. I don't suppose your being with me will change that any, but I agree that you might do well to avoid your father for a while. I am sorry that I am abandoning you like this."

The cottage was deadly quiet even as I put my hand on the door. I wondered if perhaps my mother was not present, but as I pushed the door, I saw her sitting at the family table brushing tears from her cheeks. I barely entered the room and quietly closed the door behind me.

"And there he is," my father said sarcastically. He danced around the room flailing his arms and continued, "Do you see him, Luisa? Does he not bring pride to your bosom? How could you have brought such a conniving scoundrel into this world? He stood in this very room and swore that he has done nothing to bring shame upon our family. Now look what your son has done!"

"Fernando..."

He stopped gyrating long enough to face me. "What say you, son? You gave us your oath that you have done nothing to dishonor my name!"

"Truly father, I remember taking no such oath, but all the

same, I have done nothing to bring shame upon our family."

"No, no, no!" he barked. "You are no longer part of OUR family. You have set out to start a family of your own! After I strictly forbid you to see that girl!"

"Fernando!" my mother cried out. "Tell me you did no such thing!"

"Keep out of this Luisa. This is between me and your son."

"*My son?*" she said with a distinct sternness that told me she still had plenty more in reserve. "That is the third time you have called him *my son*. You listen to me, Fernando Rodrigo Castillo De la Roca. You were no saint at his age. I have no doubt that you may have left a bastard child or two behind when we left Spain."

"Luisa!"

"Father? Mother? What is this about?"

"What is this about?" he asked, dripping with sarcasm. "What do you think this is about? It's time for you to tell the truth!"

That is what Lord Leatherby had said, but I knew not what truth they wished to hear.

"Don't be afraid," my mother said. "Your father may yell and scream like a raving lunatic and I wouldn't be surprised if he begins to foam at the mouth even..."

"Luisa!"

"But he still loves you. We both do. We just want you to know that you can trust us, no matter what news you have for us."

"Mother, I love you both as well, but I do not know what you want to hear. The world seems to have gone mad overnight. First Lord Leatherby interrogates me, and now the two of you. Over what? I do not know."

"Fine," my father said. "If you will not be forthcoming on your own, then I will ask you more directly. What did you do yesterday?"

"I went to town with Elizabeth. She is teaching me to be a better horse rider."

"And what did you do in town?"

"We went to the tavern for something to eat."

My father eyed me suspiciously and paced as he continued his interrogation. "That was all?"

"No. We met some friends there. Walter, er, Master Chamberlain was there, as were a couple of farmers that we know."

"Did you go anywhere else?"

"I do not know what you want to hear, father, but we didn't leave the town until near sunset. Where else is there to go and still get back by sundown?"

"Did you not go to the market?"

"Oh, yes! Of course! We went to the market and did some shopping. Lord Leatherby had given me some spending money."

"And what did you buy?"

"Elizabeth bought some scarves as I recall..."

My father stopped pacing and spat out, "You bought a cradle and baby toys, did you not? Did you think nobody would notice? Did you really think nobody could piece the clues together?"

I finally saw what had him so worked up, and chuckled briefly, which caught him by surprise, but it was followed by a full-fledged laugh erupting from my belly. "Is that what you have done? You've learned of some purchases that we made and without any consideration for our cause or reason, you somehow twisted it up until you assume that Elizabeth and I..."

"This is no joking matter."

"It most certainly is! You have made quite an astounding leap to a preposterous conclusion, and I find it quite amusing."

"Enlighten me then. Tell me the grand purpose behind your mad shopping spree."

"No. I don't believe I will. You are deserving of no explanation. I told you that I had not dishonored this family, but you chose not to believe me."

His tirade faded and left him speechless, causing my mother to laugh softly.

"Now," I said calmly, "if you'll excuse me, I think I shall go tell Elizabeth what nonsense you and her father have cooked up, especially since it is mostly at her expense."

I left as quietly as I had entered.

I wasn't sure where Elizabeth might go to find solace, but I was pretty sure it wouldn't be the main house. When I left her, I had left her with my horse, so I should probably start looking for her at the stable house.

"Hector!"

I closed my eyes and shook my head slowly. That was the voice of one very upset Isabel.

"Hector! I want a word with you!"

I kept walking towards the stables. "I have no time for this."

"For *this*?" she shrieked. "You will make time for *me* and then you will explain *this.*"

"When I said that I had not time for *this*, I meant quite specifically that I have no time for *you.*"

She screeched and started to run towards me. I was still aiming for the stables, but she was clearly on an intercept path. I stopped and turned towards her, holding up my palms and shouted, "Stop! I have more important matters to deal with than your unrequited crush upon me."

She did not stop, but reached me and planted a very hard slap upon my left cheek. "How could you! We were meant to be together, and you have hitched your wagon to that... that..."

"Isabel! She is the lady of the house, and you will not use slurs against her!"

"Slurs? What harm would slurs do upon her when the world learns that she carries your child?"

I shook my head slowly. "Do not believe everything you hear. I am sorry that you feel so deeply about this, but I really must find her. She does not know of these ridiculous accusations."

"You mean it's not true? Is there still a chance for us?"

"Isabel. I have told you over and over that there is no chance for us. As to the merit of the rumors, no, they are not true, but let's just keep that to ourselves until I find Elizabeth."

"Why the secret?"

"Because, and I think you will appreciate this, I do not want to marry her and I must find some scheme to get out of it, but keep that to yourself also."

"So, you do love me, and there is a chance for us!"

I sighed. "Yes, Isabel, but there is only a chance for us if you keep my secret. Tell no one, or we are finished."

I could already see the daydreams in her eyes as she started walking back to the manor, but then she turned and said, "Master Walter sent word that he wishes to speak to you."

"At Chamberlain Hall?"

She shrugged and asked, "Is that your secret place?"

I closed my eyes again, wondering what news he had. "Did he say when?"

She shrugged again and turned back for the manor.

"Thank you, Isabel."

I didn't know when Walter would be at the pond, but I was so close to the stables now, I might as well catch Elizabeth first. She was still sitting on her horse outside the stable when I arrived.

"Elizabeth, are you still riding?"

"I don't know. I know not where to go, but I don't wish to return home just yet."

"I may have someplace to go, if Winston would bring my mount out to me again."

"You may tell him that yourself." She said with a measure of mirth in her voice.

"I heard," Winston said, followed by the sound of the saddle being slapped upon Sandy's back again.

"Where are we headed?" Elizabeth asked.

"The pond," I said as Winston handed me the reins. "Someone wishes to meet us there."

I mounted Sandy and guided her to the path that would take us out to the pond.

"Are you going to tell me what your father had to say?"

"I don't want to. That is, you won't like it, but I think I must."

Silence followed as I tried to measure my words, until she pulled up alongside me and asked, "Do you plan to make me guess?"

I slowed Sandy so I could more easily watch her expression as I explained, "There is no easy way to put this. Your father and my father learned that we purchased a baby cradle and concluded that you are carrying my child."

Her first reaction was a mixture of horror and surprise, then confusion took over. "So, they plan to move up our wedding. I guess that's better than sentencing me to a convent."

"A convent? Would he do that?"

"That is what they do with unchaste noble-born women."

I scowled at the thought. "I was trying to think of a way out and thought that maybe if I just refused to accept the baby, your father would see how unfit I was to be your husband."

"He would, and then he would send me to the convent and probably banish you from the property."

I sighed. "Then my actions would have brought the shame

onto my family, for which I have already been accused."

"What if it was I who vowed to never marry you? What if I claimed you were not taking fatherhood seriously, and I had no desire to be wed to you forever?"

"Would that not have the same result? Me banned and you in the convent?"

"Perhaps," she said. "What if I merely suggest that I could do better and that I wished to have more suitors?"

"That could work if he is willing to gather suitors for you with the utmost haste. If he still wishes to send you to the convent, we could always tell him the truth."

As we neared the pond, Elizabeth pointed and asked, "Is that Walter?"

"Yes. My message was to meet him at our secret place."

"What if we tell my father that it is Walter's baby?"

"That is an option, but I think we would need to discuss it with Walter first. He is your true betrothed, but he may not want you when he learns you are no longer chaste."

I paid for my cheeky remark when she slapped her whip across my thigh and rushed forward to the pond.

I took a more leisurely pace, rubbing my thigh and allowing time for them to hold each other, but it would seem that she was already relaying what I had told her.

"Oh, they did," he said, "did they? Your father and Hector's? It would seem that I may have had a similar encounter with my own father. We had already had a small quarrel before I had come to town, and he fortunately had left me to my own devices when I had returned home last evening, but this morning, upon first seeing me, he lit into a rage."

I must say that Walter is a very good storyteller, and the telling of his story completely enveloped me as if I were there. I shall endeavor to transcribe it for this recording, as best as I can in the same sequence that it happened.

"I told you," Lord Chamberlain growled at Walter, "to stay away from the Leatherby girl! I have said so repeatedly, but I have reports now that you have been seen together in the town square."

"So, you have spies following me now?"

"No," he replied, "nothing so tawdry as that, but people do tell me what happens when they believe it to be significant."

"And do you pay them for their information?"

Lord Chamberlain shrugged and admitted, "I might compensate them for their trouble."

"There's a name for that," Walter said. "N o, a moment please, there are *two* names for that. The first is *rumor*, for that is all they have shared with you, and the second is *story*, for that is apparently all it takes for some peasant to come to you for a coin. And you share it with them like some gullible half-wit eager to swallow any tale that they feed to you."

"You cannot speak to me like that," he ratcheted up his voice and stood directly in Walter's face. "Not this time, not after what you have done."

"What have I done?" Walter asked. "What should make these rumors so different?"

"Must I spell it out? You certainly weren't concerned

about hiding her condition from the town."

"Her condition? What are you talking about, Father?"

"You don't get to call me father, not this time. I shouldn't be surprised anymore when the Leatherby blood shows itself to be so brazenly lecherous."

Walter closed the small distance between them by half and screamed directly in Lord Chamberlain's face, "Do not speak of her that way!"

"I will speak of her any way that I wish!" Lord Chamberlain looked as if he might strike Walter at any moment, but instead, he turned and stormed out of the room mumbling, "But I wasn't speaking of her."

Walter shrugged at the end of his tale. "I know not what he meant by that, but if either of you do, please share."

I also shrugged.

Walter's face had resonated the anger of his story throughout the telling, but after saying the last words that he had heard, he looked perplexed. I, on the other hand, began to see the meaning behind his father's words and looked back and forth between Elizabeth and Walter, then shook my head to clear the image that was forming.

"What is it?" Elizabeth asked. "Do you see some hidden meaning behind Lord Chamberlain's outburst?"

I saw no familial resemblance between the two of them and could not share with them that Lord Chamberlain suspected that Walter was Lord Leatherby's son. The Earl of

Leatherby was Lord Walter Leatherby the third. Has nobody ever questioned why Lord Chamberlain's son would be named after Lord Leatherby? Or why Lord Leatherby was chosen as his God Father in the first place? Was it to hide some secret scandal? Lord Chamberlain must have pieced it together. I closed my eyes and tried to force the image from my mind. That was the exact same kind of conjecture that led them to believe Elizabeth was with child.

"What is it?" Walter echoed Elizabeth. "You look as though you have figured something out."

"Nothing," I lied. "It would seem that your father took a little harmless rumor, the same as Lord Leatherby and my father had done, and turned it into a scandal."

"What rumor?" he asked.

"That the three of us were seen purchasing a baby cradle, which obviously must mean that Elizabeth is with child."

Walter started to laugh, but Elizabeth cried, "It's not funny! Why does everybody laugh at something that tarnishes my virtue?"

"I am sorry," Walter said. "I do not laugh at your situation, only at how dull witted all of our fathers can be. We must do something. We must teach them a lesson that they will never forget."

"Yes!" Elizabeth sparkled as she spoke, "We thought that we would allow them to continue believing that I was with child, but I would reject Hector so my father would have no choice but to accept you as my husband!"

"That's your plan?" Walter asked. "I thought you didn't wish to tarnish your virtue."

Elizabeth frowned. "As long as we are married, then do

not the ends not justify the means?"

"Perhaps," I said, "that might be enough for your father, but I don't think Lord Chamberlain will be so easily satisfied."

"What do you suggest?" Walter asked.

"I don't know yet, but let me think about it."

"Well, you'd better hurry," Elizabeth whined, "or we'll be married, and it will all be over."

"I won't let that happen."

Walter said his goodbyes, leaving Elizabeth and me to return the horses to the stables.

"Are we overreacting?" Elizabeth asked. "I mean, how bad would it be if we simply told my father the truth?"

"We can never divulge the secret of Agnes marriage to George, at least as long as this stupid feud persists."

"You're correct," she admitted, "of course, but we could simply say that the cradle was for Agnes."

"We could, and your father would have a laugh, but what lesson would he learn? He would still think that you and I are to be wed. No, I think we must use this situation to our advantage."

"So, you propose that we continue to let my father believe I am with child?"

"For now."

A small sinister smile stretched across her face as she asked, "And you still want to abandon me in my time of need?"

"That would certainly turn him against me."

We rounded a small stand of apple trees and saw the stables at the end of the road, with Lord Leatherby speaking with Winston.

"Look," Elizabeth said as she pointed to the stables, "There's my father. What do you plan to say?"

"I don't know, yet, what I will say. Do you think he is waiting for us?"

"It seems so."

Lord Leatherby raised his hand and hailed us. "Elizabeth! Hector! I'm glad I could run into you. I think it's time for us to talk."

A small groan escaped from Elizabeth's throat just before we were within earshot of him.

Leatherby helped Elizabeth down from her mount and watched me clumsily dismount mine. In truth, I was in far more need of assistance than she was, but he did the chivalrous thing, especially considering her supposed condition.

He smiled pleasantly as he asked, "How was your ride?" It was an obvious attempt at small talk, and judging from his sideways glances towards Winston, I believe he was only waiting for some privacy with us.

As we started up the path to the manor, he said, "I may have been a bit presumptuous with you this morning, but I feel strongly that we shouldn't waste a moment before we start you off on your new life as man and wife."

"Lord Leatherby, I understand how you might feel a need for such haste in this matter, but I've started to question if this is the right course of action."

"In this matter?" he asked, "Under the current circumstances, what other course of action could there be?"

"Well, you already know that the other Lords would oppose my being wed to Lady Elizabeth, and they would stand against you if that were to happen."

"Don't worry about me," he said with a puff of his breast, "I'll handle the other lords."

"All of them? When they come here to question my suitability, or rather my lack thereof, to be her husband? They will want to know why you would settle upon me, a gardener's son, and why you would do so with such haste."

"You think they will find out your secret?"

I pounded my fist into my other palm and declared, "I'm sure of it. And they will ask why you hadn't interviewed more suitors."

"They won't dare question my judgment. Especially not after I testify to the love I have seen between the two of you; for years even!"

"But they would. If you could just show them one or two other suitors and still claim that I was the best available, I'm sure they would have no choice but to see the reason in your acceptance of me."

"Why would you even suggest I interview more suitors? Do you not think this would be a great opportunity for you?"

"For me, perhaps, but I have no dowry…"

He raised his palms and said, "Pish posh. I have no need for a dowry from you."

"But Elizabeth does! She needs not the money, but marrying a pauper would be a grave insult to her honor."

"Then I will give you the money. I already told you that it was time for you to draw a salary from the estate. Your finances will never be a concern."

I raised my voice and tried to sound irritated. "You will pay me to marry her? How am I supposed to shoulder that insult?"

Leatherby stopped walking and turned to me. "What are you hiding? These are just excuses that you make. Why do you not wish to go through with a wedding?"

"I do not feel that I would be a fit father. She needs someone who would be a proper provider but can also show the spine required to raise a child."

Leatherby furrowed his eyebrows and growled, "You do not think you would be a fit father? Is that what you say? It's a bit late for that, don't you think?"

I saw my chance, but I hated myself already for what I was about to say. "I'm young. I may find that I still have many prospects out in the world; prospects that won't be available to me if I'm saddled with a child."

I may have pushed too hard. He curled his hand into a fist and would no doubt have hit me had Elizabeth not stepped between us.

"Father, I do not want a man who must be forced to marry me. It would seem that Hector is not the man I thought he was. I would not want to be tied to a sniveling coward for the rest of my days, so if Hector is not the right man, then perhaps the right man is still out there, if we just look for him."

Chapter Five

Leatherby was no genius by any account, but neither was he the sort of man to play the fool and be easily manipulated by others. Were it not for Elizabeth's rather harsh comments upon my character, I would either have ended up married to her, or in the stockades. He did, however, listen to her and come sunrise. He sent a post out for a matchmaker of some renown.

If my own opinion mattered for much, I would say this energetic entrepreneur that Leatherby sent for was a fiendishly clever man, with a magical gift for words, but I would still call him a charlatan. Being that I consider myself somewhat clever, I liked the man anyway, at least on some level, or maybe I was just impressed by his reputation.

Regardless of my personal feelings towards the man, I won't be the one to call him out. I am hopeful that his influence will open a door for Elizabeth to entertain more suitors, which, if everything goes to my plan, would include Walter.

Having Elizabeth declare her disdain for me may have helped our endeavor to have Lord Leatherby consider Walter among any of other suitors brought to light by the matchmaker, but it also distanced me from the process, making it more challenging for me to maintain any sort of control on the situation. If I was to succeed, and thereby the scheme which I had put into motion, there could be no question that everything had to take place more or less on schedule. That would require me to remain involved at least a while longer. I went to the manor to beg a word with Lord Leatherby.

He made me wait near the entrance, not even far enough to remove my coat and hat. Clearly, I had lost his favor. When he finally deigned to see me, he had someone show me into the main hall where he stood next to the large throne that still remained from before the unification under a single high king. He looked me up and down and said as irreverently as he could possibly muster, "What do you want?"

"Lord Leatherby," I saw how things were with him and reverted back to addressing him more formally again, "It occurred to me that until you actually acquire more suitors for Elizabeth, perhaps we should continue to maintain some sort of facade that she and I are still together. After all, I am still your plan B, or maybe plan C or D, but for us to be apart like this might draw unwarranted attention to the manor."

He huffed and went to the mantle where he made a great show of examining the shine on one of his tournament cups, "Do you really think that I am so easily manipulated?"

"No Sir."

"You think you can worm your way back into my daughter's good graces?"

"No matter what transpires," I said, "I will always want what is best for Elizabeth, even if that does not end up being me." In this, I was entirely sincere.

He moved on from the mantle to a sword which hung from the wall. He removed it and looked down the length of it, verifying its flatness, I think. I don't know if this act was meant as a veiled threat to me, but it was somewhat unsettling. He replaced the sword on the wall and grumbled, "Very well, if she agrees, but ONLY if she agrees, and I see no reason why she would agree to ever be associated with the likes of you again."

Elizabeth saw me leaving the main hall and asked, "What are you doing here? Is there a problem?"

I led her out the front door so we could speak more freely. "Everything is fine. I spoke with your father and we agreed to maintain some semblance that nothing has changed, but you must agree to him that you are willing to carry on this charade. I can't control things while being exiled from our little circle."

She giggled and said, "I gather you did not tell him that."

"Oh no, but I stressed that in any eventuality, I would still be the last resort for your groom, so we should not appear to have fallen out."

"Father has sent for a matchmaker. I'm not keen on the idea."

"It's all according to plan. Once the matchmaker introduces you to another suitor with better credentials than I have, we'll bring Walter in. Do not forget that your father is Walter's godfather."

"Eeeew," she laughed, "that makes him my godbrother."

I couldn't completely suppress a small chuckle. "Never the less, you must draft a letter to him explaining that a matchmaker has been summoned to find a suitable groom for you."

"Should I include code so he knows it's part of your plan?"

"No. We'll tell him ourselves. Besides, I fully expect Lord Chamberlain to intercept the message. I hope this will put him at ease, since he seems so highly agitated about the two of you being together."

The hardest part about the plans I had set in motion for Lord Chamberlain was waiting to learn the results. Fearing that a scene might erupt between Isabel and myself if she were to see me with Elizabeth, which might ultimately delay her from completing the task we were about to give her, I kept my distance while Elizabeth gave Isabel the note and sent her to Walter, knowing full well that it would first be read by Lord Chamberlain. We knew it would take a while, but as with all things, waiting makes it seem longer.

We considered doing something while we waited, but a horse ride seemed to increase our risk of missing Isabel's return. Even a stroll around the grounds could lose sight of the gate when she returned.

We waited in Elizabeth's room. It may not be the most seemly thing for a gentleman to be in a young lady's room, but we were engaged to be married and it seemed the least likely place to run into her father. We left the door ajar as a precaution.

I tried to sit and meditate over the many turns our endeavors had taken that were not part of my plan. What was it about affairs of the heart that introduced so much unpredictability?

Elizabeth chose to pace the room, which made my contemplation doubly hard, especially when she chose to pause and ask a question, "What if something happens to her?"

"What's going to happen to her on this trip that hasn't happened on the dozens of other times you've sent her?"

Elizabeth bit her lower lip and continued her pacing, but it was a repeatable cycle where she would pace a while, ask some inane question, and continue pacing after I soothed her concerns with an equally vacuous response.

Finally, Isabel arrived, breathing heavily. Good girl, she ran. Before she could even see me, or at least, before she could respond to my presence, Elizabeth leaped upon the poor girl.

"How was it? Who did you give it to?"

Isabel took half a step back from Elizabeth and closed the door. She eyed me suspiciously as she continued to catch her breath. "A moment Lady Elizabeth. I needs some air."

Elizabeth returned to pacing, as if she were counting off the moments it took for Isabel to resume normal breathing.

Isabel cocked her head towards me and asked, "Is this something you want me to say in front of him?"

"Yes! Yes!" Elizabeth said. "Who did you give it to?"

"Well, I told them at the gate that the note was for Master Walter, but before you know it, Lord Chamberlain himself comes to the gate to take it personally. 'I will take care of this,' Lord Chamberlain said to me. 'I will be sure to place it in my son's hands personally.' Then he snatched it from me and walked off."

"What was his demeanor?" I asked from my chair.

"Lord Chamberlain was all smiles and friendly like, but it was kind of a sinister smile, like he had something up his sleeve, if you know what I mean."

I nodded my head. "I know precisely what you mean. Was that when you started running back to give us the news?"

Isabel shook her head. "No. Actually, I had run there too, so I hung out to catch my breath with them. That was just an excuse, of course. I saw Lord Chamberlain open the note before he had even reached the hall door."

I stood and crossed the room to Isabel. "Did he seem happy after reading the note?"

"No. He wasn't happy, but he wasn't angry neither."

I glanced over to Elizabeth, who clearly did not understand his reaction any better than I.

"What was it?" Isabel asked. "In the letter?"

Elizabeth took Isabel's hands in her own. "It was a letter to tell him that I am pursuing other marriage proposals to consider against Hector's."

Isabel's eyes widened. "You mean you two don't really want to be married?"

Elizabeth and I both shook our heads, still unsure why the news hadn't delighted Chamberlain.

A slight twinkle shone in Isabel's eye.

"Was there anything else?" Elizabeth asked.

"Yes. On my way off the property, Master Walter caught up with me and asked me to deliver a message to you." As she spoke, she pointed to me.

"He said to tell you that his father had just sent some men out to intercept someone. He didn't catch the name, but that was right after he took the letter from me. Then Master Walter asked that you stand by. He should have more news for you when they catch whoever it was and for you to meet him at your regular place. You have a regular place? I thought you hated each other."

"No," I said, "we don't hate each other. Did he happen to mention when he wants to meet us?"

Isabel shook her head. "He didn't give an exact time, but he said he'll let you know."

"Thank you," Elizabeth said, "that will be all."

Isabel gave me a winsome smile as she turned to leave the room.

Elizabeth raised her eyebrows and asked, "Is there something going on between you two?"

"Just from the one of us, I'm afraid. Let's focus on the

plan. Why would Lord Chamberlain want to intercept the matchmaker?"

"Perhaps he thought his son's future too risky to leave up to a stranger's opinion and means to sway the man's search away from Walter."

"Perhaps, but while I do not fear any evil plot from Lord Chamberlain, I can see his plan interfering with our own. I shall go meet with Walter when the time comes."

Elizabeth saw me to the front door, but before I could leave, we saw Agnes coming up the steps.

"Agnes!" Elizabeth said a little too excitedly, "should you be walking this far in your condition?"

"Begging your pardon, mi Lady, but I have a message for you. Master..."

Before she could complete her message, Lord Leatherby bellowed from inside, "Who is it? Do we have a visitor?" He came to the door and saw Agnes on the steps but said nothing.

She curtsied to Leatherby and said, "Forgive me for using the front entrance, but I saw Lady Elizabeth just leaving and wanted to thank her for the fine gift that she gave me."

"You're entirely welcome," Elizabeth replied.

Leatherby grunted and disappeared back inside.

Something in Agnes' face suggested that there was more. I took her arm in mine and asked, "Can I walk you home?"

"Yes!" Elizabeth agreed. "Let us walk you home. We can

rest anytime you feel the need."

Agnes bowed her head to Elizabeth and said, "So long as we also rest when you need to, my lady."

"Can you keep a secret?" Elizabeth asked.

Agnes nodded her head profusely.

"Rumors of my condition, that you have no doubt heard, sprung solely from the act of our purchasing that cradle for you."

"No! You mean it's my fault?"

"Absolutely not!" I said. "The fault lies with certain men and their snap judgments. Now, seeing as we have left the manor behind us and we appear to be alone, was there more to your message?"

"Indeed! George wanted me to tell you to meet him at the pond."

"Not Walter?"

She leaned in closer so she could lower her voice and said, "Master Walter was given a task; ordered by his father he was. George can tell it better than I, but Lord Chamberlain intercepted a gentleman who was supposed to arrange a match for Lady Elizabeth. I didn't get all the details, but Lord Chamberlain paid the man to make a match that favored him."

"I expected as much," I said, nodding my head. "He probably tried convincing him to leave Walter out of the running. Will this silly feud ever stop interfering with people's lives?"

"I'm sure that was part of it," Agnes said, "but I think there was more. George will explain. Walter was ordered to escort the matchmaker to Leatherby House. He didn't want to do it. George said the shouting match between the two Chamberlains could have wakened the dead. That's why he asked George to meet with you and George sent me to let you know. He did tell me that Walter would take the matchmaker on a longer, more scenic route so I could have time to warn you and maybe you could get to the pond before George arrives there. He knows what's going on. I only know what he told me to tell you."

We arrived at Agnes' home and bid her a good afternoon before turning for the pond. I wished her father's farm was closer to the stables, but it wouldn't be the first time I hoofed it over there on foot.

George was indeed at the pond before us. He gave Elizabeth a quick nod of the head. "Lady Elizabeth, Hector. Walter sends his deepest apologies that he cannot be here himself."

"We know," Elizabeth said, "Agnes explained."

"I wasn't expecting you to accompany Hector, contessa."

"Come now George. It was cute when we were children, but you know I'm not Italian, nor am I a countess yet."

George smiled and said, "All the same, I don't think everything that I need to tell Hector will be pleasant for your ears."

"Oh?" she asked. "I don't think I fancy you having quite so much knowledge about our affairs that you think you know something I don't or shouldn't know."

He grimaced.

"Come on George," she said with a slightly gritty tone to her voice, "spit it out."

"Yes milady. First off, Lord Chamberlain intercepted the matchmaker that Lord Leatherby had summoned."

"We knew that," I said. "In fact, I anticipated that he would do something to guarantee that Walter would not be on the matchmaker's list of suitors."

George nodded. "Well, the Viscount did more than just that. He told the matchmaker to make up some story about you, Hector. I don't know what he's going to say, but it's supposed to sell you up real good. I think they mean to suggest that your father is not your real father."

Elizabeth sighed. "I wish I knew why Lord Chamberlain hated me so much."

"Oh, he don't hate you," George said, "he just don't want you getting together with Master Walter."

"Why on earth not?" I asked. "It would be a rise in his station."

Elizabeth suddenly whipped up her finger and pointed it directly and rather rudely in George's face. "What was that, George? I saw that! You know something! Your deception is written all over your face!"

"I heard things," George admitted. "Maybe things that Master Walter don't even know."

Elizabeth and I both waited for an explanation, but when one wasn't forthcoming, she straightened her back and put on a royal air, saying, "Your contessa demands an explanation."

"But you said that you ain't no...oh, never mind. Lord Chamberlain has it in his mind that Walter is your brother...half-brother, actually."

Elizabeth sucked in her breath so quickly, I thought she

might faint. I steadied her and said, "No. That can't be."

"I don't know what is or what isn't true," George said, "but I overheard Lord Chamberlain grumbling into his ale once, and I never told Master Walter. Please don't tell him I kept that from him."

"Of course," Elizabeth said, "your confidence is safe with us."

"Well," I said, "that certainly explains the feud between them. It might affect our strategy some too."

"What if it's true?" Elizabeth asked. She turned to me and asked, "What if my father already knew and this was why he was so eager to accept you?"

"If it is true," I said, "then I can no longer campaign for Walter to be your groom."

"What do you think?" Elizabeth asked as we left the pond. "Do you really think Walter could be my brother?"

"If Walter's mother would have had a child with your father, I don't think she would have named him after your father."

"My father is his God Father. Could that have just been a ruse so my father could have had a hand in raising him?"

"No," I said, "why would he have started the feud if Walter were his son?"

"Maybe he isn't the one who started the Feud."

That made a lot of sense. If Walter were actually a Leatherby, then Lord Chamberlain could have initiated the feud.

We reached a branch in the trail that led to my home. "I'm going to ask my parents if they know anything."

"You can't!" she gasped. "I mean, you can't just blurt it all out! Hello mother. Is my dear old friend Walter a Leatherby or a Chamberlain?"

I wrapped my arms around her as friends do. "I won't be so blunt, but I must know what they know."

My mother was kneading some bread when I entered the cottage. "Hello Mother."

"Hector! What have you been up to this morning?"

"Elizabeth and I went out to the pond."

My mother pounded the dough down on the cutting board and turned to me to ask, "Haven't the two of you gotten yourselves into enough trouble? Besides, I thought Lord Leatherby wanted you to stay away."

"We came to an agreement where I would continue to court Elizabeth in the event that he does not find a more suitable groom for her. Did you know that he has engaged a matchmaker? He should be arriving today."

"Well, you certainly are well informed."

I laughed and said, "Not about everything. I hear things. Rumors actually, but some of them can be hard to hear and are even more impossible to un-hear."

She resumed her torture on the dough and asked, "What kinds of rumors?"

"Rumors about our parents before we were born. Rumors

of things that may have occurred while Lord Leatherby and father were in Spain."

Something changed in my mother's expression. She stopped beating the dough to say, "If it's scandal you are looking for, then I suggest you ask your father, though I doubt he knows anything juicy enough to sate your morbid curiosity."

I never before had reason to doubt my mother's word, but even though she didn't actually deny knowing anything, I couldn't help feeling that she was hiding something and merely passing me off to my father so she could evade the conversation. "Very well then, I shall go ask him."

My father was tending the hedge by the stables when I found him.

"Hector! Will you be riding today? It is certainly a beautiful enough day, but I thought things between you and the Leatherbys were a bit strained of late. Will you be riding alone?"

"No, I won't be riding, and you could say we have a truce of sorts. I actually came to speak with you, Father. There has been a development."

He put aside the evil-looking tool that he was using to extract the weeds from the hedge and brushed his hands against his trousers to at least dislodge any dust before he removed his gloves. "Tell me then. What is this new development?"

"It's about the feud," I said, somewhat cautious about

being too blunt. "There are rumors about what may have gone on while you and Lord Leatherby were in Spain, and, more importantly, what may have happened upon your return?"

My father smiled and patted my back. "Rumors? Since when do you concern yourself with gossip?"

"Since I currently find myself in a mistaken arrangement to marry Elizabeth, and since the cause of that whole betrothal was the feud between Lord Leatherby and Lord Chamberlain, and…"

"What's this? How can that silly old feud be the cause of your proposing to Elizabeth?"

"For one thing, I never proposed to her. Walter Chamberlain did, but because of the feud, Elizabeth was afraid to tell her father."

My father's face grew concerned as he asked, "Walter and Elizabeth? I see."

"What do you see? Do you also know of the rumors regarding the true parentage of my friends? Rumors that may soon include me and my parentage?"

I saw something in his eyes when I mentioned the parentage of Walter. In another man, I would have taken it for fear, but my father seldom ever showed fear of anything. The suggestion that my own parentage may come into question, however, brought anger to his face.

He growled, "Who questions your parentage?"

"No one yet, but Lord Leatherby has summoned a matchmaker to find a better suitor for Elizabeth and we suspect that Lord Chamberlain has bribed the matchmaker to suggest that I am not the son of a gardener."

"Where is this charlatan? I'll teach him not to spread rumors about my family."

"He should be arriving any moment now. Walter…"

My father didn't wait for any further explanation and immediately started for the outer entrance to the Leatherby lands.

I hustled to catch up with him. "What do you intend to do?"

"Nothing pretty, I assure you."

"Father, please do not make things worse for me."

"For you?" my father yelled. "For YOU? What about me? What about your MOTHER? Will you allow this man to come into our home and besmirch your parents? Do you really think that it is all about you?"

"Of course not. I'm just really concerned that I may end up marrying Elizabeth and she deserves better than a gardener's son."

My father's cheeks blushed; something else I seldom ever saw from him.

We reached a small stone wall that marked the boundary between the Leatherby farms and the wild lands surrounding Greenshire. Father ducked down low when we saw a fancifully colored carriage with Walter's well-known pearl colored Andalusian horse tied to the back. The carriage came to a stop and Walter jumped down from his seat beside another man whose hat hid most of his face from us. He remained for a moment, talking to the man with the whip. We couldn't hear them, but Walter pointed our way before turning back away from Leatherby House.

My father remained hidden behind the wall as the carriage

approached until we had a better view of the man beneath the wide brim of his audacious hat. For the second time, I saw something in my father's eyes that was akin to fear, but it wasn't fear as much as concern, maybe even more anger. He quickly turned away and started running back towards the cottage. This was certainly a day for firsts, where my father was concerned. I couldn't recall ever seeing him actually run before. He had always been a prideful man and paraded around the grounds as if he owned them.

He must have recognized this man. I started to follow my father, thinking that I might get some kind of explanation, but since I was pretty sure he was heading back to the cottage, and I wouldn't be able to query him if I were out of breath, I kept my pace to a brisk walk, then thinking better of it, that I might learn more from the stranger, I turned towards the manor, taking an alternate route that would hopefully be out of the matchmaker's line of sight.

I hid behind one of my father's topiary lion heads and watched the matchmaker as he his carriage pulled up in front of Leatherby House. The man at the helm was near my father's age. Even from a distance, I could see the thickness of his dark black mustache, which was matched by his equally bushy eyebrows.

As he approached the entrance, Lord Leatherby himself emerged to greet him. The man removed his rather large hat and bowed low. He was a peacock with thick dark hair framing his head and large colorful plumes extending from his hat, but then, it seemed fitting that a matchmaker would be so gentle and well presented. One might even say he appeared overly fond of preening himself.

I could not hear them from this distance and was relieved to see them enter the house. I walked nonchalantly to the main entrance, on the pretense that I was there to speak with Elizabeth.

The doorman smiled and nodded towards me but didn't bother to open the door for me. Neither did he try to prevent me from opening it for myself, so I entered, unhindered, and waited near the door to the library, where I could hear Lord Leatherby and his guest.

"Thank you for coming so promptly," Leatherby said.

"How could I not?" the man asked with a lyrical lilt to his voice. "It is not every day that I am summoned by a nobleman for my services. Noble women, yes, but rarely the men. It is also quite fortunate that I happened to be in England and it was something of a miracle that your summons even found me. How may I be of service to you, Lord Leatherby?"

"It's my daughter Elizabeth. I fear she is not getting the best suitors from which to choose."

"Ah yes," the man said, "it can be challenging out here in the country. I gather you do not visit London often?"

"No," he replied, "not since my wife died. I fear that I may have been neglectful as a father."

Elizabeth came down and as I heard her approach, I put my finger to my lips and said, "Shhh. The matchmaker is here."

She nodded as she now understood why it looked like I was hiding behind the bust of the first Lord Leatherby, because I was.

"Tell me," the matchmaker said, "has your daughter had her eye on any potential suitors thus far?"

"No," Leatherby said, "at least none of consequence. I fear she may be infatuated with the gardener's son. They grew up together."

Elizabeth gasped, and I held my hand to her mouth to keep her silent.

"Ahh," the matchmaker said. I could almost see him shaking his head back and forth from the acidic tone to his voice. "I see it all the time with today's young people not understanding their station. It's even worse when the help doesn't respect their betters' station. I wonder why you haven't sacked the young man."

Throughout his last statement, I could feel Elizabeth tense up and thought she might fight me to storm into the room to give her father and his guest a piece of her mind.

I think we both jumped when we heard a new voice whisper between us, "Excuse me, Lady Leatherby." It was Mrs. Brindle, the housemaid. "Begging your pardon, ma'am, but there's a woman here to see you."

Elizabeth nodded to Mrs. Brindle, then looked expectantly at me, as if I would magically know who was at the door.

"You go," I said.

She shook her head, not wanting to leave our perfect little spy post.

I also didn't want to leave and suggested, "Perhaps you should bring her in."

Elizabeth nodded and told Mrs. Brindle, "Show her in, but do tell her to be quiet, please."

Mrs. Brindle looked ill at ease to be part of whatever scheme had us skulking about, eavesdropping on Lord Leatherby, but as uncomfortable as she was with my relationship to Elizabeth, she was equal parts loyal to Elizabeth and would do anything to prevent her being forced to marry me, so she nodded her head and left for the entrance.

Mrs. Brindle brought Agnes to us, saying, "... and I caution you to keep your voice down. No doubt young Hector is up to no good and has dragged my Lady Elizabeth into his nefarious schemes, and you should be careful to not get too caught up in whatever he is brewing."

Elizabeth gave Mrs. Brindle a look that was half humorous and half scolding as she whispered, "That will be enough, Mrs. Brindle. You may go about your business now. I'm sure Agnes can show herself out when she is done here."

"Just as well," Mrs. Brindle mumbled. "I didn't want to hear none of it anyways."

Elizabeth pulled Agnes in close between and asked, "What news have you?"

"Not so much, I think, just that Walter is going to the pond to speak with you both."

"Agnes," I said, "I don't know how long we will be here, but can you go to the pond for us to tell Walter that we will be there, if he'll only be patient enough to wait for us?"

She smiled and said, "I likes the pond. The swans and ducks especially."

I know not exactly how much we missed of the conversation between Lord Leatherby and the matchmaker while talking to Agnes, but when we returned our attention back to them, I detected an odd tone in Lord Leatherby's voice. It sounded like a bit of deception as I heard him say, "As I have already explained to you, I cannot sack the boy."

"But why not?" the matchmaker asked. "Has he some leverage on you?"

"No, no," Leatherby chuckled, "nothing so sinister. It is merely because he is not technically in my employ. His father is. I thought we already said that he is the gardener's *son*."

"So, sack the gardener. They can't be that hard to find."

"The gardener," Leatherby explained, "is my oldest and dearest friend. He shall not be sacked."

"Is that so? Why, or rather, how has the Earl of Leatherby come to be such close friends with a commoner? Should I meet this man? He must be quite extraordinary."

"I assure you that he is, but there is no reason for you to meet him. He is nobody to you."

"What is his name, then?"

Something in the matchmaker's voice told me that this was his game all along. He had been steering the conversation around me the whole time he was here, and now he has latched his focus upon my father.

"I should like to know him," the matchmaker continued, "if I ever come across him by sheer chance."

"His name is Fernando. He's Spanish."

"Just Fernando? No surname?"

"Of course he has a surname," Lord Leatherby said, obviously stalling. "It's de la Roca."

"No!!!" the matchmaker said with an exaggerated astonishment. "Not the same de la Roca that spirited himself and a certain lady friend of the court away from Spain to escape the inquisition?"

"Shhh!" Lord Leatherby said. "Please keep your voice down, and I would appreciate it if you did not share that information with anyone. He is here under my protection." Leatherby then put some gravitas into his voice as he warned, "And I do mean my complete protection. I would not take kindly to anyone that brought harm to my dearest friend."

"Of course!" the matchmaker whined. "You misunderstand my excitement. The story is that a certain Fernando de la Roca slipped out of Spain with a very special lady of the court who was with child at the time, and not just any child, but a bastard fathered by none other than King Philip himself. If the gardener's son to whom your daughter is already betrothed is the same child born to the lady who came with Don Fernando de la Roca, then I don't see how you could ever use my services. I could never find anyone better than a Spanish Prince, even if he is a bastard prince."

Elizabeth looked at me with wild, unbelieving eyes.

"Stop looking at me like that," I said. "None of this is true. This is the tale that Lord Chamberlain paid this charlatan to cook up against Walter. Speaking of Walter, let us go meet him now."

Elizabeth and I quietly slipped out the main entrance, but just as we reached the far end of the front court where a path split off to the pond, I heard the jingle jangle of metal chains as someone was approaching and saw my father dressed in that official-looking uniform again.

"Walter may have to wait," I said as I pulled her with me to hide behind a copse. "My father is up to something."

"Why is he dressed like that? He looks like a member of a royal court. Are you sure there is nothing to the matchmaker's story?"

"How long have you known me?"

She gave me that look like it was a stupid question. "You know perfectly well that we've both known each other our whole lives."

"And in that span of your whole life and my whole life, how long have you known my father?"

She rolled her eyes and refused to answer.

"Has my father ever been anything other than the gardener in your whole life?"

"No, but perhaps you can explain to me why your father is wearing that official looking uniform."

I had no answer.

"You can't, can you?"

"I cannot. Perhaps we should go listen to their conversation."

The matchmaker exited the manor before my father ever reached the door. Hearing my father was not difficult as he yelled, "Augustus! You slimy worm of a cow patty. What in Hades are you doing here?"

The matchmaker removed his hat and made an exaggerated, but disingenuous bow, saying, "Don Fernando. How good it is to see you alive after all these years, but you know I do not like being called Augustus. Nobody has called me that since my school days. You may call me Giovanni."

Elizabeth gasped and asked, "Your father is a Don?"

"Shhhh. I wish to hear them."

My father's voice reverberated around the court, "You would take an Italian name to hide your impoverished childhood. You were a pretentious insect when we were children, and I can already see that you are unchanged today."

Giovanni put his hands over his heart and said, "You wound me deeply. I thought we were old friends."

"We may have been friends as children, but you know perfectly well how that ended. Did you truly think I would ever forgive you for your part in that?"

Giovanni stood his ground, staring intently into my father's eyes, but said nothing.

My father pointed to the ground and demanded, "Why are you here, so far away from home?"

"I am here plying my trade as a maker of matches for the nobility. I was summoned here to find better suitors for the Lady Elizabeth Leatherby and the young Master Walter Chamberlain. It would seem that Lady Elizabeth has gone and accepted a proposal from a gardener's son. Can you imagine that?"

My father visibly bristled at Giovanni's comment.

"And," Giovanni continued, "I believe I have already found the perfect match for young Walter Chamberlain."

"It comes as no surprise," my father finally said, "that you should come to take up a woman's profession."

"I wasn't fortunate enough to inherit a title from my parents as you did, so I found a trade that I am actually quite good at."

"You may not have inherited a title," my father growled, "but I can see that you have inherited your father's foppish ways. Do you also have a penchant for young boys as he did?"

Giovanni's temper showed as he growled, "That was never proven."

"None the less, you are here under the pretense of being a matchmaker, woman's work if there ever was, and I can see from your attire that it suits you well, but I do not believe for one instant that you are sincere in this work. You were always a scoundrel, and I'm certain this is just some flowery way for you to steal from the nobility."

"I assure you," Giovanni said, "I am quite sincere in my efforts."

This time it was Fernando who bowed. "My sincerest apologies, then. I hope you have found her the perfect match." My father smiled and said with a sarcastic undertone, "Perhaps you can find someone more suited to her than a gardener's son."

"It's uncanny," Elizabeth whispered, "how your father sounds just like you, or is it you who sounds like him?"

"Shhh."

The matchmaker smiled wryly as he chuckled. "You don't fool me. Remember that I know you; I know the *real* you and the son of The Most Excellent Marquis of Avila is no more a gardener's son than I am the Duke of Normandy."

My father took a step backwards and shook his head slowly. "Long have we known each other, and even though much time has passed since we called each other friend, I never thought you were so evil as to put our lives in jeopardy. If news of our exile reaches Spain, we will be hunted. Do you really want that on your conscience?"

"Fear not, Don Fernando. I have no need to divulge your whereabouts. Rather, I have just informed Lord Leatherby that I have found a most excellent match for his daughter. I have presented him with someone even better than the son of a Marquis."

I knew the lie that the matchmaker had said, but I also understood how he now twisted the truth to confuse my father into thinking that I would no longer be the best suitor for Elizabeth. If I had shown myself and told him the truth, he probably would have run the man through with his blade, but that would not help Walter or me. I pulled Elizabeth by the hand and said, "Let's go find Walter."

Walter looked anxious as he sat on a boulder by the shore and flipped a flat stone in his hand. Skipping stones across the pond was something we did prodigiously as children. He jumped a bit when I stepped on a twig.

I nodded to him. "Sorry, I didn't mean to startle you."

"No matter," Walter said. "I was just deep in thought. What kind of tale did the matchmaker weave for Lord Leatherby?"

"He said that I was a prince. A bastard prince from Spain, fathered by King Philip."

Walter chuckled. "That sounds like my father. Aim high if you are going to take aim at all."

"Not so high as you might think," Elizabeth added. "It turns out that our dear Hector's father knew the matchmaker from their childhood, and Mr. de la Roca is actually a Marquis in exile from Spain. The matchmaker addressed him as The Most Excellent Marquis of Avila. He also called him Don Fernando."

"Woah," Walter said as he pointed at me. "You're a Marquis? Should I bow to you now? Are you to be forever known as Don Hector de la Roca?"

I laughed. "If you bow to me, you will find yourself shamefully pushed onto your backside, possibly in the pond as well."

"Seriously though," he said, "even without the matchmaker's tall story, how am I to compare with a Marquis? Now you really are the better match for Elizabeth."

"First of all," I explained, "you are not to be compared to a Marquis. You are up against a prince. How you will combat that, I do not know. The second thing, however, is that you and Elizabeth love each other. I will not stand in the way of true love."

"Wait a second," Elizabeth said, "have the two of you forgotten the most important thing that the matchmaker said? Even if Don Fernando is the Marquis, he is in exile and therefore has no land to go with his title. The Chamberlains have land, so you, Walter, have land with your title!"

"But," Walter added, "you said that Hector is now a prince!"

"A bastard prince!" I exclaimed. "Also, with no land to accompany the title."

"This is getting so complicated," Walter moaned. "I should return to my father. If the matchmaker knew your father from before, then he may also tell my father the truth about who you really are."

"The truth," I said, "is that I am the gardener's son, but your point is well taken, and I'm not so sure now that your father does not already know who we really are. Our parents seem to be keeping a lot of secrets from us."

"I wonder," Walter said, "how many more secrets our parents are keeping. My father believes that Elizabeth and I are brother and sister."

"Nonsense," I said, "not that he believes it, I mean, but it can't be true. I think our parents must suffer from some malady of the mind."

"Perhaps," Walter added, "but now we learn that you are a Marquis, or is that a prince?"

I sighed. He was never going to let this go.

"No matter," Walter said. "I should return to my father immediately and learn what the matchmaker has reported to him."

Elizabeth hugged Walter, and I embraced his hand with strength and reassurance, but it was a confidence that I did not totally feel in my heart.

For his part, Walter tipped his cap and snickered as he backed up two steps before turning around and walking away.

Elizabeth also giggled.

I was too slow to pick up a stone to toss at him.

Chapter Six

As Elizabeth and I left the pond to head towards the manor, she asked, "Should you go with Walter and question the matchmaker? We only heard his conversation with your father by eavesdropping."

"You think I can't use what we have already learned without exposing that we were hiding in the bushes?"

"No," she said, "it's not that. I wonder if you could use that silver tongue of yours to catch him in a lie that we could use against him. Maybe you could persuade him to support Walter."

"I would love to convince him to support Walter." I pounded my fist in my hand and added, "But Walter and George are more the physical persuading type than I am."

She laughed and said, "You must really be a Marquis. You are far more genteel than any of the nobles around here."

I smirked and asked, "So you accept me now as the gardener's son?"

She gasped and stopped to curtsy. "My apologies Don Hector. I meant no disrespect." She only held her serious expression for a moment before she broke out giggling and added, "You must already be aware that you are far nobler than any of the other noblemen around her, including my father."

I pretended to pull a cap from my brow and bowed low, saying, "Mi Lady Leatherby does me too much honor."

"My course is clear," I said. "You have persuaded me to go speak with the matchmaker, and perhaps I'll gather George and Walter to be my henchmen when I do."

"Anon," she said, pointing to the front courtyard, "Look!"

My father, in his uniform, stood stiffly in front of the manor while Lord Leatherby came to meet him. We returned to our previous positions behind the hedge to watch and listen.

"So," my father said, "I see you have come to your senses and engaged the services of a known matchmaker."

Leatherby glanced from my father to the matchmaker, who was climbing into his carriage, then back to my father. "Do you know him?"

"Know him?" my father asked, with an overly innocent tone to his voice. "Who does not know of the great matchmaker, Giovanni?"

Elizabeth poked me in the arm and said, "So that is where you get it from."

My concentration on my father's conversation burst as I gave her an inquisitive look and simply muttered, "What?"

"Your father sounds just like you when you are weaving one of your tales."

My eyes widened further in a look of utter incredulity. "Do you mind? You have already said that before. Can we please listen to them now?"

"Does it alarm you," my father continued, "that I would have heard of the great Giovanni?"

Leatherby sounded relieved as he nodded his head and said, "No, of course not."

"Good then. You should not be alarmed to learn that he told me what he found."

Leatherby did indeed look alarmed.

"Fear not," my father said. "I will not tell of the great fortune he has found for you."

Now Leatherby's face morphed from alarm to confusion. "He told you? And this does not upset you?"

"What is there that should upset me? He uncovered a suitor that can only enhance Elizabeth's station and when she is wed, we can still remain here in hiding, undisturbed."

"Luisa and you would remain in exile, then?"

"Why wouldn't we?"

Leatherby's look of confusion only grew. "But Hector..."

"Yes, yes," my father said. "Hector will remain as well. I dare say that with a royal in the family, you may even one day have enough clout to end our exile so we could live freely as Marquis and Marchioness."

"And this doesn't bother you? I mean, Luisa..."

"You are confusing me, my friend. I don't know why you should look so concerned. I was going to suggest that we toast Elizabeth's fortunes, but considering the state you are in, I wonder if you should really get some rest. We can celebrate tomorrow."

Having concluded what he had to say, my father clicked his heels together, nodded his head towards Lord Leatherby, then turned sharply and marched; he actually *marched* back to the cottage.

Lord Leatherby stood there, watching my father leave with his mouth hanging somewhat agape.

Lord Leatherby returned to the manor and Elizabeth stood from behind the hedge and asked, "Does your father now approve of our match? I thought he was against it, but he gave no indication that he would try to foil the match made by Master Giovanni."

"I do not believe that my father understood the plan. Giovanni told him that he had found a suitor for you that is the son of the King of Spain. He never explained that I was the same person of which he spoke."

"Do you think my father believes that you are a prince?"

I shrugged. "I've never known your father to be particularly gullible, but sometimes, people believe what they want to believe. Whether he considers this nonsense to be true, I do not know, but I think I shall speak with your father to find out."

"Now?"

"Yes, now. I have a feeling that if he believes this tall tale, he will receive me at any time I want, and if he refuses me, then perhaps that is all the answer that I need."

"As is usual," she said with an admiring smile, "you are correct. Perhaps you really are a prince. They, too, are never wrong."

"Nonsense," I said as started walking across the court towards the manor. "Royals are frequently wrong, but there are scarce few people who are willing to tell them so."

Someone must have told Lord Leatherby of our approach as his form appeared back in the doorway, which he had only just crossed. "Hector, my dear boy, come in! Come in!"

Elizabeth kissed her father on the cheek and said, "Hello father. You seem unusually cheerful today. Have we had some good news?"

I grasped his hand and said, "I almost hate to bring this to you while you are in such good spirits, but we've heard some disturbing news. Rumors, actually, but they have the taint of rumors born in truth and smothered in secrets."

Leatherby smiled as he released my hand. "You have always had a great gift for words. Not that of a poet, of course, but of a nobleman, or maybe a royal who was tasked with delivering speeches all day long."

"You are too kind, and yet again, I hate to rain dark upon your bright smile, but I must know if there is any truth in these scurrilous stories that have been bandied about. My first instinct, upon hearing them, was to deny them completely, but then, as I pondered some of the speculations regarding Elizabeth's many suitors for her future husband, and specifically how our parents have reacted to these conjectures, I could not help but wonder if there was a grain of truth in the suspicions."

Leatherby invited us into the foyer with a gesture of his hand. "I know not what you are asking me, but color me intrigued."

His expression looked more pained, almost more fearful than intrigued. "My mind is a jumble of unbelievable drivel, and I can barely bring myself to say it. Very well, I shall be frank."

"Please do. This sounds quite serious. Let us sit in the library to discuss it."

Elizabeth started to follow us, but a look from her father told her that this would be man's talk and she excused herself.

"Have a seat," Leatherby said as he turned over two glasses at the bar. "What can I get you?"

"I must admit that a Whisky would ease the telling of these tales, especially when they are somewhat scandalous and sordid stories about, shall we say, the truth regarding a mother and her child."

It was rather odd for Lord Leatherby to pour and serve a drink for a lowly gardener's son. I had a sinking feeling that he was buying the whole prince story, but perhaps that would help with the questions I was to ask him. He was quick to hand me a fine crystal tumbler, which I wasted no time in sipping. It was a far finer and smoother liquid than I had ever sampled before. "You know that, Elizabeth," I said, jumping into my explanation, "and Walter and I have known each other since we were toddlers."

Leatherby's face grew dark as he said, "I will not have that name brought up in my house."

"I'm sorry, sir, but Walter is your godson, and he was

named after you."

Leatherby winced at the second mention of his name.

I took another sip and continued, "I know not what has led to the feud between you and Lord Chamberlain, but I've heard rumors that Elizabeth and Walter are actually brother and sister. Is that why you feud with the Chamberlains?"

Leatherby's face echoed surprise, as if that was news to him. "Then it is a rumor that you bring to me? That Elizabeth is not my true daughter?"

"No, I mean," I had to think fast. Why would he jump to the conclusion that Elizabeth was the one born to the wrong father? "Is that why you feud?"

"Is that not reason enough?"

"And is that why you would never sanction a betrothal between Walter and Elizabeth?"

"What?" His face grew dark and angry. "There can be nothing between them and I already told you. I do not wish to hear that name in my own house."

I sighed. "So, you think there is something to these rumors then? You don't have to answer that. I mean, I believe that you already have. Thank you for the drink. I will show myself out."

Leatherby knew something, but he proved unwilling to disclose it to me. Worse yet, it sounded like he had a completely different take on things from what Chamberlain believed. It would be truly funny if both of their suspicions were correct;

that Elizabeth was actually a Chamberlain and Walter was a Leatherby. That would mean that they were not brother and sister and could marry without any great scandal, or at least without sin. As I say it in my head, it doesn't sound so funny, as they would be tragically separated for no reason.

My gait wasn't particularly swift as I hoofed it back to the cottage, even though I was feeling a bit peckish. Too many thoughts were firing off in my brain for me to start the next round of questioning just yet.

I knew my father would have to change out of his Marquis uniform before he returned to his gardening. I shook my head at the utter absurdity of that thought. I was still trying to process the thought that he was a Marquis, but there was no way to rationalize his removing his Marquis uniform so he could work as a gardener. My father worked for Lord Leatherby, in spite of the fact that his rank was superior to the earl's.

He was still lacing up his boots when I entered the cottage. "Father? May we speak for a moment?"

"Of course," he said. I haven't heard his tone so light and friendly in a very long time.

"Walter, Elizabeth and I have been hearing a lot of crazy rumors. There seems to be a lot of confusion regarding who our true fathers are. I wouldn't normally put any stock in rumors, if it weren't for the fact that I've been able to verify that both Lord Leatherby and Lord Chamberlain appear to believe that there may be some truth in them."

The expression of joy that was on his face only moments ago soured some. "I would never call the Lords dim-witted, but they are men of action and tend to possess simpler minds. As such, they could probably be convinced of anything."

I recalled the conversations that took place between my father and both Giovanni and Lord Leatherby and wondered if my own father might be a little simple in the head. "I asked mother earlier, and she told I should speak with you."

"About rumors?" He asked.

"Precisely," I replied.

"I know not what light I could shed. You say the rumors are regarding your parentage?"

"Questions have been raised, yes."

He frowned and grabbed the vest he liked to wear in the garden. "Walk with me. I have to tend the gardens."

I grabbed a chunk of rye cake to settle my stomach. "Isn't it rather late for gardening? The sun is almost set."

"I have fallen behind my time while tending to some personal matters. Today must be a day for personal matters, as you also have been dealing with some scurrilous rumors. Do you think it matters whose seed brings life to a child? Is not the child's father still the one who raised him?"

I was a bit shocked to hear my father say this. It was neither a common nor a very well accepted opinion. "What you say has much wisdom, but does not the true parentage carry more significance when dealing with nobles?"

He bent down on one knee and started removing weeds. "Ahh. Nobles, yes, and especially royals, who tend to put much more stock on their lineage."

Again, my father's opinion seemed from another time, one that may not even have come yet. "So, you're saying that the act of raising a son makes a man more of a father to him than the fathering of him did?"

"You should be careful what you ask, or even think. Questioning whether or not I am your true father can bring shame upon your mother."

"I meant no insult to her." He thinks I am talking about us. I am starting to wonder many more things about all of our parents than any child ever should. "Thank you for explaining it to me. I shall ignore any further rumors that I may hear."

"That is wise, especially if you hear any nonsense from that charlatan who calls himself Giovanni. I knew him once, and he was never to be trusted."

I nodded my head to him in sort of a curt bow of the neck and moved on. The picture being painted was not very clear, and it wasn't shaping up to be particularly pleasant.

Walter was happy to join me to visit his father; otherwise, I doubt that I would have been received at all had I been alone. It was clear from Lord Chamberlain's expression and his demeanor that he wasn't particularly pleased to see me, but I think he was mostly concerned about what kind of intrigue would have prompted me to visit him in the first place.

I bowed to him and said, "Lord Chamberlain. I am so pleased that you would take the time to see me."

He made a dismissive little coughing sound in his throat and said, "Yes, well, it is taking my time, so what say we get on with this?"

Walter rolled his eyes and said, "Come now father, you weren't doing anything of importance."

Lord Chamberlain glared at Walter, but said nothing.

"Very well," I said, taking charge of the conversation. "The feud between the Leatherbys and the Chamberlains has gone on since Walter and I were quite young. The cause of it has been a mystery to us, but it has put a strain on our ability to remain friends, and I include Elizabeth Leatherby as part of our circle of friends. We have recently come across some unsavory stories about our parentage and were wondering if you might be able to shed some light on the subject."

Chamberlain turned his gaze to Walter, and didn't look too happy to hear the question. As I watched the uncomfortable stare, I wished more than ever that I could have spoken with Walter's mother instead of his father.

"Are you certain," he finally spoke, "that you want to hear the truth of this matter?"

Walter, who had eagerly wanted to know mere moments ago, did not look so sure after hearing his father's question, and the tone with which it was delivered, but he nodded his head and said, "Yes, father. We would like to know the truth."

Something in Chamberlains face told me that he was about to fabricate a lie. He turned to face me and said, "Your father is not who he says he is. In fact, if the rumors be true, he may not even be your father. Your mother was with child when she arrived from Spain. She was a lady of the court in Spain. You may have guessed as much from her refined manners."

This was not what I was hoping to hear, but his face had

already told me that he wasn't going to reveal the truth.

"I can see," he continued with a nod of his head, "that you were not expecting this revelation. Perhaps you should speak with your mother. She obviously knows more on this than I."

"Thank you, sir, I will, but what you say is true: I was not expecting you to speak on my own lineage. I wanted to know why you think Elizabeth and Walter are brother and sister."

"What?" he asked defensively. "I never said any such thing."

"But you have," Walter said, "and we want to know why. What have you done?"

"I have done nothing, and I will not sully the memory of your mother with such innuendo."

So, it would seem that Lord Chamberlain does not question Elizabeth's lineage, but instead is suspicious of Walter's.

Walter's eyes welled up, as if to tear, but he controlled his emotions and refused to cry in front of his father. I took his elbow in my hand and said, "Come, Walter, this gets us nowhere."

He looked somewhat blankly at me, and I nodded my head towards the door. In truth, I learned quite a bit, but it was just another piece that still didn't fit the puzzle.

The walk back from the Chamberlains was thankfully long enough that I could rehash and digest what Lord Chamberlain had said. Walter walked with me for a short ways, and the expression on his face showed that he was equally confused by the collection of suspicions our parents have concocted.

After we had said our goodbyes and Walter had turned back towards his home, I marked the position of the sun and cursed the day for being such a waste. I considered having another talk with Giovanni, The Great Matchmaker, but that just invited my gut to burst out laughing at his use of 'The Great Giovanni' for his name. I'm sure the birds in the nearby trees thought me quite mad when I suddenly exploded in such a raucous sound.

Each one of our fathers sang a different tune, and each of them seemed to doubt the legitimacy of their own offspring. Was this some kind of madness that all men suffer? I like to consider myself a man already, but I have no desire to join this sorry club of doubt and insecurity. I can think of only one person left to question, but I will spare my mother from any of the doubts that my own father may have.

It was early for the evening supper, but I could already smell the pleasant fragrance of my mother's soup stock on the stove. My father, the Marquis, should still be tending to the grounds somewhere, and I was grateful to see him absent as I entered the cottage. "Hello Mother."

"Hello dear," she said from the table, where she was kneading some dough. It seemed to me like she was always kneading dough. If my father is a Marquis, then she is, by marriage, a Marchioness, yet I always catch her working dough or mixing batter. She glanced up from the dough she had been working and said, "You have that mischievous look in your eye again. Dare I ask what you have been up to?"

"I've been interrogating Lord Leatherby and Lord Chamberlain."

"Interrogating?" she asked. "Is that a proper thing for you to do with the nobility?"

"Something is afoot, I tell you, and I have found that people are often more compliant to questioning when they have something to hide, and both lords were hiding something indeed."

"Oh? What have you uncovered?"

"For one thing, I have learned some of the truth about you and father."

I noted a slight reaction in her posture; a mere tensing of her hand muscles and the slightest turn of her head. She had probably been waiting for this day to come for a long time.

"And what have you learned?" she asked.

"For one, I have learned that father is not a gardener."

"But he is," she replied. "Do you not see how excellent the grounds are under his care?"

"Well," I corrected myself, "he is not a mere gardener. He is a Marquis of Spain. He is, in fact, Don Fernando, The Most Excellent Marquis of Avila, and we are all here in exile."

She backed away from her cooking and faced me. "Perhaps that was him once, but no more. He relinquished his title when we fled from persecution."

That was the most truth I have received yet from any of the parents. "Well, I think the Lords both know this, and perhaps that helped me attain audiences with them."

She returned her attention to her bread making and said nothing.

"When you came her from Spain, had you a chance to

know Lady Leatherby and Lady Chamberlain?"

"Oh yes. They were our only confidants, that is, they also knew who we were and why we were in exile, but we had all agreed to never speak of it again."

"So you were close friends?"

"We all were. In fact, Lord Chamberlain watched over both estates and had sworn to be Lady Leatherby's champion, should the need arise."

"You mean, while Lord Leatherby and father were in Spain?"

"Your father and I were already in Spain. Lord Leatherby had come to purchase some horses and had struck up a friendship with your father."

"Were you and father already married?"

"No," she said, "we had not even met yet. I met Lord Leatherby on one of his visits to the court."

"The court? Do you mean the King of Spain's court?"

"Yes. My family had long been friends of the King and his family."

I hated to think it, but her story was weaving itself into the lie being broadcast by that charlatan Giovanni. "So you knew King Philip?"

"I did; quite well in fact. He was a very charming man, when he wanted to be."

"And it was there that you met Lord Leatherby? And all this was before you met my father?"

She stood away from her bread again and asked, "Where is all this leading?"

"It's all innuendo, but it might be quite a scandal," I replied. "It would seem that Lord Leatherby has doubts that

Elizabeth is his true daughter, and Lord Chamberlain has doubts that Walter is his true-born son."

My mother closed her eyes and shook her head. I thought I saw her swallow a chuckle just before she said, "Men can be such idiots."

"It gets worse," I said.

"Don't tell me your father is one of those idiots."

"I will not speak ill of my father, or my mother for that matter, but the matchmaker hired by Lord Leatherby was paid a bribe by Lord Chamberlain to claim that I am actually the bastard son of King Philip."

My mother's cheeks reddened. I wasn't sure how to interpret that.

"Oh dear," she muttered. "Your father may run this matchmaker through if he ever learns that."

"About that," I said hesitantly. "It would seem that the matchmaker and father are already acquainted. He told father that he had found a match for Elizabeth, and that the match was the son of King Philip, but I do not believe that father realized that he was speaking of me, as if you had been with the king in that way, or I have no doubt that father would have gutted the man right there."

"How do you know so much? Where is it that you hear so much gossip? You should place less stock on the rumors that you overhear."

This time it was I who blushed. "They are not all rumors. I have ears and have heard some of these exchanges myself."

The expression on her face did not bode well for my father when he returned, which should be soon.

"So," I asked, "you believe the fears of the Lords to be

unfounded?"

"Of course I do. If either Lady Leatherby or Lady Chamberlain had lain with another man, they would have confided in me. These men and their stupid egos are to blame for these unfounded rumors."

"And," I added, "the feud as well."

My mind raced between all the many suspicions our parents were so easily induced to draw for themselves. It did not make for an easy night's sleep, nor did it speak well of our fathers' abilities to reason.

I have generally liked to think that a new day brings new opportunities, but then, I also believed that I could control the course that my life would take, and the past few days have been anything but controlled.

The morning and the weather were certainly full of promise, despite my dreary attempts to slumber, so I tried to draw upon them to feel hopeful for the coming day. I left the cottage and headed towards the manor and Elizabeth, but apparently she had the same idea as we met in the middle, her accompanied by Agnes.

"Good morning," I said.

"Good morning to you," Elizabeth replied. "Walter and George, wait for us at the pond."

"Oh? Has something happened?"

"Not yet, but it's like you said yesterday. You could be more persuasive with Giovanni if you had Walter's and

George's muscle behind you."

I tried not showing any irritation as I replied, "I thought we said that in jest, but you told them what I said?"

"No," Elizabeth said, "I did not."

"It was me," Agnes said. "My George and Master Walter have already thought it was time to do something about the matchmaker."

"Do something? They wish to threaten him if he does not change his tune?"

Agnes nodded her head. "And worse. At least, that's what I overheard them talking about when I said they should get you to talk sense to the man first."

"You did the right thing," I said. "But I must admit that I don't like the sound of it when you say, 'and worse.'"

Walter was on his usual boulder, staring wistfully out over the pond, but he sprang up from his perch at the very first crack of a twig beneath my feet. His voice was like a rapid drummer as he spat out, "You are not going to believe what I just heard."

"Slow down," I said, "if you talk so fast, we won't be able to understand you. What did you hear, and was it from a reliable source?"

He took a deep breath and asked, "What do you know of how your mother and father met?"

I whistled at the question. News travels fast as I had just learned that from my mother on the previous evening. "My mother was a lady of the court of Spain when she met my father. Please do not repeat the same ridiculous scandal that is being spread by that fake matchmaker."

"But *HOW* did your mother meet your father?"

"Lord Leatherby introduced them."

"Well, my father overheard me telling George of your family title and he called me into his office. In privacy, he said that Lord Leatherby had never intended to introduce them that way. In fact, he had been courting your mother before accidentally introducing her to your father."

"What?!?" Elizabeth exclaimed. "He was already married to my mother."

"Perhaps not," I said. "He has made claims to have only been promised to her, and by arrangement, even."

"On top of that," Walter added, "he's a man and..."

Elizabeth raised her voice a pinch as she asked, "Is that how you feel? He's a man, so he's entitled to sow his seed where he wishes?"

Walter realized his error and shook his head. "I didn't mean me, only that maybe that's what a lot of men like him do."

"Men like him? You're talking about my father!"

"Sorry."

Elizabeth scowled. "Is this what you are to be like when you inherit your father's title?"

"Excuse me," I interrupted, "but as entertaining as this is, I think we need to focus on the facts of what Walter has learned. I believe he had learned some fascinating new facts about my mother. I hope it is not to be more nonsense about her and King Philip."

"No," Walter said, glad to change the subject, "it has nothing to do with King Philip. Apparently, your father was in the tavern, mumbling into his ale something about Lord Leatherby and loyalty. My father was there and the two of them got into the drink pretty heavily. My father confessed doubts about my mother's fidelity and your father confessed that he suspected that Lord Walter Leatherby may in fact be your true father."

I was stunned. "My father doubted my mother? That can't be."

"According to my father, your mother was with Lord Leatherby before she had ever met your father, so there was never any question of her disloyalty."

"Wait!" I said, with a little too much force. "Why would your father suddenly share all this with you? Why now?"

"After you questioned him, he must have figured out that we were starting to learn about all this stuff, but I think the real reason was that he wanted to create a scandal for Lord Leatherby."

"That would do it," I said sadly.

"The real question," Walter said, "is why would your father be friends with him?"

"Yes," Agnes said. "Why would the Marquis of Avila stoop to being Lord Leatherby's gardener?"

"Unless," Walter said carefully, measuring his words, "Lord Leatherby was somehow blackmailing him."

Elizabeth looked at Walter as if she wanted to shoot darts from her eyes. "What did you say?"

"I'm not saying that I believe that," Walter back pedaled, "but do you have another suggestion?"

"Isn't it obvious?" she asked. "Don Fernando came here to escape religious persecution. He is living here in exile to protect his family. Do you honestly think that he would do that if he believed that his wife bore another man's child?"

"He would," I said. "First of all, he loves my mother very much and would forgive her anything. And second, we had the strangest, but most touching conversation, where he admitted that raising and protecting a child made a man more of a father to the child than being his sire would have."

"He actually said that?" Walter asked.

I nodded my head.

Walter whistled and said, "That's practically an admission that you are Lord Leatherby's son."

"No it is not," I replied.

"Think about it," Walter continued. "He has given you access to all the same tutors as Elizabeth. He doesn't make you work. I'm surprised he hasn't given you a stipend for being part of the family!"

I sighed. "He recently did give me a monthly stipend."

"See?"

"No," I barked. "I don't see. The stipend was for my marrying into the Leatherby family, and Lord Leatherby would never approve of our betrothal if I was his son and we were brother and sister."

"He would," Walter said, "if he didn't know you were his son."

"Or," Elizabeth said with a tear cresting onto her cheek, "if he didn't believe I was his daughter."

"Stop that!" I snapped. "My mother was quite adamant that you and Walter are entirely legitimate. She knew your mothers quite well and they would have confided in her if there had been any irregular coupling going on. And Lord Leatherby's behavior is quite consistent with him believing that I am a Marquis."

"So what do we do?" Elizabeth asked. "Do we educate them on how silly their suspicions are?"

Walter nodded enthusiastically. "That might help end the feud and clear the path for our marriage!"

"It might," I said, "but that's not what we are going to do. We *are* going to teach them a lesson, but first, we are going to visit Master Giovanni."

Agnes and Elizabeth both rolled their eyes when George and Walter each smiled and punched their fists into their open palms.

Winston readily obliged when Elizabeth asked him to saddle a horse, but his displeasure was obvious when he realized it was for me. His disdain only grew worse when he saw Walter and George already on horses. I could practically hear his mind concocting all the many kinds of trouble that we planned to get into, and whether it would come back to get him in trouble.

When I mounted my horse, Elizabeth came to me and said, "Do be careful."

"With these two by my side?" I asked. "I don't believe I will be in any danger."

She snickered and said, "I meant for you not to get Walter into any trouble. Talk to the man, but don't do anything rash."

Walter smashed his fist into his palm again and asked, "What do you consider too rash? Just kidding. We will only convince him to consider his actions."

I nodded to Elizabeth and asked, "What do you plan to do while we are away?"

"Me? I'm going to walk Agnes back to her home and we'll probably talk about the coming baby."

I stroked my woefully bare chin and glanced over to Agnes, who was with George, probably asking him to stay out of trouble. "You should study Agnes, and learn what it is like to be with child."

Elizabeth stepped back and asked, "What?"

"As I said before, we must teach our parents a lesson. Knowing how to act like a woman with child may serve a useful role in that endeavor."

"Oh," she said, blushing slightly that she had taken my meaning the wrong way.

Walter appeared amused by the last exchange. He leaned over in the saddle, bringing his face down far enough to kiss Elizabeth on the cheek, which thoroughly deepened her blush. "Someday, perhaps, it won't require your acting skills to appear that you are with child."

Her blush was now an unmistakable crimson as she slapped the haunches of his horse and said, "You should ever be so lucky, you cad!"

I laughed out loud and followed him away from the stables. "Let us head over to the tavern where I expect we will find that charlatan deep into his ale."

George trailed behind as we entered the small village, although I know not how much longer I might call it small without getting disbelieving stares. Even the wooden arch of bent saplings had been replaced with a rather impressive stone archway. Sadly, the soot from the burnt coal that clung to buildings and the ground may have said more of its growth beyond a mere village than anything else.

I twisted around in my saddle and saw a change in George's disposition. His face was intent on what we were about to do, but it was more than just that. "What is it George? What is this man to you?"

George brought his horse up next to mine, presumably so he wouldn't have to shout. "He means nothing to me personally, but the feud stands between me and Agnes, and the baby. Fixing this so Master Walter can marry Lady Elizabeth could end the feud and allow me to live happily with my family."

It was a sensible answer, and it was a sentiment for which I would have to take into account, once I had a plan in place. Walter had already entered the tavern, and poked his head out the doorway to say, "Will you two stop fooling around? He's here."

George leapt off his mount and flashed to the door, only to stop abruptly and turn to look at me with an awkward expression on his face. He bowed, and with a nod of his head, said, "Don Hector, after you."

Before I could react, he winked and flashed me a smile. I could only wag my finger at him and say, "One day, your sense of humor will get you in trouble. Now step aside, peasant." I winked back at him and entered the tavern to join Walter with a semi-conscious matchmaker.

"Look at him," Walter said. "I don't think he'll be much good to us like this."

"You didn't think it would be easy," I asked, "did you?"

George pulled the matchmaker's head off the table and pulled an eyelid open. "Oi. Master Giovanni. We'd like a word with you."

A moment of semi-consciousness passed through the drunkard as he rolled his eyes around to look at us, then curled back for a view of the back of his eyelids.

George lifted him up from the table. "I may need a hand with him. I stepped in to help, but Walter pushed me aside and said, "I got this."

I looked at him curiously and said, "Please don't tell me this is because we've learned that I'm a marquis."

"No," Walter said, "it's because we are the muscle, but your being the marquis is just as good of a reason as any, I suppose."

George snickered and said, "You just might have to get used to it, Don Hector."

Together, they lifted the matchmaker's not inconsiderable heft and walked him out the door.

Walter and George carried Giovanni between them with the matchmaker's arms wrapped around each of their shoulders. The drunken lout managed to move his legs enough that they didn't have to drag him.

Giovanni turned his head towards Walter and slurred, "I know you. You're the Chambermaid... Chamberman... the viscount's boy."

Walter grimaced and turned his head away from the matchmaker's breath.

Looking at George, Giovanni said, "I don't know you. Did you need a wife too?"

George smiled and said, "No thanks. I already have one of those."

Giovanni flopped his head back over to Walter and said, "But you do. I have the perfect girl for you."

Walter gave him a half smile as I pointed to a small clearing on the edge of a stream and said, "Over there, on the log."

They guided him to the spot I selected and sat him down.

Walter poked and prodded his cheeks. "Maybe this wasn't such a good idea. He's so drunk, I don't think he'll feel anything."

"Great," I said. "I really was hoping to talk to him."

George snickered. "Good luck with that."

I slapped his cheeks just enough that I hoped it would snap

him awake. "Master Giovanni?" He rolled his eyes back and flopped his head around. I slapped his cheeks again with just a little more force. "Master Giovanni?"

"I'm Giovanni."

"Drink this. You'll feel better."

I gave him a potion that was supposed to help revive him from his drunken stupor. I suspect that he thought it was more alcohol when he slammed it down and thanked me, but his eyes fell shut, anyway.

"I got this," George said as he hooked his arm under Giovanni's. "Walter, take his other arm."

They dragged him up onto his feet. George led them to the edge of the stream, where he dropped him onto his hands and knees and dunked his head into the cold water. Giovanni instantly thrashed to get his face out of the stream, but George dunked him two more times. I suspect that the second dunking was sufficient, and the third was just for good measure.

When they pulled him back to his feet, Giovanni sputtered, "What is it? I didn't do it."

George and Walter dragged him back to the log to face me.

"Master Giovanni," I said formally. "Why did you tell my father that I am a prince of Spain?"

"You're a good boy," he said, "and you deserve the girl. I made you look good."

"But you lied."

George slapped his cheeks to keep him alert.

"Don't you love her?" he slurred. "Everyone says you are already betrothed to her. I sealed the deal for you."

"You didn't have to do that."

"Don't you love her?"

"I've come to face the fact," I lied, "that she loves Walter. I won't stand before her happiness."

George slapped him again; something for which I believe George derived a bit too much pleasure.

"She can't have Walter," he said, shaking his head. "That just can't happen."

"Why?" I asked. "Because Walter's father paid you to keep them apart."

"No! I mean, yes, he paid me, but I'm an ethical man of business. Affairs of the heart are my stock in trade."

"Then why did you tell the lie that I am a bastard prince?"

Giovanni shrugged and said, "It was just a little white lie, but I stand by my word that you are meant for Lady Elizabeth."

"But they are in love," I said. "Why do you interfere with their love? What greater affair of the heart can there be than the love of two young people like them?"

George went to slap him again, but Walter stopped him, preferring to get a few blows in himself.

"They can't marry. It would be a scandal. The church won't allow it."

"What?" Walter asked. "Why wouldn't the church allow it?"

"Because incest is a sin." He tried signing the cross on his head, but only managed to rub his nose.

I closed my eyes and shook my head. "Are you referring to those ridiculous rumors that they are brother and sister?"

He opened his mouth to speak, but stopped short.

"That's right," I continued. "Those outlandish lies must

stop. They are *not* brother and sister. Do you hear me? Their fathers can be idiots sometimes. You must fix this!"

He shook his head and said, "Even if what you say is true, they are still not right for each other, but I have found the right girl for him. This is what I do for people and I have my reputation to think about."

Walter raised his hand again to slap the drunkard again, but I stopped him, fearing he had more on his mind than keeping the man conscious.

The matchmaker's insistence that Elizabeth and Walter were not right for each other was a twist that I had not anticipated. I had hoped that we could enlist his aid to match the two of them together, but I may need to devise a new strategy. His declaration that they were not right for each other did not come with any reasons. For all I knew, he may have consulted Tarot cards or astrology, neither of which did I subscribe to. I was not against, however, using such baseless superstitions to enact some sort of revenge against our parents. In all likelihood, Walter's supposed match had some political gain for somebody and was not based on their compatibility as a couple, which, by the way, had zero bearing on noble marriages in those days.

It might have helped me to know who this mystery woman was that was so perfect for Walter, but I couldn't extract that information in front of Walter. Perhaps it will come out as I start to take action against our parents.

Chapter Seven

I recall thinking, while the events were still unfolding, that I had created an absolute mess of things. That Elizabeth would end up married, I had no doubt, but it now looked like she would end up bound to a husband as surely as a beast is tied to its master, and much of it would have been my doing.

But now, with the perfect clarity of hindsight, I know that I not only was clueless as to how bad things actually were; I had absolutely no idea exactly how out-of-control things would eventually spin.

I had a thought in the back of my mind, that I might include Elizabeth in all my plans, but I couldn't help feeling that if I simply fed her what she needed to know and pointed her in a direction, she would give a more convincing performance.

It was as if I were two different people arguing the merits of these ideas in my head, all while I continued to walk blindly up to the manor. I should make a note to ask my mother if such madness runs in our family.

Mrs. Brindle snapped me from my reverie, an act which I find happening with more and more regularity. "She's not here."

I took a moment to sweep the cobwebs from my mind before replying, "What makes you think I haven't come to see you?"

She didn't even bother to snicker, but instead cocked her head to the side and put her hands on her hips, waiting for the next cockamamie thing I might say. When I made no further reply, she said, "I heard about your father being a Marquis. I guess that changes things on how I has to treat you, but if you don't really need nothing, I got the ballroom to clean."

"I understand. Is there some special reason, an occasion perhaps, for which you've been directed to clean the ballroom?"

"Heaven's no. I just need to dust it and tidy it up so it's not so bad when we needs it."

I nodded my head and started to leave, but turned back and asked, "When we need it? When have we ever needed it?"

"You might be surprised to learn that there was a time, before Lord Leatherby brought your mother and father here, when we used to host some mighty fine fancy balls."

"Really?"

"Oh yes," she continued. "We had kings and queens here

in our heyday."

It struck me hard that it all ended when we came. Lord Leatherby sacrificed some of his station to help my father hide here. Things will probably change now. Not only has my father been exposed, but Elizabeth's upcoming nuptials will most likely engage the ballroom again. "Thank you, Mrs. Brindle. Do you know where the Lady Elizabeth might have gone?"

Mrs. Brindle shrugged. "To town maybe; she was heading towards the stables. Might be she just wanted to ride, though."

I imagined in my head the kinds of balls that Leatherby might have thrown before our arrival. Kings and queens had come here. How much had he sacrificed to help my father's exile? His sacrifice seemed even greater, considering my father's noble status. I couldn't think of any nobler thing than the status Lord Leatherby risked on my father's behalf.

Winston saw me approaching the stables, but his face didn't register the disdain that I had grown accustomed to seeing. He sprinted up to me and asked, "Shall I ready a mount for you?"

"Possibly," I replied. "Has Lady Elizabeth been this way?"

"Yes, sir. She didn't say what she was planning, but I saw her head towards town. I'll get a horse ready for you."

He ran off into the stable, leaving me to wonder if he had ever called me "sir" before.

I still hadn't completely decided what I planned to say when I ever found Elizabeth, but at least the torturous arguments in my head had subsided. This was my first ride into town alone, but in some ways, I found it not so different from riding with someone. While riding with Elizabeth gave us the privacy to speak freely, riding alone afforded me the quiet time to sort out my own thoughts, but that privacy turned out to be short-lived.

I wasn't in a particular hurry, but once my horse knew we were heading to town, she picked up the pace slightly into a comfortable trot. As I rounded a stand of trees, I saw the familiar brightly colored carriage of Giovanni, who had apparently just left Lord Leatherby. My father was correct when he called him a pompous poof, but I had a private inkling that he may actually know something of his craft. He certainly defended himself as a true practitioner of the art.

I pulled back on the reins slightly as we pulled alongside him. He tipped his hat and said, "Good morning, Don Hector!"

I cringed at the title, but it is something I may never be able to escape. "Good morning, Giovanni. Were you visiting Lord Leatherby this early in the morning?"

"I did indeed. He had asked me to come by so I could talk with him about some of my other services. You know, my job doesn't end when I bring two potentials together."

"You don't say. I had a feeling there was more to you than first met the eye. I must admit to having some fascination in how you practice your craft."

"Is that so?" he asked. "You don't mean to steal my business, do you? I'm told that you are a very clever boy."

"Not at all," I assured him. "I like to consider myself as a man of science and I've seen enough of these traveling seers who believe that they can divine the future and arrange couples by tossing bones or reading tea leaves. I suspect, however, after watching you a bit, that your craft is founded in something more substantial than witchcraft."

"It is true what they say, that you are very clever. You are correct when you suspect that my craft is more science than witchery, but there is also a bit of artistry, if I do say so myself."

"Tell me more. When a client comes to you with a son or daughter, how do you find the perfect mate for them?"

"You are sure that you are not after my job?"

"Absolutely not! Now that my title has been exposed, I will no doubt find myself with new duties that will leave me little time for matchmaking. Besides, someday I may have a son or daughter and be in need of your services."

He smiled broadly at the prospect of matching the off-spring of Don Hector, a future Marquis of Spain, even if I was in exile. I cringed at the thoughts that had just run through my head. He narrowed his eyes at me as he asked, "And you're not trying to find some flaw in my techniques? Something that might lose me my commission?"

"No sir. You have nothing to fear from me. I merely am fascinated with how you go about pairing up a couple."

"The first thing I do is get to know my clients, both the parents and the child. I try to learn about them by talking to their friends and the staff. I keep records of all of them. You never know when they will come in handy."

"Ahh!" I exclaimed. "That explains the size and apparent weight of your carriage. There must be more, however. Friends and staff may tell you about their personality, but you serve the nobles. Certainly, if you keep records, you must also record their lineage."

"Indeed. During my travels, I take a moment to get a peek at the parish registers to record the births."

"But those are locked and require three keys to open!"

He eyed me suspiciously and said, "You are certainly well informed. The parish birth records are indeed locked."

"Yet, you manage to get past those protections? Perhaps my father was right to treat you with so much suspicion."

He raised his hands to show me his palms. "Slow down, Don Hector. It is not as sinister as you may think. Many parishes are too small to afford the three clerks required to protect the registry chests. One parish parson is far easier to bribe than three. Sometimes it requires gold, but other times, it only takes an excess of drink to loosen the locks on the chests."

I couldn't quite decide if this made him crafty or villainous. "And I suppose you manage to copy down whatever you can for your own records."

"Those that I can't copy, I try to remember and record later."

"Well," I said with a big, although not entirely genuine, smile, "it was a great pleasure to speak with you, but I don't want to keep you from your tasks any further. I'm actually going into town looking for Lady Elizabeth."

"Perhaps I'll see you there. I'm actually expecting someone very special today, and plan to wait in town for their arrival."

He piqued my curiosity, but asking more would have appeared invasive, so I merely said, "Good day, Giovanni."

He smiled and tipped his hat while simultaneously flicking the reins to get his horse moving.

If I thought the two voices in my head that kept arguing about whether or not I should confide my ideas in Elizabeth were annoying, the new wild imaginings that were zooming through my thoughts after visiting with Giovanni were downright terrifying, but exhilarating at the same time, and I knew I was going to act upon them.

I entered the tavern, not to find Elizabeth, but to plant the seed of an idea and see if it might germinate.

"Hector! Can I get you your usual?"

I smiled and nodded my head at the attractive bar maid. "Thanks, Nelly, that would be fine."

She smiled brightly, perhaps a little more attentively than she ever had before. "I'll be right back. Find yourself a seat."

I scanned the mostly empty room and selected a table near

enough to some other patrons that I might be overheard.

She arrived promptly with a fresh mug of ale. "I wasn't sure you'd be having the same drinks as before, if the rumors be true."

"You know what they say; even the wildest rumors can have a shred of truth to them."

"Aye," she replied. "Truth is that I wasn't even sure you'd be drinking here no more, what with the generally poorer quality of our beverages and you being an aristocrat of sorts." She looked around suspiciously to see if the proprietor might have overheard her.

"I'm still the same person I was last week," I assured her, "although if rumors be true, there may yet be a few surprises to come out in our little hamlet."

She sat down next to me and said, "Wasn't it you that just said all rumors had a shred of truth?"

That wasn't exactly what I had said, but it was what I had hoped she would hear. "It would seem that, in his younger days, the King may have sown a few wild oats, and one of them may have taken root right here, or near enough."

"No! We has a royal bastard living amongst us?"

"It would also seem that, of recent, the king has been seeking his bastards out. I don't know if he's just not happy with the brood he has for his official heirs and is looking for a better sort, or if he just wants to get them all out in the open so they can't up and surprise the current heirs claiming their own rights to the crown."

She bought it. I could tell, and telling her was as good as telling everyone. To top that, the booth next to us had become uncommonly quiet during the telling and I'm quite sure this little gem of a rumor would spread like a wildfire.

Nobody who had ever seen the world would have mistaken Greenshire for London or York, but there were plenty of locals who might have thought of it as quite the up-and-coming city. Up and coming, it may have been, and perhaps one day it might become more than just a small local town, but as it was buried in the country and was not betwixt any major metropolitan hubs, there was little chance of it ever reaching those lofty goals.

As such, new arrivals to our hamlet tended to raise a bit of curiosity. It hadn't been that long since Giovanni had ridden in with his gaily colored coach with its festive streamers and garishly festooned horse to draw it. He made quite the impression upon his arrival, so it was quite the event when another visitor came to town, this time in a dazzling, but elegant, closed cover carriage. Clearly, this was someone of substance and class; so naturally, everybody wanted to know what business they could possibly have in Greenshire.

The first assumption on everyone's tongue was that they were lost and needed directions, but that notion was quickly forgotten when Giovanni rushed out of the pub to greet them. "Lady May, Lord Cranston...Lord Cranston?" The excited man hadn't even allowed them to step out of the carriage before he had greeted them. I took a seat out front of the tavern and snickered at his excited clumsiness.

An exceedingly attractive young maiden stepped down from the coach. I had to swallow a full-blown guffaw when I saw the utter disdain upon her face as she glanced around the square. "My father no longer attends these ridiculous arrangements. For the life of me, I wonder why he continues to allow them, given how they never work out."

Giovanni removed his hat and bowed low. "Your father has never before had a match made for you by the Great Giovanni."

She rolled her eyes and said, "My father, the Baron, has truly worked his way down to the bottom of the barrel, then, hasn't he?"

I had to cough loudly to cover the laugh that threatened to bellow up from within me.

Ignoring her insult, he took her hand and guided her to the tavern entrance. She didn't look thrilled and made not even the slightest attempt to hide her feelings.

"Giovanni," I said as I leapt from the seat I had taken to observe their arrival, "who is this enchanting creature that you have brought to our small hamlet?"

He clearly looked at me as if I was interfering with his business, but he smiled anyway and said, "Don Hector de la Roca, this is the Lady May Cranston, but she is not for you. You are already betrothed."

I must admit that her look of disappointment was a welcome stroke to my ego. I bowed to her and said, "None the less, it is my great honor to be the first to welcome you, Lady May, to Greenshire."

Giovanni coughed and said, "Giovanni was first, but you are a good second. I have brought her here to meet Lord Walter."

I struggled to hide the cringe I felt when he said 'Lord Walter'. Lord Chamberlain was adamant that he should only be called 'Master Walter', but fortunately, Chamberlain was not here at present.

Giovanni continued, "Is he here yet?"

I nodded my head and said, "You will find him inside."

Giovanni nodded his head and took her in. It would be some time later that I learned of Lady May's reputation and her nickname of Lady May Not. I recall thinking at that moment in time that her introduction was going to complicate my endeavors to bring Elizabeth and Walter back together, but as I later learned, it wasn't necessarily so.

While Giovanni was engaged with his matchmaking between Lady May and Walter, I took the opportunity to wander over to the livery where Giovanni's carriage was parked and his horse was being fed.

A dank, musty smell clung to the interior of his carriage. A crate of bottles with corked stoppers was placed in the front, presumably so he could reach them while on the road. I had thought the man too much of a drunkard to appreciate a fine wine, but corks were a rare commodity and only to be found in the better vintages. These were probably payment from his noble clientele, although I could easily imagine him pilfering these from a wedding that he may have had a hand in arranging.

Next to the crate of wines, on the right side of the carriage, were two large chests which I found to be filled with clothing. One of them was a rumpled pile of dark-colored blouses and trousers, the same you would find with any common thief or vagabond. The other chest, however, had much finer clothing, neatly folded and layered. No doubt, these were his nobility costumes that he used for meeting with his elite clients.

The left side held three more chests filled with papers and scrolls. Most of them were neatly tucked away, but a few lay conveniently on top and were the very items I was interested in finding. They concerned the records of Greenshire, and both the Leatherby and Chamberlain households. I considered taking them, but decided it was too soon to expose myself, and chose to commit them to memory instead.

Judging by the placement of the documents, I got the feeling that Giovanni was particularly interested in Walter's lineage. The documents covered not only births and marriages, but also land holdings, and one of them in particular said that the Chamberlain estate had fallen to a lesser heir when the foremost Chamberlain was a daughter with only a single male child that had apparently failed to impress.

I didn't know how this information could have helped Giovanni do his job, but I had an idea how I might use it to start a rumor that perhaps the current Lord Chamberlain wasn't the rightful heir. My purpose wasn't to hurt Walter's claim, but since Lord Chamberlain had practically denied Walter's claim already, this could hardly make matters worse for him. My true thought was to show the folly of rumors in general, since the whole silly feud was based on ridiculous rumors.

I did not want to spend too much time rifling around Giovanni's belongings. For one thing, my plans relied on my ability to start some alternative theories and rumors, so being caught in the matchmaker's files could bring too much light to any plans I hatched. Plus, I wanted to return to the tavern before Lady May did something to spoil my plot.

Having committed his documents to memory, as best as I could, I returned to the tavern and there they were, Giovanni, Walter and Lady May, all sitting together at the grandest table in the house, grandest meaning it was larger with a polished surface that was kept relatively clean. Walter waved at me and beckoned me to join them.

"Lady Cranston," he said, "I would like you to meet one of my dearest friends since childhood."

She smiled a bit too warmly and replied, "Yes. I have already had the pleasure of meeting Don Hector when I arrived."

"Excellent! We've known each other since we were babes, but his Excellency is a sly one who hid his true title from us until just recently."

She looked astonished. "Why on earth would anyone hide their title?"

"In truth," I said, "and Walter knows this, I was unaware

that my father had brought a title with him. I think there are those in Spain who would not wish to know of our well-being."

"You're in hiding?" She asked.

"We're not criminals," I said in defense of my father, "but my father did find asylum here with Lord Leatherby. He won't speak of it, but I surmise that the church and their inquisition did not take well to those who did not follow the teachings of Rome."

"Ahhh," she said with a knowing nod of her head. "Politics. I do not agree with the old way of thinking, but my father is not so modern, and he continues to try to find me a mate, as if I were a prize filly fated only to bring him an heir."

She glanced ever so slightly over to Giovanni during the last of her statement.

"I'm parched," I said, "anyone else?" The simple statement brought a new round of ale from the ever attentive Nelly, who had been just close enough to catch when we needed service. I winked at her to show my appreciation, then turned to the table and said, "Giovanni, I'm sure that you have much more important things to do than listen to us prattle on all night."

He looked concerned, so I added, "Do not worry, man. I am not after your job. I merely wish to speak more privately with my old friend and our new friend."

Giovanni stood and bowed awkwardly, then left.

Lady May laughed lightly. "Are you sure you only just recently learned of your title? You dismissed him with the grace and power seldom seen amongst even the most seasoned nobles."

Walter lifted his glass as if to toast and said, "Hector here was raised as the gardener's son, but you are correct in assessing that he is the noblest soul I have ever known."

She clapped her hands lightly and smiled the most genuine smile I had seen on her since her arrival. "I think that's wonderful! Not just that Don Hector was the noble son of a gardener, but that you, Lord Walter, have seen him as your equal even believing that he was but the son of a gardener."

"Then you misunderstand me," he replied, "for I was never Hector's equal. He is quite extraordinary and I can only aspire to one day be his equal."

"And what about you?" I asked. "You did not seem so thrilled to be brought to this country tavern, yet you have expressed, dare I say, a somewhat disdainful opinion of noble life?"

"That's not it at all," she said. "I adore noble life, and I don't mean the finer trappings that come with it, although many of them are nice and I would not want to live in squalor, but I believe nobility is in a man's, or woman's, actions. I don't think people should be fated to a life of poverty just because of their lineage."

"Wow," Walter said with a genuine level of admiration, "you truly are a modern woman. Let us drink to that!"

We joined our mugs together, and it was as if a heavy blanket was lifted from the table. We could truly speak freely, at least between the three of us.

"So, Lady May," I said as I wiped the foam from my lips, "you do not appreciate being sold off to the highest bidder?"

"The highest bidder?" she asked with a laugh, then she

looked to Walter apologetically and said, "Sorry, Lord Chamberlain..."

"Stop right there," Walter said. "My father might just barely tolerate people calling me Lord Walter, but I'm quite sure he would not take well to my being called Lord Chamberlain. He is Lord Chamberlain, and will remain so until he is laid to rest."

"Lord Walter then," she said with a curt nod of her head, "and I mean no disrespect by this, so please don't take it the wrong way, but you are hardly the highest bidder. My father has become quite desperate in his search to marry me off."

Walter frowned impishly and asked, "How could I take that the wrong way?"

She looked alarmed until I said, "He's joking. You'll come to learn that he has a sly sense of humor."

"Well," she continued, "as I was saying, my father wishes to have me married, and has tried finding me a suitor many times."

I nearly choked on my ale. "Nobody would have you?"

"Impossible," Walter added.

Now it was Lady May that smiled impishly. "My father may consider me to be only a pawn, but I prefer the queen's role. Had I been inclined to be married off to just any man, the matter would have been settled long ago, but I have my ways, and when the match doesn't suit me, and it never did, I can be quite unapproachable when I want to be."

"You are a schemer," I said, showing my own modicum of admiration, "and I gather, a chess player."

She blushed slightly and nodded her head. "Guilty on both counts. I have been educated as well, in reading and politics.

Should I ever find a suitable man, I could help him run things."

"That would be a rare man indeed," I said.

She nodded her head demurely and said, "So you see my plight."

"Walter," I said with an air of authority, "why don't you show Lady May our market? She can meet some of the real people of Greenshire."

Lady May didn't look quite ready to leave, but I assured her, "Fear not. We will have more opportunities to speak. For now, I have some webs to weave."

She looked me directly in the eye and nodded knowingly. I have no doubt that she completely understood the nature, if not the details, of what I was planning to do.

With them gone, Nelly returned to buss the table.

"What do you think of her?" I asked.

"Of who?" she asked. "I wasn't close enough to hear what you was saying."

"Nelly..."

"It taint my place to have such an opinion."

I smiled broadly and said, "You liked her, didn't you?"

"I did. I do. She's a real down-to-earth girl if you asks me, despite her upbringing."

I smiled broadly and said, "She might be a real lucky girl, if she can latch onto Master Walter as a husband."

Nelly looked confused. "He's a good enough boy, I suppose."

"Sit down," I whispered, "please."

She took the nearest chair, knowing I was about to reveal something juicy.

"The thing is that catching Walter could go either way. Did you know that Lord Chamberlain might not be the rightful heir to Chamberlain Hall?"

Her eyes widened as she gasped, "No!"

"It's true. Apparently, they skipped a first-born daughter, even though she had already given birth to a son. Do you believe that? It's not like we're talking about the crown. The Chamberlain holdings are only a viscounty after all."

"Is someone contesting it? Do you mean that she could tie up with Master Walter and end up a pauper?"

"It's possible," I said, "but the pendulum could also swing the other way. There's a possibility that Walter could be one of the long-lost bastards that the King is looking for."

She sucked in her breath, unable to reply.

"So you see, Walter could be quite a gamble for her."

"No," Nelly said. "Walter would be a gem indeed. She won't care none if he's a pauper. She already expressed her disdain for tying nobility with blood."

"But what if he's the King's bastard?" I asked.

"Then she still has the catch of her life. They would no doubt get some stipend to buy them off and not claim the royal title."

I nodded my head as if she had explained it to me. "You are really quite brilliant. It's a wonder you don't own this place."

"One day," she said, "maybe I will."

"I must go." My job here was done. Soon the town would be buzzing with the new gossip.

I had scarcely left the tavern when I saw Elizabeth approach on a creamy white colored Andalusian horse which was brought over from Spain when Lord Leatherby brought my mother and father here.

She waved from her mount and said, "Hector! Winston told me I might find you here."

I had to think fast, because I certainly was not the only one she was going to find here. "If you'll excuse me, I was just leaving. I hope you are not too tired to ride back with me."

"Nonsense," she said. "As long as I am here, I may as well peruse the market."

I must have stood there too long with a dumbfounded expression on my face.

"What's wrong? Is my father expecting you back?"

I shook my head no.

"Your father then?"

I croaked out a weak, "No."

"Fine then. Walk with me. Agnes said there were some new colored silks that I should see."

I needed to snap out of it, but at the moment, I was no longer in charge. I took the reins of her horse and tied it off, then helped her down. She immediately started walking to the market square with me in tow.

"You're awfully quiet," she said. "Is something vexing

you?"

Before I could answer, Walter and Lady May exited one of the larger booths. Walter waved and called out, "Elizabeth!"

Elizabeth started to return his greeting, but paused when she saw Lady May. "Who is that?"

"That is…"

Walter pulled Lady May by the hand and said, "Lady Elizabeth Leatherby, this is Lady May Cranston."

I found my voice and said, "Lady Elizabeth and Walter are betrothed."

Lady May jerked her hand from Walter's and said, "But I thought I was brought here to meet Lord Walter. In fact, I am quite sure I recall Master Giovanni telling me that the Lady Elizabeth was betrothed to you, Don Hector."

"Technically, yes," I replied, "but that was just a ruse…"

Elizabeth stepped in to finish my statement, "until we could figure some way to get my father and Lord Chamberlain to end their silly feud."

The anger that had registered on Lady May's face only a moment ago had melted away to be replaced by quite a hearty laugh. "Oh, this is priceless. The three of you are playing a wicked game with your parents, while your parents have some kind of feud getting in the way?"

"Yes," I said.

"That's the sum of it," Elizabeth added.

I explained, "It wasn't something that we planned to do…"

Elizabeth continued my thought, "but when my father discovered my betrothal ring, I panicked…"

"and," I continued, "she told him the ring was from me. I immediately thought the idea was folly."

"It's true," Elizabeth said. "Hector thought the idea of me marrying a gardener's son was ridiculous…"

"And it was," I said, "but for some reason, her father was delighted, and that was before we even learned that my father was a Marquis."

A spark of surprise entered Elizabeth's eyes. "My father must have…"

"… known all along." I finished, with the same shock to my voice.

Elizabeth and I shared a mild look of shock and sudden understanding. When I turned to Walter and Lady May, they were also staring at us with the same surprised look. "You see it too? How he must have known all along?"

"Yes," Walter said, "I see it too, but that's not why I'm staring at you. It's the way you two…"

"… keep finishing each other's sentences," Lady May said. Then she and Walter turned to each other and laughed out loud.

Lady May slapped her hands together in a single loud clap and announced, "Whatever you are up to, count me in. I love the intrigue and the drama you are creating."

Walter snickered and said, "I get the feeling that you would love anything that might make a fool of our parents."

Lady May shrugged and said, "They created the rules. I think it's high time we question them. What can I do to help?"

I smiled broadly and said, "I have some ideas on that, but we must all be prepared for the plans to change in an instant."

Lady May rubbed her hands together and smiled mischievously.

I tented my hands like a monk in prayer and said, "Lady May, I..."

She thrust her hands out towards me and said, "Can we dispense with the titles when it's just the four of us? Please call me May."

"Are you sure?" I asked. "I mean, may I May?"

Walter and Elizabeth laughed, but May just gave me a blank stare.

"Oh," I said, "I suppose you've heard that one before?"

"More times than you can count."

"Well, just so we are all on the same page, I've dropped some rumors that the King had taken a lusty tour through these lands, before any of our births, and may have left a bastard or two in his wake. I've implicated Walter as a possible prince, but I've also suggested that Lord Chamberlain may not be the rightful heir to the viscounty. It turns out that there was a first-born daughter who was skipped for succession of Chamberlain Hall."

"That's true," Walter said. "My Grandda had an older sister."

May groaned. She clearly hated the patriarchy. "How does building him up and down at the same time help?"

I pointed at Walter and Elizabeth and said, "The whole silly feud between their families is based on unfounded rumors and suspicions of infidelity."

May nodded and said, "So you give them a choice of rumors to choose from that have opposite consequences."

I nodded.

"So," May asked, "What do the people know about me?"

"Only what Giovanni has told them."

She smiled sinisterly. "He only knows of my father. Nobody will speak of my mother."

This piqued my curiosity. "What was wrong with your mother? Please don't tell this to anyone, but I snuck a peek at Giovanni's notes, and I saw nothing about your mother in them."

The three of them cocked their heads and gave me a look of surprise that lasted but a few seconds before she replied, "Nothing was wrong with my mother, except that she wasn't born of noble blood."

I looked at her curiously and asked, "If your father was so open-minded and modern that he would marry a commoner, why does he insist on getting you a noble marriage?"

"Because he loved my mother dearly, but he was ostracized for marrying her. Trade deals with other houses fell through and she was blamed and humiliated by other families until the day she took her life."

Walter put a warm, friendly hand on her shoulder and said, "I'm so sorry."

"Thank you," she said, "but the fact that she is kept such a secret means she could have been anybody."

"Yes," I said, catching on, "your mother could have been a princess from another land."

Elizabeth curtsied and said, "Your Majesty."

May giggled and said, "I mean, maybe, if it could help."

May, Elizabeth and Walter had gone together to see some of the new silks, while I tried to think of ways to introduce May's mother into the plot when Nelly came out of a of a farmer's stalls just across the aisle from me.

"Nelly!" I exclaimed. "It is so seldom when I see you outside of the tavern. Does this mean you have a new love interest?"

"Ha!" she laughed. "Garrick thinks I'm his dog that he can send out to fetch things for him."

I glanced up and down her figure. "But your hands are empty. Are you fetching fresh air for him? Lord knows the tavern could certainly use it."

She laughed again and said, "I just delivered his order for more wheat. Same thing, if you asks me. How's the new girl doing? She looks pretty chummy with Master Walter. Warn't he sweet on Lady Elizabeth? Or did you come in and steal his lady from him?"

"Hardly. Ever since word got out that Walter might be one of the King's bastards, he's been getting letters of introduction from royals all over Europe. She's a princess, royal on her mother's side."

"You don't say. Well, I better be getting back to work. Garrick kicks dogs, you know."

And easy as that, I had laid out another tidbit of my master lie.

As I watched Nelly walk back to the tavern, Elizabeth called from behind, "What's this? His excellency Don Hector de la Roca is flirting with a local barmaid?"

It was clear that she was teasing. I resisted turning to face her, and continued towards the tavern, until I heard May add, "I must get to know this town better. First the Lady Elizabeth is betrothed to the gardener's son, and now the notorious Don Hector is spending time with a barmaid. I must applaud you on your freedom to love here."

"But he's MY Don Hector," Elizabeth whined in a clearly fake baby cry.

I sighed and turned. "I hope you are enjoying your laugh, but I was busy setting our plan in motion."

"Which plan would that be?" May asked. "I do have the feeling that you might have multiple plans in mind, and none of them end with you actually caught in any woman's snare."

"I'm just trying to find happiness for Elizabeth and Walter."

May pointed towards the tavern and asked, "By flirting with her? I don't think Elizabeth looks very happy."

Elizabeth and May could only hold their sour expressions for a moment before bursting out laughing.

I wagged my finger and said, "The two of you are going to ruin everything with your shenanigans."

Walter had stood off to the side, enjoying the teasing, but it was getting late and he said, "Perhaps we should get inside and have enough to drink that all of this gaiety won't seem out of place."

I nodded and headed for the tavern.

Once inside, Walter went to secure one of the larger tables, but I took his arm and said, "Let's sit in the shadows and listen."

Nelly was happy to serve us wherever we sat, but she had to ask, "Why are you hiding in the corner here?"

I smiled and lied, "I'm expecting someone who may be in a foul mood and I don't want him to see me."

The late crowd had not arrived yet, but the early revelers were getting a start on the evening's frivolity. The general noise rose with both the size of the crowd and the volume of drink consumed.

Walter tapped me on the shoulder and asked, "Did you hear that? I swear I heard someone say that I was a royal bastard."

I smiled broadly and said, "Give them time. By evening's end, I expect that every one of us will be royal by rumor."

The evening was progressing splendidly, until, that is, my father stepped in. He wasn't wearing the courtly uniform I had seen him in before, but neither was he wearing his gardener overalls.

I stood and called to him, "Father!"

He came to our table and everyone immediately stood and nodded their heads to an unrehearsed chorus of, "Excellency."

He sucked in his breath, and I thought he would object to the title, but before he could speak, I said, "Please join us. You are looking quite formal tonight. Allow me to introduce you to the Lady May Cranston. Your friend Giovanni has brought her here to meet Master Walter. She is quite a delight, as you shall see if you join us."

May extended a delicate hand and said, "Your Excellency. It is indeed a pleasure to make your acquaintance. Don Hector has told me almost nothing about you, and I hope we can take this opportunity to rectify that."

My father took her hand and held it to his lips. "It has been long since I have heard the gentleness of the court." He then nodded his head and took a seat.

"In truth," I said, "Giovanni has shared almost nothing about her father, Lord Cranston, but her mother is an even bigger mystery."

"Oh?" my father asked. "It is a shame when such a well-mannered young lady is born to a scandal."

"It's not that," Elizabeth said. "The rumor is that her mother was a princess."

"Only a rumor?" My father asked. "Do you not know if your mother was a princess?"

I explained, "Lady May never had a chance to..."

May kicked me slightly under the table, as she bowed her head and made a sad expression, "My mother died when I was young, and there was a scandal, but the staff was not allowed to share it with me."

"I see," my father said, "sometimes it is best to let the sleeping dog lie."

"It was a long time ago," she continued, "and my father did a grand job of raising me. I wish I could have known her, but I can't complain without tarnishing the job that my father had done."

My father nodded his understanding. "It would seem that my old friend Giovanni may know his craft better than the credit I gave him. I should speak with him the next time I see him."

As if on cue, Giovanni began to sing loudly as he sloshed a mug of ale around the table where he sat.

My father laughed and said, "Perhaps I'll wait until the next time I see him sober."

I laughed and raised my mug. "Let us toast to my father's patience as he waits to speak with a sober Giovanni."

To my surprise, my father actually defended his old friend. "He's a man, and he has apparently done well in his work. He deserves some time to rejoice and relax."

We all smiled and toasted his patience.

The ride home left me too much time to think, and I had far too many things running through my mind. Not only about the schemes I laid out in town, but also how exposing my father's title had changed our lives.

I didn't exactly know what the change was in my father, but he seemed more personable. In removing his gardener guise, he seemed to have also freed his own personality to come out on display. I had always known him to be a friendly, loving man, but that was at home with his own family. Outside of the cottage, he was reserved and never sought any kind of recognition, except in his gardens. They were magnificent, but the truth is that no matter how spectacular a nobleman's gardens are, the gardener is just a hired hand and would seldom get any real praise for his work.

Elizabeth rode ahead, allowing my father and me to ride side by side. As much as she often acted the vacuous aristocrat, she sometimes made very astute observations, and at the moment, she deemed this a good time for us to bond outside of the home.

My father cleared his throat slightly, to break the silence that had preceded it. "That May girl seems to be a very nice young lady. Do you know where she will be staying?"

In all the time I had known him, he had never referred to a noble person with such familiarity. He must have also shifted back into his own noble personality. I shall have to see if I like this new person. "I do not know, but I'm sure that Giovanni would have secured adequate accommodations for her."

"Yes," he replied. "I guess he would have. I must compliment him when I see him next."

"When he is not drunk," I added with a snicker.

Lord Leatherby was out in front of the manor, looking quite agitated. "Elizabeth! My darling girl! I am so glad to see you!"

"What is it Father? What is wrong? Has something happened?"

"Wrong?" he asked. He was hiding something. I could hear it in his voice. "What could possibly be wrong? You have returned and you are in the company of my dear friend Don Fernando and my adopted son Don Hector. I hope, Don Fernando, that you don't mind my calling him my adopted son. He has always seemed so, and he and Elizabeth were so much like brother and sister, growing up together as they have. Tell me, is Lord Walter with you?"

Elizabeth and I looked quizzically at each other before I answered, "He is not, Lord Leatherby." I used his title since he had addressed both my father and me as Dons, not to mention calling Walter a Lord rather than the somewhat derogatory Master.

Elizabeth climbed down from her mount and gave the reins to Winston before asking, "What is with you, father? Since when is *Lord* Walter or any Chamberlain welcome on Leatherby lands?"

Leatherby bowed his head and said, "Please forgive this foolish old man. I never should have allowed that silly feud to go on so long."

I chuckled and whispered to Elizabeth, "He knows."

She barely acknowledged my remark and asked her father, "How would the Chamberlains know that you have come to your senses after all these years, and why would that compel *Lord* Walter to come here himself?"

That was the second time I noted how she stressed the word 'Lord' in reference to Walter.

"I may be an old fool," Leatherby said, "but I'm not stupid. I know that you and Lord Walter have been seeing each other behind my back. I hear things."

"This is excellent news!" I said as I climbed down and gave the reins to Winston. "Elizabeth and Walter are an excellent pair."

Elizabeth opened her mouth to speak, but my guess was that she wasn't sure what she was arguing about. She turned to me and whispered, "I don't understand what is going on."

I smiled and said, "I think I do. I started a rumor that Walter might be one of the king's long-lost bastards."

Her face twisted up, and still speaking privately to me, she said, "Oh, is that it? Walter was not good enough for me because we loved each other, but now that my father thinks he may be royal..."

"Easy!" I said, trying to calm her down. "Isn't this what we wanted?"

She scowled and mumbled, "It was. Now I'm not so sure."

I took her in my arms and reassured her, "Don't fret about it tonight. Sleep well and see how you feel in the morning."

She nodded her head and went inside.

I bowed as a nobleman and said, "I bid you good night, Lord Leatherby."

My father chuckled and said, "Good night, Walter."

My father and I turned to head back to the cottage.

Chapter Eight

For someone with absolutely no responsibilities, I found myself utterly swamped with things to do and too many places where I needed to be simultaneously. In particular, I was spending far too much time planting the seeds of rumors at the local tavern where I also hung around observing their growth.

The sun had barely started to warm the air when I headed off towards town. My father was already up and working in the gardens. He had fully acknowledged his title as the Marquis, or perhaps I should say he resigned himself to regaining his title, yet he still rose before dawn to tend the gardens. Was it habit now? Knowing him all my life counted for naught. I was only just learning to know the man. He may have felt some sense of pride in what he had created and wasn't willing to relinquish it until he found a suitable successor.

Winston was still fetching my horse when I saw Giovanni's cart pull up to the manor.

"Winston? I'll be right back."

Lord Leatherby anxiously greeted Giovanni in the courtyard. "Thank you for coming so early. I want you to arrange a match between Lady Elizabeth and Lord Walter."

"But…"

"I know what you are going to say. Elizabeth is already promised to the gardener's son."

I was grateful that they had not gone inside. It was far easier to spy on them from behind the hedge, and if I was to spread rumors throughout the land, then I must also admit that I was a spy as well.

"You do know," Giovanni said, "that Don Fernando is no mere gardener."

"I know this, but that is how the people have seen him for many years and I think Lord Walter would be a much more suitable match."

"The matching of souls is a solemn responsibility to me. I cannot override the science and art in what I do on a whim."

"I will pay you. Handsomely, I should add. Just see to it that they are put together."

Giovanni sighed. "I can put them together, but that may not be the course that nature will take."

"Do that then. Put them together and you will be rewarded."

I slipped quietly back to the stables, as any master spy would do, and mounted my horse with the thought that if I left promptly, I might beat Giovanni back to town without him ever seeing me.

I aimed my steed towards the town, but stopped abruptly and slipped down from it when I saw my father heading towards the manor. "Here," I said to Winston as I handed the reins back to him and said, "I'll be right back."

"Yes, my lord."

I closed my eyes and sucked in my breath to tell him not to call me that, but just shook my head instead and scurried off to a better vantage point. Maybe this spy stuff was going to my head.

"Don Fernando!" Leatherby exclaimed. "Have you come for breakfast? You know you are always welcome."

My father nodded his head in a kind of mini bow and said, "No, I actually wanted to let you know I would be going to town this morning."

"Tut tut," Leatherby said. "You need not inform me of your comings and goings. I don't think anybody still thinks of you as a servant."

"Call it a courtesy," my father said.

Now it was Lord Leatherby's turn to bow his head. "I hope all is well."

"Of course. I was just hoping to speak with my old friend Giovanni."

"Giovanni?" Leatherby asked. "You just missed him by a hairsbreadth, but I thought you no longer considered him your friend."

"This is why I wish to speak with him. I fear I may have wronged him."

"You should hurry, then. He has promised to arrange a meeting for the Lady Elizabeth and a new suitor. I am almost inclined to follow him myself and see how it goes, but I fear that such an action may be over watching my daughter."

"It is hard for us not to be too protective of our children, is it not?"

"If you hurry, you might catch him."

"I think I shall enjoy the ride. Where could he go, but the tavern?"

I sprinted back to the stables and leaped onto my horse, then galloped towards the exit before my father could catch up to me.

Have I mentioned that I had been spending far too much time in the tavern? I wasn't drinking, mind you, but if I wasn't spreading innuendo, then I was observing how they spread on their own. I usually did my spy work from the shadows, where only Nelly knew I was there. She loved the intrigue, and even though she wasn't a core member of our inner circle, she involved herself any chance she could.

It was still early when I entered the pub and Nelly quickly swept me to a poorly lit corner, saying, "You'll have to do your spyin' from here today. Your usual shady corner is taken."

"This early?" I asked.

"Yeah. They arrived last night and haven't shown no signs of leaving. They is dressed like merchants, but I seen their daggers on their belts and I don't think they is who they says they is. I wouldn't be surprised if they has swords hidden away under their cloaks too. They is nice enough to me and hasn't acted like cutthroats, but who was I to know?"

She sat me in a corner opposite from them. I could make out their outlines, albeit barely, as they stirred and drank their ales. The light was too dim to make out any colors. That was what I must have looked like when I sat there. It's probably what I looked like in my new corner as well. "Who do they claim to be?"

She sat down next to me so she could lower her voice. "Come to think of it, they hasn't said who they was, but I can tell you that they talks like they is important. Kind of educated like."

"Thanks Nelly."

"Should I bring you your usual?"

I nodded my head.

"If they says anything, I'll be sure to let ya know."

I glanced around the room at the empty tables. It was still early, but I had at least a good view of the entire establishment while at the same time feeling safe in my shadowy corner.

This was not the kind of establishment that would have farmers and ranchers in the middle of the day, and certainly not this early in the morning. But there was Giovanni, sitting at one of the center tables, looking more suspicious than usual. I say suspicious because he wasn't drinking, and he was wearing one of his finer costumes. Did I mention that he wasn't drinking?

Then there were those four gentlemen in the corner, scratch that. They weren't exactly dressed as gentlemen, but they might have been. They seemed too disordered and undisciplined to be soldiers, and they definitely weren't wearing uniforms. Perhaps they were merchants, but since when do merchants travel in packs of four?

I had a perfect view of them, but was far too distant to hear them, although I couldn't actually see them speaking much. Two of them appeared to be resting, and may actually have been napping. One of them tapped another on the shoulder as I heard the door open and close to my right.

My father strode in and walked straight to Giovanni's table. Giovanni looked alarmed and said, "Don Fernando, please excuse me, but I'm rather busy today."

My father showed his palms in a sign of peace and said, "This will only take a moment. I fear that I have wronged you. I have slighted your profession and brought question to your voracity. For that I apologize."

Giovanni was caught speechless only for the ticking of a clock. "Excellency, this is so unexpected. I think I can spare a moment for you. Would you care to sit?"

My father joined him at the table and said, "I have seen and heard enough to believe in the fruits of your work and I was wondering..."

Giovanni folded his hands together and broke the silent pause. "Yes, Don Fernando? What were you wondering?"

"Now that our identities are no longer a secret, I was wondering if you could find a suitable match for my son Hector?"

Giovanni smiled slyly. "Do you think he needs my help? He is such a clever boy, much like his father."

My father chuckled and said, "I think his cleverness comes from his mother."

"Was it her idea to take sanctuary in England under the guise of a gardener?"

"No," my father admitted. "That was my doing. I wonder sometimes if I have done Hector a disservice."

Giovanni touched my father's sleeve. It was a familiar gesture that would not be tolerated by two men doing business. "From what I have witnessed with my own eyes, your son is far nobler than most children who were raised into their nobility. I think that how you raised him as a gardener's son has made him a better man."

My father placed his hand atop Giovanni's, which was still on his sleeve. "You do me too much credit, but here I am, the Marquis of Avila, with a son who was raised as a servant's boy. How is he ever to wed into society?"

Giovanni sucked in his breath. "I thought you were jesting. Are you truly asking for my help?"

My father's face turned stern and noble. "I am. In your official capacity as a matchmaker, can you find a proper bride for my Hector?"

Giovanni smiled, almost a sinister smile, and said, "Fear not, Don Fernando. Giovanni will find the perfect match for Don Hector, and for you, my old friend, there will be no charge. It will be my honor and my pleasure."

My father stood and clicked his heels. "Thank you, Giovanni. I shall await word from you as to when arrangements can be made."

The sinister smile never left Giovanni's face. "You shall get it. I promise you. Word will come."

I hadn't even noticed the three boys standing by the door until after my father had left and Giovanni had signaled for one of them, and that was only after he had folded three of the documents he had been writing and pressed his seal onto the freshly dripped wax.

My spy skills must need some training or I would have seen them skulking by the entrance. I knew the boy that came forward. He was an unremarkable lad named Tommy, who was often seen working on one of the farms. I could guess his age at around twelve years old. He was probably the farmer's son, but he could have been a homeless boy working for scraps when the farmers could afford it.

Giovanni handed the three documents to Tommy and pressed a coin into his hand as he whispered some instructions to him. The boy enthusiastically nodded his head and ran out. The coin would have been far better than the scraps he might get from a farmer.

The mysterious strangers in the corner followed Giovanni's every movement and whispered amongst themselves. I thought for a moment one of them was going to get up to follow Tommy, but one of his brethren held his arm and he remained seated. These were not merchants. Perhaps their interest was in Giovanni, or the coin that he kept. Up until a few moments ago, my father had described him as a scoundrel and these men had the look about them of men who might take an interest in such a rogue.

Giovanni continued working on four more documents. After folding them as he had done with the first, he again used his seal and wax to fasten them and called up each of the other boys in turn. More whispered instructions and a coin sent the boys off through the door with two documents apiece.

Something was most definitely afoot, and Giovanni was at the center of it. I was sure that it would reveal itself in due time, or he wouldn't have employed the three boys to deliver the documents, which I presumed were part of his craft and based on the official seal he used, were probably invitations.

It struck me that if spying does not work out for me, I could employ myself as a watchman to protect the people and investigate crimes, since I seemed to have some aptitude towards the craft.

I shook my head to brush off that particular reverie. I was definitely spending too much time in the tavern.

The four strangers in the corner did not appear interested in leaving, except perhaps to piss, and they took turns doing that. I didn't know what could be so intriguing about our little tavern, but I was convinced that they were here for a purpose and were absolutely interested in something.

I, on the other hand, could not lounge around all day. Even without any official duties at Leatherby House, I did at least need to greet my mother once in a while. Plus, as good as the food sometimes was here, they rarely served anything other than left-overs for the mid-day meal, and anything my mother prepared was far better, anyway.

As I got up to leave, Nelly blocked my way and asked, "What's this? You're not staying for a bite?"

I was unprepared to respond, and my jaw fell slack.

She giggled and said, "I'm just teasin' you. You can do a lot better than what I'll be serving for this meal today. Except for that fancy fellow Giovanni, I think we're still reusing the meat from two days ago. Did you know that he brung in his own cooks? I thought there would be a row about it, but I suspect some coins changed hands to keep the peace."

I kissed her on the cheek and said, "Keep notes for me while I'm gone?"

She smiled broadly and said, "I would if I could."

I knew she couldn't read or write, but it made her feel a

little more important when I treated her as if she could. "No, No! Nothing on paper that anyone might find." I tapped her on the temple and said, "Just keep your notes up here and tell them to me when I return."

She winked and slapped my bottom. "Has you gotten more plump in the seat since you been made a Don?"

I shrugged my shoulders and left. Maybe I should have a talk with her about whether such contact is appropriate in public, given my new title, but in truth, it kind of gave me a warm feeling inside. I can be a nobleman and still be one of the people.

I had scarcely reached my horse when I saw Walter and May leaving the Mall together. I left the horse tied up and crossed the road to them wagging my finger. "The two of you are up to something."

May looked appropriately, if not genuinely, perplexed as she asked, "Don Hector. Whatever do you mean?"

"Just Hector between us, and I shall call you May, if I may, May?"

She giggled. "Of course."

"You caught us," Walter said, "but you really must hear May's idea. Go ahead and tell him."

"We learned that Lord Leatherby is now in favor of Elizabeth marrying Walter."

"Did you hear that?!" Walter exclaimed as he punched me in the shoulder. "Something about some ridiculous rumor about me being one of the king's bastard whelps."

I clapped my hands. "This is excellent news. It would seem that my plans are working, but what has this to do with the mischief that you two seem so intent upon?"

"Because," May said excitedly. "Why should we make it so easy for them? First Lord Leatherby thinks Walter is not good enough for his daughter, but now he thinks better of his decision. Placing so much emphasis on Walter's lineage sounds just too much like my father wanting the perfect sire for his mare. They are treating us like livestock."

She was far feistier and more modern than I had ever given her credit for being. Perhaps I was just then seeing how she earned the nickname I saw in Giovanni's files of Lady May Not. "So what, exactly, are you proposing?"

She hooked her arm around Walter's and said, "Walter and I will become an item. That is why I was shipped here, after all."

I winced slightly when she said, "shipped."

She caught my glance and said, "It's okay. You tend to get used to it when you are raised from a young age, knowing that you would one day marry a man and give them sons. It's assumed that we are to give them sons, but to be perfectly honest, I'm not sure I would want to raise a daughter to these expectations."

"You are truly a stand out individual," I replied. "I can't recall anyone, man or woman, with your grasp of the real politics behind the diplomacy. You would make a fine leader if ever called upon."

She laughed, but it was a cruel, heartless sound. "As if a woman could ever lead in this world, but we digress. I thought that if Walter and I appeared to become very close, then Lord Leatherby may learn that his plans to sell his daughter to the highest bidder may have failed." With that, her face changed instantly from a hardened, bitter woman to a soft, desirable young lady.

I bowed low and said, "Lady May, I think your plan is a marvelous one and I shall do nothing to interfere. In fact, I shall only enhance it." I did not add that after watching her morph her face as I just had, that I would not dare do anything to cross any sorceress of such extraordinary powers.

"So," I asked, "are you heading to the tavern? There's not much going on there at the moment."

"We are," Walter replied, then he held up one of the dispatches that I had seen Giovanni give to the two boys. "We have apparently been invited to lunch with Master Giovanni."

May held up the other matching invitation and waved it back and forth, saying, "Summoned may be a better word for these invitations."

"Then you are in luck. He is there now and appears to be doing some business. I shall not hold you. It is time I check in with my mother, anyway."

May looked shocked. "You still check in with your mother?"

Walter chuckled and said, "You haven't tasted her stewed beef."

"Well then," May said, "We shall not hold you either. Eat well."

I had nearly reached the estate's outer gate when I saw Elizabeth emerge, but she wasn't riding the brilliant white Andalusian that she normally rode. She was in an open carriage with Winston at the reins. As we neared each other, I saw the purpose of the carriage. She wore a very fine dress, like those she would reserve for a ball, if her father had only held them anymore. The glint in her eye told me she was rather excited for the opportunity to dress so finely.

"Good morning," I greeted her.

"Good morning," she replied, unable to suppress the smile that beamed across her face. "I think it's finally happening. Father spoke to Giovanni on Walter's behalf, and now I have an invitation to join him for lunch, in an official capacity, no less."

I grimaced and leaned close to say, "There is something you should know then. Walter and May have cooked up a scheme to make your father look somewhat foolish."

"Why on earth would they do that?"

"They only wish to teach him a lesson about, as May put it, selling his daughter to the highest bidder."

The smile was gone from her face now. "What does that mean?"

"Only that your father did not come around to accepting Walter until he heard the false rumor that Walter might be the King's bastard."

She frowned now. "One of your schemes, no doubt."

I grimaced again and shrugged my shoulders. "Do your duty and meet with him. Do not let their fake affections bother you. It's actually a decent lesson that all of our parents could learn from."

She sighed and admitted, "Yes. I can see how that would work, but I was so excited that the invitation might be to join Walter and myself."

"Be excited then! In the end of all of this, you will be matched with your love, and our parents will have learned a lesson in true nobility."

"You are right," she said, her voice a little brighter, then she pitched up her volume and said, "Winston? Carry on."

My father would normally be in the garden doing whatever gardeners do. I think I was lucky that he did not take me to the fields to learn his craft, especially given what we have learned about our true lineage. Not that gardening isn't a worthy profession, but it was never something to inspire me. He wasn't in the gardens at present. I entered the cottage to find him with my mother, beaming from ear to ear and waving one of those invitations that Giovanni had sent out.

"What are you doing with that?" I asked.

"A correspondence came for you," he said.

"It did? For me? And is that it that you have already opened and read?"

He seemed to delight in torturing me at the moment and waited a good pause before bringing up his other hand and saying, "No, the one I wave in my hand was addressed to me, but you have this other one of your own."

I snatched it from his hands and ripped it open. It was one of the documents from Giovanni. I couldn't let him know that I had been spying on his little meeting with Giovanni. "What is this? Why is he addressing me with his concerns?"

"Forgive a proud father, but it is time for you to reap the benefits of our heritage."

"What do you mean? Why do you speak to me as if you were giving a speech?"

"Not a speech," he replied, "but a toast. A toast to your wedding."

"My WHAT?" I did not mean to raise my voice, but it happened all the same. "Father! What have you done?"

"I spoke with my old friend Giovanni and asked him to arrange a suitable match for you."

"Without asking me first?"

"It is time," he said.

It was only then that I noticed my mother holding one of my father's uniforms. It was not like the black one that I saw him wear to confront Lord Leatherby, but it was not so different, save for being bright red. "What is that for?"

"This is for you," my mother said, beaming with the same pride that my father wore. "You have been summoned by Giovanni to a dinner where you should meet someone worthy of your station."

"Now I have a station? After all these years as the gardener's son?"

"Yes," my father said in a calm, soothing voice. "You have always had a station, no matter what guise I wore. Have you not benefited all these years from the same tutors as Lady Elizabeth?"

"Because I was close to her age, and Lord Leatherby is a modern, fair minded man."

"Those are all true," my mother said, "but you are also Don Hector Reynaldo Castillo de la Roca, son of Don Fernando Rodrigo Castillo de la Roca, The Most Excellent Marquis of Avila."

"Let us not forget," my father said, "that you are also the son of the Marquess Luisa Esmerelda Castillo de la Roca. Now put this on and go meet with Giovanni."

My jaw fell slack as my mother pushed the uniform into my hands. While I was plotting my schemes, they were plotting schemes of their own.

"Put that on," my mother said, "and go."

"But, Mama..."

"Don't mama me. You're a grown man now. Go meet your potential bride."

"That's right," my father said. "Keep in mind that whoever she is, she is only a prospective bride. If you don't like her, you don't have to marry her."

I looked again at the invitation. There was no indication of who I was to meet, other than Giovanni.

"Go on now," my father said. "Change clothes and go to town."

"But I'm hungry," I said in a childish whine. I didn't know why I suddenly sounded like a small child, but it also felt kind of like they were treating me like a child.

"Well, it's a good thing," my father said, pushing me towards my room, "that it's a dinner invitation. Hurry up and change if you are so hungry."

There was no use fighting it. I went to my room and put on the very bright red uniform. It left me feeling like a game fowl just begging some hunter to shoot me, or worse yet; I was a color blind matador inciting a rabid bull to gore me to death. I exited my room and showed my parents that at least I was an obedient son. The uniform fit surprisingly well, considering that it was probably one of my father's old uniforms. Even as fit as he has kept himself, I doubt he could fit it today.

I was quite sure that I heard them proclaim their pride in me as I left the cottage, although their voices were private whispers between only themselves. Today would be the first day in a very long time that I did not anticipate how things would unfold. This shall be interesting, if nothing else, although terrifying would be a more appropriate description of how I felt at the time.

When I entered the tavern, I saw Walter and May at a table off to the side. Even through the mild haze that forever hung in the air, I could see pleasant expressions on both of their faces. Elizabeth, on the other hand, sat at the center table with Giovanni and she was not amused in the slightest.

Walter saw me even before the door was closed behind me. How could he help but to see me? This uniform shone like a beacon through the night and I swore I could see a red cast reflected in the haze.

I approached their table and said, "Walter, May, have you convinced Giovanni to endorse your charade?"

Walter shook his head no.

May volunteered, "Remember, he had sent for me just so I could meet Lord Walter, so here we are."

"Ahh," I said, "I expect he needs to put the two of you together to fulfill his contract. I hope that playing the part is not too taxing on you."

"Not at all," Walter said. "May is a spirited conversationalist. I believe that we shall remain friends no matter how this all resolves."

"It is always good to have friends," I added.

"Speaking of which," May interjected, "I think your friend Lady Elizabeth could use your council."

"Actually," Walter said, "I think she needs you to come to her rescue."

May giggled, but I saw the truth in Elizabeth's eyes. "Very well then, I know my duty."

As I turned towards Elizabeth at Giovanni's table, I noticed that the four strangers had taken a striking interest in me. After conferring with each other, one of them stood to leave the tavern. Clearly, I could not be a spy in this peacock of a uniform. I quickly sat down at Walter's table and said, "Walter, don't ask questions, but quickly keep to the shadows and sneak out to follow that man and tell me what he does."

I could see that Walter's first instinct was to ask why, but instead he slipped out of the chair and slid his back up to the wall, where he quietly left.

"What is it?" May asked.

"I'm not quite sure, but I've been watching those fellows in the corner all morning. There's something not quite right about them."

"How marvelously intriguing!" she said, "But why don't you follow him yourself?"

I pinched the red fabric of my suit and shrugged.

She laughed and said, "Of course. He's not in any danger, is he?"

"I don't think so."

Nelly quietly slipped into a seat between May and I. "Did you see that? That's the second time that one up and left when it warn't his turn to pee."

"When was the other time?" I asked.

"That was when the Giovanni fellow set up at the center table. If I recalls correctly, he almost left after you left this morning, but the other blokes pulled him back."

I scratched my chin and said, "Thanks, Nelly."

"There's something else," she said.

May and I both leaned in close, but Nelly was silent until May said, "What!?! What else is there?"

Nelly was clearly enjoying our rapt attention and said, "They was scratchin' out little notes every time afore that one left."

Walter returned, panting. "It was a bird. They have a crate of birds in the livery, and he let one go."

"Did he attach anything to the bird?" I asked. "Like a note maybe?"

"Oh," Walter said, "is that what he was doing?"

"So," I said, more to myself, but aloud just the same, "they're not merchants."

Nelly nudged me in the ribs with her elbow and said, "So you isn't the only spy in the house, eh?"

"Shh," I said, "let's keep that our little secret."

Elizabeth looked distressingly impatient when I finally arrived at Giovanni's table. I shrugged meekly and asked, "Am I early? I can wait until you are finished with Eliza...Lady Elizabeth."

"No, Don Hector," Giovanni said, "you are perfectly on time, and may I say how smashing you look in your court clothes."

"I'm on time?" I asked as I glanced over at Elizabeth, but she only shrugged.

"Please," Giovanni said as he motioned to a seat opposite Elizabeth, "sit down and I will explain how this works."

I took the seat he had indicated and asked Elizabeth, "Do you know what this is about?"

She shrugged again and said, "He refused to tell me anything."

"Nonsense," Giovanni replied. "I told you I would explain it later, and now it is later. Each of your fathers has engaged my services to find suitable prospects for the two of you.

Normally, this would entail a grand ball where multiple prospects would come forth for you to choose from, but apparently, these lavish affairs have gone out of style at Leatherby House."

Elizabeth sighed. "I've told father many times that we should return to hosting events..."

"I've heard her personally," I added, "but I think Lord Leatherby was afraid that he couldn't prevent certain families from attending..."

"So," Elizabeth finished for me, "he chose to simply stop hosting them."

With us sitting at opposite sides of the round table, and Giovanni essentially in the middle of us, his head had to swivel back and forth to follow the conversation. "It would have been more convenient," he said, "if the tradition had not ended, but no matter. Here we are. As you can see, I have already set Master Walter to sit with Lady May so they may get to know each other."

Elizabeth grunted at the mention of the two of them together.

Giovanni smiled broadly and said, "And don't they look pleasant together?"

"Are we to take turns?" Elizabeth asked. "Do you expect Lady May and I to trade places to sit with Walter? I already know him quite well."

Giovanni shook his hands in the air as if they were saying no. "Not at all. I have another table set aside for the two of you..."

"The two of US?" I asked. "Did you mean for Lady Elizabeth and I to sit at a table together..."

Elizabeth finished for me again. "... when we are practically brother and sister? We've known each other..."

"... since we were babies!" I said. "You can't possibly be suggesting that..."

"... the two of us could be a couple!" she finished.

Again, Giovanni's head was on a swivel. "What could possibly give me that idea?"

We both looked at him blankly.

He smiled and said, as if it were an adequate explanation, "It's not as though you were finishing each other's sentences."

We looked at each other, not sure what to think.

"Have you not noticed?" he continued. "It is like you are married already."

"No!" I said. "It is like we already told you! We are..."

"... brother and sister."

Giovanni shook his head. "But you are not. Perhaps I should introduce you. Lady Elizabeth Mariana Leatherby, Countess of Leatherby, daughter of the Earl of Leatherby, it is my extreme honor to introduce you to Don Hector Reynaldo Castillo de la Roca, future Marquis of Avila, and son of The Most Excellent Marquis of Avila, Don Fernando Rodrigo Castillo de la Roca."

"That all sounds very grand," I said, "but certainly, by now, we have lost our titles to Avila."

"Well," Giovanni said as he raised his index finger in a gesture of something interesting to come, "there are two schools of thought on that. There are quite a few who consider your father a hero for standing up to the inquisition."

"But he didn't stand up to it. He snuck out in the dark of

the night, and not even on his own. He had Lord Leatherby to help him."

"Nonetheless, his people adored him and prospered under his rule. The church would have you believe that he was a heretic, but the people of Avila will tell you that the church didn't approve of how much sway he had with the crown."

A pause followed before I asked, "And what of the other school of thought?"

"That would be the inquisitors," he replied. "Your father's escape was an embarrassment to them. I think they wished to gain control of the whole nation, but they couldn't even control a single Marquis. They probably still want him dead. Now, enough about your family history. Go to the table I prepared for you and enjoy a marvelous meal."

Elizabeth chuckled. "Have you not eaten here?"

Giovanni returned her smile and said, "I made special arrangements for today. Go now. Go on!"

Elizabeth and I sat quietly at our new table, unsure of what we were expected to talk about. I could see, from across the room, that Walter and May had no such trouble. Giovanni looked quite pleased with himself as he sat alone at the center table, looking like a man who had just been crowned king.

"Look at him," I said. "He certainly looks quite pleased with himself."

"The nerve of him," Elizabeth growled.

It was only then that I saw her gaze riveted on Walter.

"I mean," she said stoically, "I understand the plan, and it's a worthy scheme, but must he enjoy playing his part so much?"

"I meant Giovanni. He seems far too pleased with himself."

"HA!" she barked a little too loudly, then in a meeker voice, "He's a buffoon. He sets them together, completely oblivious to the charade they play. And then he has the audacity to sit us together at the same table, even after we explained to him that we are practically siblings? What does he want of us?"

I didn't want to feel mean towards Elizabeth, but I struggled to withhold the mirth I felt from observing her jealousy.

"I thought," she continued, "he was supposed to be a professional! Has he not worked with nobility before? How could he match a brother and sister together?"

I shrugged and said, "I know not, but it is not like there is no incest among the royals."

She shot a look at me that said I should not jest and continued her rant. "We had everything under control. We had it all planned out."

"That's right," I said. "We were going to match Walter and May together to teach your father a lesson."

"Yes!" she said. "No! Not like this. We were only playacting."

"Is that not what they are doing?"

She shook her head and replied, "I know not. He looks truly happy and engaged with her."

"Engaged?" I asked.

"That's not what I meant! They are talking; really talking."

"Are we not talking?"

"No," she said. "We are plotting and scheming."

"And making jealous little observations."

She looked like she were about to hit me when the door burst open and Lord Chamberlain marched in. Giovanni leapt quick as a cat out of his seat to intercept Chamberlain.

Chamberlain spotted Walter and May, but Giovanni skillfully guided the man to the center table. "Lord Chamberlain. Please sit with me while the prospective couple gets to know each other."

Lord Chamberlain started to offer up an argument, but followed Giovanni to his table instead. Nelly was quick to the table where she poured something a bit finer than their usual ale; something that was no doubt from Giovanni's private stock.

Giovanni had arranged the seating, so Chamberlain's back was to Walter and May. Lord Chamberlain craned his neck around and said, "She's a lovely girl. I was skeptical at first, but I must say that you are certainly worth every penny."

Giovanni nodded his head in appreciation and said, "She is quite striking, and she has a sharp head on her shoulders, but perhaps you can give them a moment of privacy while we discuss their future."

Elizabeth's mood, which already balanced precariously between anger and disappointment, grew fouler when she heard Lord Chamberlain's remarks. "Why does he hate me so? Is their silly feud not between him and my father?"

"I believe the feud is based on the many rumors surrounding your births."

"Why would he question whether I am a Leatherby? Does it matter to him so much? Are you suggesting that he had lain with my mother? I wish my mother were here to defend herself."

I patted her hand to soothe her. "I think he questions whether he is Walter's true father. I also firmly believe that all their suspicions are baseless."

"So what if Walter was a bastard? I would love him just the same."

From the corner of my eye, I detected some movement coming from the table with the four strangers, and I swear they became deathly quiet. "Keep your voice down," I whispered. "It would make a great deal of difference if Walter was actually Lord Leatherby's son and your half-brother."

She snapped her hand out from under mine.

"I do not believe it is so, and that is not what I am saying at all, but I suspect that Lord Chamberlain may wonder it."

"What a distasteful thought," she whispered. "We look nothing like brother and sister."

I took a sideways glance at the strangers and observed them craning their necks to hear us. "A game is afoot. You cannot listen to what people say about either of you, and most especially what I'm about to say."

She looked alarmed. "What you're about to say?"

I raised my voice just enough over a whisper, but not shouting and said, "If Walter is one of the King's bastards, then Lord Chamberlain may want something for raising him."

Neither Walter nor his father gave any indication that they had heard me, but the four strangers certainly did as they put their heads together nearly as soon as the words had left my lips. I don't know who these strangers are, but they seemed terribly keen on the rumors circulating our hamlet.

Just when I thought we couldn't have any more drama, my father strode in wearing his official black uniform. He was all smiles as he strode in, but his smile evaporated when he saw me sitting with Elizabeth.

"What is this?" he demanded from Giovanni. "I thought I was clear with you to find my son a proper match."

Giovanni's eyes were keen on the dagger that was tucked away in my father's waist. "Don Fernando, won't you join us?"

My father started turning towards our table when Giovanni pleaded with him, "Please, Don Fernando. Let us discuss this before you make a scene."

It was already too late. The scene was created, but it certainly could have been much, much worse. My father closed his eyes and paused mid-stride, then turned back to join Giovanni at the center table.

"They cannot be together," my father said.

"Why not?" Giovanni asked. "They are quite compatible and have known each other for years. Many fine long-lasting marriages were born in friendship."

"They just can't," my father said.

"Do you find her unsuitable?"

My father shook his head and said, "She is a fine young lady. I have known her practically since she was born, but they simply cannot be together. They are like brother and sister. It is unseemly."

Giovanni held his ground. "They are well suited for each other. They are both quite clever with even temperaments..."

My father rose suddenly from the table and shook his fist. "You are not listening to me! They are more like brother and sister than you know!" He stormed out of the room.

I saw the tears crest Elizabeth's eyes and make their way down her cheeks. "Why does everybody hate me?"

"Everybody doesn't hate you," I said quietly to her. "I don't hate you. Walter doesn't hate you. In truth of fact, I don't believe that anybody actually hates you!"

"But..."

"But our parents have fallen prey to some rather salacious rumors, yet, aside from the feud between the Leatherbys and the Chamberlains, they still managed to love us."

The tears fell in earnest now. "I can't be Walter's sister and yours too, yet they act as if it were so."

My focus on Elizabeth's pain almost let it slip that one of the strangers in the corner had left his table immediately after my father left, but I did not miss him leaving the tavern, rather stealthily, out the back door. I feared for my father's safety as I tried recalling if my father had worn his sword, for the stranger that followed him most certainly had one.

I turned my attention back to Elizabeth and said, "Let us not forget the plan. We will teach our parents a lesson for believing in such nonsense."

Her tears stopped. "Yes. I thought it was just play, but this is no game. We will make them twist in the wind before we are done with them."

I smiled feebly and nodded my head. I thought for a moment how I may have created a monster.

Chapter Nine

I am quite certain, as I reminisce on these events, that my mind may have embellished a few small details here and there. One of those things might be how my father's voice seemed to reverberate around the tavern long after he had gone, but that, of course, is nonsense. That he stormed out is undeniable, and when he did, he was followed by one of the strangers. Not that I could have done anything about it, but I feared for my father's safety. To the best of my recollection, he did not have his sword at his side as he had when he had spoken with Lord Leatherby in front of Leatherby House, and the stranger I saw following him most certainly did. Had my father been armed, I could tell you with utter certainty that I would not have had any concerns for his life, but I was quite sure that he was not armed, save for a dagger that was mostly ornamental.

Other eyes and ears in the tavern had also noticed my father's departure. How could they not? He was not a quiet man when his temper was riled. With time, however, the tavern had returned to its normal level of chatter and clinking goblets.

It was only a brief moment of peace, or at least what a tavern would consider quiet, until my father burst back into the room looking quiet uncharacteristically upset. The stranger did not enter behind him. What had he done?

My father darted directly to Giovanni's table and pointed an accusing finger at him. "You have done this! You have alerted the crown as to my whereabouts and now we are all in jeopardy!" He turned to me and barked, "Come, Hector. We must go NOW! Out the back!" He turned back to Giovanni and growled, "I make you this promise. If blood is shed, yours will be mixed among it!" He shouted again, "COME, HECTOR!" and darted out the back.

I knew when my parents had sprung the surprise invitations on me that this day would not go as I had planned, but I had no inkling of what had just transpired or what was about to happen. I stood and shrugged my shoulders as I shared a quizzical look with Elizabeth, who also looked frightened.

Four unknown Spaniards burst in through the front door. When did strangers start traveling in fours? They took a quick look around the room, and when they spotted me, one of them darted directly to me and grabbed me by the collar.

"Alvaro," one of the other Spaniards said with the unmistakable voice of authority, "Look at him! He is too young."

"But," Alvaro said, "he wears the uniform of Spain!"

I smiled meekly and said, "Would you believe it? We are playing with costumes tonight. It is a small game that we like to play. See my princess, who is seated at the table?"

Alvaro let go of my collar while the man that had reprimanded him came much closer until he was inches from me, looking me dead in the eyes. He hardly moved as his eyes traced the contours of my face. He said nothing other than a barely audible, "Hmmm." then turned and went to the center table where he looked down his nose and said, "Well, if it isn't the great Giovanni."

The other Spaniards laughed.

From the corner of my eye, I saw the fourth stranger slip quietly back into the Tavern's shadows and along the wall towards his friends.

"Tell me," the leader of the Spaniards said, "what brings the great Giovanni to such a small village? For that matter, what brings you to England at all? Have the nobles of Spain finally had enough of your meddling in their affairs? Have you been reduced to scouring such small hamlets to find matches for lonely farmers now?"

I expected some bluster from Giovanni, but he remained quiet, which, considering the fear in his eyes, was actually showing a fair amount of bravery.

"Where is he?" the Spaniard demanded.

"I'm sorry," Giovanni replied, "but where is who?"

"You know who."

The fourth stranger had rejoined his comrades where they put their heads together in an animated discussion with a great deal of shoulder shrugging.

Giovanni had regained much of his composure at this

point and said, "I'm sorry, but you look hell bent on blood and I have no desire to point out some random man for you to slaughter. If you'd like to be a little more specific, perhaps I could help you."

The leader's face darkened, and he growled, "Where is Don Fernando?"

Giovanni looked as if he was searching his memory.

"You are only stalling!" the leader barked. "Tell me where I might find The Most Excellent Marquis of Avila! Tell me now or I will gut you like the pig that you are!"

They wanted my father. These men who seemed hell bent on blood had come to the tavern specifically to find my father. I dared not shout what I was thinking: *don't tell them!*

"Oh him," Giovanni said, still maintaining his composure. "You just missed him. He was here mere moments ago, but he left with about a dozen caballeros."

One of the four strangers, in fact, the one who usually held one of his comrades back from leaving, and the one I assumed to be in charge, stood and asked, "Who is this Don Fernando that you seek? Perhaps we may be of some assistance."

The leader of the Spaniards looked suspiciously at the stranger, but then bowed and said, "Forgive me. I am Mateo Gabriel Moya. I am a captain of King Phillip's royal guard. And you are?"

The gentleman returned Mateo's bow and said, "Well met. I am Sir Charles Westemere. I am also a captain in the King's guard. So, who is this Don Fernando?"

"Don Fernando is a nobleman from Spain, who we believe may have been kidnapped many years ago and brought to this province. The King wishes to see him again."

Sir Charles walked out of the shadows until he was just in front of the table where he had been sitting and said, "Tell me, Captain Moya, do you often find kidnapped individuals lounging about in taverns?"

"No we do not, but we have reason to believe that *this* man," he pointed to Giovanni, "who is well acquainted with Don Fernando, might know something of his whereabouts, and I can assure you that he *is* often found lounging about in taverns, as you say."

"It would appear," Sir Charles said, "that you were correct, since he just told you that the poor man had just left, and you might be glad to know that the man who just left did not appear to be held against his will in any way."

Mateo briskly bowed his head. "It would appear so. We must look elsewhere."

Sir Charles smiled broadly and reached out to shake Mateo's hand. "It certainly would seem so, and may I commend you on your command of the English language."

Mateo accepted his hand and said, "Thank you, Sir Charles."

When they released their grips, Sir Charles said, "I don't need to remind you that you are in England now, and as one of King Phillip's guard, you are expected to conduct yourselves as envoys of the Spanish crown."

Mateo's cheeks reddened some as an indication that he understood the nature of the understated reprimand hidden within Sir Charles' words. "I understand completely. Please excuse us for interrupting your evening."

The tenseness of those moments seemed to have been diffused until my father burst back in from the back. He skidded to a stop when he saw the Spaniards already in the room and me on my feet. I can only assume he was wondering why I had not followed him.

Two of Sir Charles' companions rose from the table and rested their hands on the hilts of their swords.

Mateo dropped to a single knee, followed quickly by his companions. "Your Excellency. King Phillip sends you his compliments. He was quite relieved to have only recently learned of your rumored safety."

My father approached the Spaniards and asked, "Mateo? Is that you? Has the King sent you to come and apprehend me?"

Mateo rose and said, "No, Your Excellency, the King asked us to find you and warn you that the church has sent their guards to capture you."

Sir Charles stepped forward and said, "Not on English soil, they won't." He turned slightly and said, "Vince, send a bird at once."

Mateo motioned for his men to rise and said, "We were sent not only to warn you, but to protect you if need be, with Sir Charles' permission, of course."

Sir Charles went to look out the door as he asked, "How much time do we have?"

Mateo shrugged. "Hours perhaps, but maybe days. They are the churches soldiers and travel heavier than we do."

"And," Alvaro added, "they like to drink a bit on the way."

My father straightened out his uniform and said, "Captain Moya..."

"Excellency," Mateo said, "how long have we known each other? Please call me Mateo, as we did when we were children."

My father nodded his head and replied, "Agreed, if you can stop calling me Excellency."

"Don Fernando, then," Mateo said, "but never just Fernando."

"Mateo," my father continued. "As you can see, I am unarmed. If the inquisition is coming for me, then I must return home to get my sword. I will not go with them quietly."

"Nor would we allow them to take you," Mateo said.

"In the meantime," my father continued, "would you stay and watch over my son Hector?"

Mateo gripped my right arm with both of his hands and said, "Infante. It would be my very great honor to protect you, but we are sworn to protect his Excell...that is, Don Fernando, your father."

Sir Charles gripped the hilt of his sword and said, "We can watch the... the... did you call him infante?"

My father bowed his head and said, "Sir Charles, please allow me to introduce you to my son and heir, Don Hector Reynaldo Castillo de la Roca."

Sir Charles gripped my arm and said, "Well met."

Mateo would not allow my father to open the tavern door to leave. "Franco, open the door and see if it is all clear."

Franco pulled his sword and opened the door cautiously, and there in the doorway, reaching for the latch, was the looming figure of Lord Leatherby. Franco assumed a defensive stance, but seeing Lord Leatherby, I shouted out, "Easy! He is a friend."

Elizabeth cried out, "Father!" and ran to wrap her arms around him.

Leatherby scanned the room and asked, "Are we at war? We appear to have quite a few swords scattered around the room."

"No, my friend," my father said, "not yet anyway. These men are King Phillip's guards. You may remember Mateo from our time in Spain."

Mateo clicked his heels and said, "Lord Leatherby. I was only a private in the army, but I certainly remember you."

Leatherby gripped his arm and said, "Of course I remember you. I remember most of Fernando's friends, especially those who liked to drink into the wee hours of the morning."

Mateo nodded his head and admitted, "That would be me when I was younger, anyway. My taste for duty has grown some beyond my taste for the drink."

Leatherby entered the tavern so they could close the door. "Sir Charles. I haven't seen you since Teaksbury and the Flemming wedding."

Sir Charles only nodded.

"You have come at a good time," my father said. "It would seem that the church of Spain has learned of our little deception and has sent soldiers to find me and either capture or kill me. I do not know which. Mateo was sent to warn me and provide some protection. I do not know what has brought Sir Charles here, but his presence is most welcome."

"It's a somewhat delicate matter," Sir Charles said, "but we have heard rumors that someone in this area has claimed to be one of the King's bastards. We have come to ascertain if it is some charlatan who is masquerading as such, or if it might truly be one of the King's youthful indiscretions."

"Hmmm," Leatherby said, "I too have heard such a rumor, and that is what has brought me here today. The rumor I heard claimed Master Chamberlain over there to be one of the King's own."

Sir Charles glanced over at Walter and said, "We can sort that out later. For now, I think we should prepare for the threat of violence from the church's soldiers."

"Yes," my father said, "I was just going home to get my sword."

"Excellent idea," Leatherby said, "and you should stay there at home, or at least at Leatherby house. I may not have a garrison, but I do have some fortifications that we may use."

"No!" I shouted. "The soldiers are coming HERE, and from what we are told, they may be drunk. We need to protect the people of Greenshire and especially of this Tavern. We can lay in wait here and ambush them when they arrive."

"Don Hector is correct," Sir Charles said, "and his idea to ambush them is sound."

"Very well then," my father said. "I will return with my sword."

Lord Chamberlain had been quiet long enough. He jumped up and slapped my father on the back, saying, "I'll accompany you. We can escort Elizabeth and this other young lady to Leatherby House."

"Is that wise?" I asked. "You plan to return with swords. All the strength and might will be here in the tavern. Is it not a safer place to protect Elizabeth and May than at home with no guards to protect her?"

Leatherby scrunched up his face, but grunted his agreement.

Before they breached the door, I shouted out to them, "Walter and I could use weapons as well."

Lord Leatherby joined them at the doorway and said, "Then you shall have them. I'll see to it."

There was a part of me, the same part that likes to fix things and control the narrative, that wanted to go with my father and the other Spaniards. There is so much I could discuss with them; about my father; about my heritage; about my title even. Mateo knew my father as a child. They said so themselves. He could probably tell me about my grandparents, even.

My feelings must have been written all over my face as I heard Giovanni say, "Your father is in good hands. I have known Mateo since we were still on our mother's breasts. He is a good man."

I had forgotten that Giovanni had also known my father when he was young. "Did you know my grandparents?"

"I did. Your grandmother liked to swat us on the backsides with her broom. I don't think that broom had ever been used to sweep the floor. She had servants for that. And I think her broom was special with inlaid carvings in the handle, but it was such a long time ago and my memory may have embellished those details."

"I would like to hear more, some day, but right now, I think I should do what I can to keep the women safe."

I motioned for Elizabeth to join me. "Let us go sit with Walter and May. This is no longer a time for separate companionship. We may need to prepare for combat."

Sir Charles slapped his hand on their table and said, "Don Hector is correct again. We should gather the couples together so they would be safer. Please allow us to give you our table. It is furthest from the door and would be the easiest to defend."

I nodded and motioned for Walter and May to join us. "When Lord Leatherby returns with weapons for us, we can take up positions by the door."

Sir Charles put his hand on my shoulder and said, "I

admire your resolve. You have demonstrated remarkable leadership qualities, but I think it would be best if my men and I take up the forward positions while you and your friend remain behind to guard the ladies."

He was right. I could probably provide more comfort to Elizabeth and May if I were seated at the table with them, although May had already pulled a dagger from some hidden fold in her skirt. She was going to make someone a formidable companion, assuming we live through this night.

We may have been over anxious. The soldiers could have stopped along the way to drink themselves into oblivion.

Sir Charles and his men eventually found a table near the door where they didn't exactly relax, but they sat and watched the entrance.

A local craftsman came in and Sir Charles was quick to his feet. Sir Charles wanted to relieve him of his weapon, but he refused and an argument broke out. Neither man went for their swords, but a scuffle ensued and Sir Charles' men went to his aid.

Walter jumped into the fray and explained, "This is John the blacksmith. He is from Chamberlain Hall and is welcome here. He actually makes some very fine swords if you are ever in the market."

Sir Charles' men released John's arms. I could not hear what he said, but Sir Charles patted him on the chest and raised a hand to get Nelly's attention, so I assumed he was buying him a drink.

During the fracas, six more strangers entered the tavern and seated themselves at a far corner table where they disappeared into the gloom and smoke. I don't think Sir Charles or his men had spotted the newcomers, which was kind of sloppy on their part. Perhaps a protection detail was not a normal part of their duties.

I stretched my lips in a sly half grin as I recognized that I was doing it again; I studied the room and was deducing how well everyone was doing.

Walter returned to the table and asked, "What? Did I say something wrong? You have that look on your face like you know something that nobody else could possibly know."

I laughed and said, "It is nothing. I was just enjoying how everybody has their role to play in this drama."

Elizabeth shot me a cold hard steel look and exclaimed, "How can you make light of this?"

"Relax princess," May said as she slashed her dagger in the air, "you'll be safe."

"Let us review the facts," I said. "We are expecting a handful of soldiers who will most likely be drunk and looking for a brawl. We already appear to have enough fighting men to handle a few drunken soldiers, but we are also expecting Lord Leatherby and my father to return with what I am sure will be their best weapons. And if that were not enough, you have Lady May, the mistress of death, to protect you."

May laughed, and Elizabeth followed suit.

"Giovanni!" I shouted. "Why don't you..."

Elizabeth finished my thought and shouted, "... join us so Lady May can protect you with her fierce dagger!"

Giovanni looked confused, but came to sit with us all the same.

John the smith sat at the center table where Giovanni had been all day. Nelly fetched her finest ale for him, courtesy of Sir Charles, and things appeared for a moment like it would be business as usual in the tavern. Perhaps the Inquisition soldiers really did stop to get drunk and pass out along the way. We could be here till sunrise without ever seeing them. I was already feeling a bit peckish and didn't relish the thought of missing my evening meal.

"What if they never come?" Elizabeth asked.

"Are you reading my mind now?" I asked with a wink.

Giovanni flashed me a wry smile and jotted something down in his notes.

"You may joke all you want," Elizabeth said, "but we could be stuck here all night. I wish we had taken up my father's offer to wait at Leatherby House."

"And what if they do arrive?" I asked. "Who is going to protect Nelly from a bunch of drunken Spaniards?"

Elizabeth shot me a burning glance and asked, "Why the sudden concern for Nelly?"

"I have the same amount of concern for Nelly today as I did yesterday."

Walter snickered and said, "Nelly has always been sweet on Hector."

Giovanni took more notes.

May stabbed the point of her dagger into the tabletop. "I bet that smith could protect her pretty good. Especially if they come in drunk as you expected."

The door burst open and the first inquisition soldier walked in. His sword was still in its scabbard, but his hand was on the pommel and he walked to the center of the room with the steady grace of a man who was most definitely not drunk.

Sir Charles rose to greet him. His hand was also touching the pommel of his sword. "Good afternoon, friend. You don't have the look of a man from around here."

The Spaniard sized up Sir Charles and his friends as first one, two, then six more of his companions entered behind him. "And you do not have the look of a man who tends the bar at a local tavern. Neither do you look terribly like the proprietor of such an establishment." Like Mateo, his English was impeccable.

"No sir," said Sir Charles, "I am not, but I am a man of adventure, and I'd wager that you and your friends have also seen your share. I'll buy you and your friends a round of drinks if you would just regale us with one of your daring tales."

The Spaniard bowed and said, "I thank you for your gracious offer, but we are not here to drink."

Sir Charles shrugged his shoulders and looked around the room. "You and your men are clearly somewhat weary from your travels, and you come into a tavern, but are not here to drink?"

The Spaniard laughed and said, "When you say it like that, it does sound a bit comical. One might even consider it suspicious, but we are here on official business. We are here on behalf of the Spanish Crown. We are looking for a wanted criminal and have only recently learned that he may be hiding here among you."

"Oh my," Sir Charles said, "is he dangerous?"

I was very impressed with how Sir Charles piloted the conversation.

"Yes, sir," the Spaniard replied. "He is considered to be very dangerous. His name is Fernando, Fernando De La Roca, but the coward may be using an alias to hide from us. Do you know of any Spaniards living in these lands?"

Sir Charles looked as if he were searching his memory. "A Spaniard you say, and dangerous too, well, he must be VERY dangerous for King Phillip to send you here. How is he, by the way? You know I've met him. I was part of our king's entourage, but I had a moment to speak with him in person. I never thought he was the kind of man who would ever take an interest in something as trivial as a single wanted man."

"King Phillip did not send us personally. Our orders came from his holiness, Bishop Beltran on behalf of the crown. We are here on church business, you see, which is why we have sworn not to touch the spirits until our mission is complete."

"Ow," Sir Charles said, "just hearing that makes me parched. Nelly? Another Ale please."

Nelly brought him a fresh mug, and he made a show of drinking it in front of the Spanish delegation.

Several of the Spaniards seemed to be quite mesmerized by Sir Charles' mug of ale and the foam it left across his upper lip. He smacked his lips and wiped the foam on his sleeve, then exhaled a satisfying, "Ahhhh." The Spaniards licked their lips and glanced over at their commander. I could almost hear their thoughts pleading with him to allow them a sample.

The commander, who still had not relinquished his name, stared intently into Sir Charles' eyes. He was not fooled at all by Sir Charles' theatrics.

One of the soldiers, possibly the most diminutive member of their company, could not bear to watch Sir Charles and scanned around the room, looking for anything to keep his eyes off that foaming mug of ale. His eyes finally landed on me and my bright red beacon of a uniform. He pointed, frantically exclaiming, "Capitan. Mire! Mire!"

Now at least, we knew the commander was a captain in the Spanish army, and he looked my way and said, "So, Sir Charles. You could not recall any other Spaniards in the area, but here sits one, in all his glory. Forgive me, please. I do not know how I could have missed such a blindingly red uniform when I first entered. That is an official uniform of the office of the Marquis, is it not?"

Sir Charles glanced over his shoulder as if he had not

noticed me either. "I'm an adventurer, remember? I'm not actually from around here either."

The Spanish Captain took a step towards me, but Elizabeth swiftly flew out of her seat to stand in front of me, with her arms raised in front of her, as if to block him by the chest. "I am Lady Leatherby. You are on Leatherby lands at present and he is my guest and under the protection of my father, Lord Leatherby."

Giovanni smiled at her and made more notes in his journal.

Sir Charles deftly took Elizabeth's hand and traded places with her. "As you can see, he is just a local boy playing dress up with his lady friend. They are young and in love. Did you never play with costumes when you were young?"

The Spaniard showed his palms in mock surrender and said, "Apologies, but he does not look so young to me. He does, however, look like a Spaniard, but he is far too young to be our fugitive. I am curious, however, how such an authentic-looking costume has found its way here for you to play 'dress up'."

My father came in with Lords Leatherby and Chamberlain through the front entrance.

"What is this?" Lord Leatherby demanded, and in a moment of déjà vu, asked again, "Are we at war now?"

The Spanish Captain turned towards the door and said calmly, "No declaration of war has been issued."

My father stepped forward and said, "Sebastian. They would send you. How eager you must have been to answer their call."

The captain bowed and said, "Fernando, my old friend."

My father pulled his sword halfway from its scabbard and said, "I am Don Fernando, The Most Excellent Marquis of Avila, and you will address me as such."

"Fernando," the captain said, boldly ignoring my father's reprimand, "we do not need to resort to bloodshed. My orders were to bring you in alive... if possible, and you can certainly see that you are greatly outnumbered."

My father relaxed his hand on the hilt of his sword, but did not slide it back into its home as he squinted sideways at the captain. "Have you forgotten so much of our youth? You were never my equal, either in title or in strength at arms. Even Giovanni over there had bested you at arms. What care have I that you have these men at your back? What kind of man would follow a mewling mouse like you, anyway?"

I was surprised that my father was talking to this man. Even surrounded by soldiers, he had a remarkable temper, and I would have expected him to pounce on him without any warning. It wasn't until I saw Mateo and his men quietly slip in through the back door that I realized that my father was just distracting the captain. Mateo handed swords to Walter and myself whispering, "Stay behind us."

Captain Sebastian laughed and said, "It has been a long time, Fernando. God and the church have seen to it that I am more fit and more proficient than I was when you knew me last."

Mateo stepped out of the shadows and announced, "But

it would seem that God has failed to teach you humility, an oversight which I would be too happy to remedy, and also, you seem to have lost your advantage."

Sebastian shouted, "Mateo! Why am I not surprised to see you here?"

"Perhaps," Mateo said, "it is because you are not surprised that the TRUE King has sent us to warn and protect the Marquis and his Infante."

"His Infante?" Sebastian asked. "Well, that explains the red uniform, at least."

Four more Spanish soldiers slipped in through the front door and Sebastian said, "As you can see, I still have you outnumbered, and I do intend to return Fernando to Spain to face the Inquisition."

Mateo growled, "DON Fernando will not be returning with you, and if you insist on shedding blood, you will not be returning either!"

My father drew his sword further from its scabbard. He and Leatherby were surrounded by about five Spaniards, and even with the support of Mateo, I did not see this ending well for my father. I stood, slowly at first, as if in a daze, but then with more vigor, I raised the sword that Mateo had brought me from Lord Leatherby's stores and said, "I think your advantage in numbers is not so great as you may think."

Walter also stood, as did John the smith, who added, "Fernando, that is, Don Fernando, is a righteous man and a good friend of mine. You might think twice before you act."

Sebastian laughed. "I can tell from your apron and the soot on your hands that you are naught but a blacksmith and WE are trained soldiers who do not cower to blacksmiths and children!"

"Do not underestimate me!" I growled. The fever of the moment was taking over my actions and my words.

Something in my father's expression changed when he saw me. Growing up as a gardener's son, especially one that apparently had the privilege of never having to work for my keep because of my secret title, I had done nothing special to earn his pride, yet he had always been proud of me, but this; this moment with me raising arms to defend him; this was something very special that could not be ignored, and I saw it in his face.

In the heat of my own words, I had forgotten that Lord Chamberlain was even there, but he stood with his hand clearly gripping his sword and announced, "I am NOT a farmer or blacksmith, and you may find the bite of my sword more than you are bargaining for."

I never thought that I would see the day when Lord Chamberlain would come to the defense of my father and Lord Leatherby, but there he was. I glanced over at Walter and saw a new twinkle of energy in his eyes.

Sir Charles gently put his hand to my chest and said, "Take your friend and retreat to the corner so you can better guard the women. We are trained soldiers and we can handle this rabble." Sir Charles did not even know me, yet I saw the same pride in his face that my father had just shown. Perhaps he has children and hopes one day to see the same bravery in them.

I nodded my head and backed away to our corner table. "Nelly!" I shouted. "Come sit with us."

Sebastian snarled at me, "That's right, little boy. Back away to the women's table where you can feel safe. Maybe the women will even praise you for your bravery, but they should rather scold you for being so foolhardy." He turned back to my father and said, "So now where do we stand? It would seem that I once again have the advantage on you Fernando, well if you are going to be perfectly honest, I always did have the advantage, because your little boy in his pretty red costume could never match with me or my men."

One of the men that had snuck in when Mateo and his men were questioning John the blacksmith stood at his table. His hand was fondling the pommel of his sword. "If it is only numbers that you respect, and not the skill of your opponents, then I suggest you count again, but you may find that you do not have enough fingers to complete your census, so allow me to help you. You are on English soil now and no longer have the advantage of numbers." As he spoke, three more armed men rose at their respective tables.

Sebastian's cheeks darkened, and I thought him about to burst with uncontrollable anger, but instead, he sucked in a deep breath and closed his eyes as he exhaled it. "I am not here to draw blood, but this man," he pointed to my father and continued, "this man is a fugitive from Spain. He is wanted by the courts to face trial for his sins against the crown."

Mateo stepped forward and said, "That is quite an over statement Sebastian. I am the Capitan General of the King's guard. King Phillip has my ear and sent me here personally to protect Don Fernando from you and the church's brand of treason!"

"Treason?" Sebastian growled. "How dare you! I am here at the behest of the crown!"

Mateo slammed his fist on the table and pointed his other hand directly at Sebastian's face, growling, "I am here representing the Crown. I am here at King Philip's personal request. You are here for the inquisition. You and your church friends want nothing more than to take over the crown and rule Spain as if it were your own. My disgust for you is immeasurable and if it were up to me, I would gladly run you through right now."

Sebastian was clearly incensed. "This man is a criminal fugitive who fled his land and his country to escape the righteous trial by God!"

Mateo laughed. "This man, to whom you refer, is The Most Excellent Marquis of Avila. He is loved by his people, but was forced to flee his homeland to escape persecution by the inquisition simply for not being a slave to the Church of Rome.

He came to this country seeking asylum, and it would seem that he has found it and while he was here, he raised a son, who as far as I can tell, has better moral fiber than you or any of your church friends."

"Asylum?" Sebastian screeched. "From this backwater province of England? I spit on your asylum. This man has been hiding here associating himself with blacksmiths! Does that sound like asylum? He may have befriended a local count or maybe an earl, but he is no friend of the King of this land and therefore, I do not recognize his asylum! He is coming with me, and I will shed blood to take him. You, Mateo, are a diplomat and no match for my soldiers. I suggest you step aside and recognize that the true advantage is mine."

Three more strangers stood at their tables as one of them said, "I am a trained soldier." The second of them added, "We are all trained soldiers." The third capped it off with, "We are the King's elite guard and we do not take kindly to strangers coming into our land uninvited with the intent of foisting their laws upon our citizens."

"But he is not your citizen! Already it has been explained that he used to be the Marquis of Avilla."

"He still is!" Mateo barked. "The King has refused the church's requests to relinquish his title. His people still remember and revere him. He is still Don Fernando Rodrigo Castillo De La Roca, The Most Excellent Marquis of Avila!"

"Bah!" Sebastian spat. "He is in exile. He consorts with blacksmiths. I wonder what lowly menial tasks he performs so he can hide his title."

"So you admit he has a title!" Mateo said, taking the statement as a victory.

"Answer the question!" Sebastian barked.

Lord Leatherby stepped forward and said, "Very well. I will answer your question. I invited my very good friend Don Fernando to come stay on my lands. Nothing was demanded from him, but he has a great love for gardening and he also owns quite a miraculously green thumb. He is a proud man and insisted that he would only accept my generosity if I allowed him to keep my grounds. He is by far the best groundskeeper I have ever known."

"So," Sebastian said, with as much disdain as he could muster in his voice, "you must be the lowly nobleman that I knew would be involved."

Elizabeth stepped to the front of the table alongside me and forcefully said, "He is Lord Leatherby, the Earl of Leatherby, and you will speak civilly when you speak with him or of him!"

"Ahhh," Sebastian said. "The Lady Elizabeth, as I recall? She speaks again to protect her father."

Leatherby started to pull his sword fully from its scabbard, but my father stopped him.

"I am Lord Leatherby, as my daughter just said, and I am the Earl of these lands, and you, sir, are no longer welcome here."

"Fine," Sebastian said. "I will take my prisoner and go."

"You will do no such thing," Leatherby barked, pulling his

sword another inch from its home. "He is my guest, and I have granted him asylum within my borders!"

Sebastian shook his head. "You do not have the authority to grant asylum to a Spanish Fugitive!"

The final of the new strangers stood and announced, "But I do. I have heard quite enough. I have seen the love and loyalty of *my* people towards Don Fernando, so I grant him asylum within the borders of England."

Sebastian opened his mouth to object, but stopped when everybody who was not within striking distance of the Spanish soldiers' swords fell to their knees and cried out in unison, "Majesty!"

One of the strangers pulled his sword completely free and pointed it directly at Sebastian. "As I told you, WE are the King's elite guard, and as Lord Leatherby, one of my king's loyal subjects has said, you are no longer welcome here. We will escort you to our borders, where I assume you have a boat waiting."

More of the King's guards brandished their weapons and the Spanish soldiers either dropped theirs, or pushed them back into their scabbards.

Everyone's attention was on either the Spanish soldiers or the King, except mine. I noticed some movement from the back of the tavern and saw several more strangers enter and take up hiding places behind the tavern bar. They wouldn't hide if they were either Mateo's or the King's men, so I must assume they were hostile. I needed to alert Mateo, but while Walter and I were tucked away in the corner, guarding the women, I could never get his attention. Especially with everyone's attention on the center of the room. I gripped the hilt of my sword, prepared to spring into action. Walter saw this and put his hand on his sword as well. I tried indicating the bar with my eyes, but I'm afraid I just looked like some drunk trying to flirt with someone for a free drink.

Chapter Ten

Sebastian was crushed. I saw it in his face and his posture. Even his voice was that of a desperate, defeated man. He had found his fugitive, but he was being forced to return home without him. At least he could tell the church that he was forced to leave by the King of England himself, which in the world of excuses, had to rank right up there near the top.

Mateo collected their weapons and told the King's guards, "I will accompany them back home personally, and will only return their weapons after we have reached the opposite shore."

The captain of the guards looked apprehensive, but Sir Charles said, "Mateo is the captain of King Philip's guards. He has shown us true honor, and I trust him."

"Very well. I am Sir Nicholas, and captain to captain, I trust you as well."

Mateo clicked his heels and nodded his head. "Well met, Sir Nicholas."

Sir Nicholas glanced over at the Spanish soldiers and asked,

"Can I trust their honor? Will they leave England willingly, or will I have to bind their hands?"

Mateo snapped his fingers and shouted, "Sebastian! Sebastian! A word, please."

Sebastian was already halfway out the door when he heard his name and turned. "What do you want? Is this your chance to rub my nose in my failure? Are you plotting how you plan to take credit for my defeat and crow about your great victory?"

Mateo sighed. "Such a poor loser. I only wish to speak with you. Please join us."

Sebastian scowled for a moment, then joined Mateo and Sir Nicholas.

"Sebastian, this is Sir Nicholas. His men will escort you back to your ships. I will also accompany you, but he was wondering how far he could trust you and your men?"

Sebastian sneered, but said nothing.

"That's what I thought. I told Sir Nicholas that your hands and feet should be bound for the journey, but he thought you should be shown more respect than that. So I give you a choice. Produce a bible and swear an oath upon it that you will freely return to Spain without causing any more harm to anyone. If you do not do this, then you and your men will have your hands and feet bound for the journey."

Sebastian frowned and shook his head. "You can't be serious. I give you my word that we will not try anything."

"That's not good enough," Mateo said. "Produce a Bible. I know you carry one with you. Swear an oath upon it that you will try nothing as you are escorted back to Spain. Swear an oath to your God like you have never done before."

"MY God?" Sebastian asked. "Is he not your God too? And how am I supposed to produce a bible out here? Do you think I can afford to carry one with me everywhere I go? Do you have any idea how much they weigh?"

Mateo remained quiet for a moment. "Are you done? Have you no more excuses to make? I am perfectly comfortable in my beliefs. I pray to the God of Rome and to the trinity, but I sometimes wonder if you pray to the Inquisition as if it were a new God."

"That is blasphemy!" Sebastian roared with disgust.

"None the less, I know you do not travel without your bible, no matter how large or how heavy it is."

Sebastian's eyes darted around the room, but he said nothing.

"Produce the bible," Mateo ordered, "or be bound."

Sebastian motioned for one of his men to retrieve the tome. His eyes finally settled on the floor in front of his feet as we waited.

"You see?" Mateo said to Sir Nicholas. "He can be reasoned with."

Sir Nicholas looked as if he would prefer to be excused from the argument between the two Spaniards.

The King stepped forward and said, "Before you escort these men back to their country, I'd like to better understand what they are doing here."

"Indeed," Sir Charles said, "in fact, I was wondering how you got here so swiftly, I only sent the bird about the soldiers mere hours ago."

The King's cheeks reddened. I believe that my mouth may have fallen open some upon the realization that this King, a man known to preach how his lineage was assigned and blessed by God to be king, was only human after all.

"It would seem," the King explained somewhat quietly, "that the Queen had intercepted one of our earlier correspondences."

"Oh," Sir Charles said, "I see. I would not want the Queen angry, especially with me, your majesty."

The King smiled some and said, "Fear not, she is not angry with you. In fact, I would say that she was not really angry at all, but was rather amused and took every opportunity to tease me about the subject."

"So you came here to escape her?"

"Heavens no," the King said, "well not entirely. I wanted to hear the evidence for myself so I could put an end to these rumors. Finding the Spaniards here just made it all that much more interesting. As to my mission here, I see at least two strapping young lads. Do they have fathers? Have you been able to positively determine their lineage?"

"Not yet, sire. This young man in the red Spanish uniform is Don Hector; the son of Don Fernando, who we've already learned is in exile from Spain with his family."

I was struck dumb. I had just been introduced to the King of England, and my mouth had already been hanging open with nothing to say. After a moment, frozen in fear, I managed a clumsy bow and said, "Your majesty."

"Young man," the King said, "Is Don Fernando your father?"

He asked me a direct question. I could not skirt the issue and must be equally direct with him. "Yes sir. He has raised me since I was born, and my mother swears he is my father, and she should know."

My father stepped forward a bit and said, "If I may, your majesty, perhaps I can shed some light. I met Lord Leatherby while he was visiting the court in Spain. I was the Marquis of Avilla..."

"You still are," Mateo said with a slight bow.

My father smiled and nodded his head in acknowledgment. "I am the Marquis of Avilla and I spent a great deal of time in the court with King Phillip. I was a single man in those days and the King often chided me for not taking a wife, but I was young and adventurous, which was how I had met Lord Leatherby. We had grown quite close during those days, as we rooted out some bandits that had been terrorizing my land. It was he who had introduced me to my wife, but that was not his intention. She was a lady of the court and they had been together romantically when I had wooed her away from him. I count myself fortunate that he did not hold a grudge for my stealing her."

The King pointed to Lord Leatherby and asked, "Is this how you recall things?"

"It is, Sire."

"So," my father continued with a shrug, "as to my son's parentage, I know not who sired him with any certainty, but I love Lord Leatherby as a brother and I love my wife tremendously. I love my son enough not to question things, but I may have made a mess of things if I ever suggested any doubt about whether I was his true father."

The King glanced over to Sir Charles and shrugged. "Could these rumors have blossomed into rumors that I might be the boy's father?"

Sir Charles returned his shrug and said nothing.

"I would appreciate it," my father said, "if nobody present were to tell my wife that I ever harbored any such suspicions. It is bad enough that my son has heard my confession."

A tear gathered in my eye as I hugged my father and whispered, "That you raised me as your own with such uncertainty makes you even more of a father to me."

Leatherby cleared his throat and said, "I may not be completely without blame. As Don Fernando has already recounted, we met while I was on a trip to Spain looking for horses to bring to England."

Sebastian rolled his eyes and muttered, "Joto." He looked embarrassed when he realized that I heard him.

Leatherby continued, "While I was out of the country, my wife stayed with Lord Chamberlain."

"Don't you mean your intended?" my father asked.

Lord Leatherby blushed and said, "That was what I told you to keep you from stealing Luisa from me. Please don't hate me for it."

My father scowled, but said, "I probably would have done the same."

"Anyway," Lord Leatherby continued, "I was gone for

about a year, during which time Elizabeth was born. My dear wife died in childbirth, and perhaps it was my grief, but I not only blamed Lord Chamberlain for her death, I questioned whether Elizabeth was mine. Lord Chamberlain swore that her birth came after only eight months of my absence, but she was such a small baby when I returned..."

Elizabeth stood and gasped, "Father!"

Leatherby was crying now as he looked upon her. "I never let my suspicions affect our relationship. I raised you as my own. You ARE the Lady of Leatherby House."

"Everything was fine," he continued, "until she seemed to become infatuated with the young Master Chamberlain, at least, that is, until she became betrothed to Don Hector. I thought everything was going to work out at that point."

"I can't believe you!" Elizabeth cried. "I was never truly going to marry Hector! He is like a brother to me!"

Leatherby's cheeks were stained with tears now as he asked, "And who is young Walter to you if not your brother?"

The King plopped down in a chair and said, "Someone bring me an ale. This reminds me of a comedy at the Globe, except I fear it may end up a tragedy."

Chamberlain stood, and I thought I detected a tear in his eye as he said, "You thought Elizabeth was mine? I knew you were insanely jealous, and that you thought I had been with your wife, but I swore to you then that I never had, yet you never believed me and bedded my wife in revenge."

"I what?!?" Leatherby exclaimed. "Never! I never did such a thing!"

"If what you say is true, then I have succumbed to your jealousy, which was most contagious, for I believed that Walter was your son, especially after my wife insisted that we name him after you."

May chuckled and said, "The King is right. This is like one of the Bard's tales."

Mateo overheard her and shook his head, saying, "Nobody has been killed yet."

She smirked and whispered, "The night is young yet."

"Wait a second," Walter said, "you forbade me from seeing Elizabeth because you thought I was Leatherby's son?"

Chamberlain nodded his head and hung it in shame as he admitted, "It would be unseemly for you to marry your sister."

"And you," Walter said as he pointed to Lord Leatherby, "disapproved of our union because you thought she was my father's daughter?"

"Again," Leatherby said timidly, "your sister."

May tugged on Mateo's sleeve and asked, "Who do think will die first? Shall we wager on it?"

The King appeared thoroughly amused as he clapped his hands and said, "This is all very intriguing, but I did not come out here because you doubted the legitimacy of your own children."

"Aye," Leatherby said. "I think I know why you are here. There have been other rumors. I know not where they came from, but it's been said that one of the boys may have sprung from your own loins, your majesty. I do not know which of the boys, however."

Chamberlain heaved a mighty sigh, almost a small cry as he said, "I've heard the rumor that my own boy, Walter, might be the King's bastard, and if I'm to believe my old friend Lord Leatherby, how am I to discount this rumor?"

"You could start," Walter said, "by trusting in the fidelity of my mother. Shame on you for ever falling prey to such idle gossip. My mother was a saint, is a saint, and she should be glad to not be here to endure this slander."

This left no doubt that tears had crested from Chamberlain's eyes. He hung his head in shame, or perhaps to hide the tears, but I saw them.

"My son speaks the truth," Chamberlain cried. "His mother was a saint. I knew her to be faithful, yet I doubted her. The sin was mine."

"That is all very touching," the King said, "but I fail to see how all of this turned this boy into a royal bastard."

The strangers that had been hiding behind the bar stood and a strong woman's voice said, "Yes. I'd like to know that as well. I'd also like to know why my husband took so seriously, a rumor that he might have a bastard child in this province."

Again, men around the room either bowed or fell to a knee

and muttered, "Your Majesty."

The King looked momentarily flustered and quickly hid the surprise from his face, but not so fast that I hadn't already noticed it. "Ahh," he said, "the Queen is here and has joined us in this game. I came here merely to ascertain how such a rumor, which is obviously false in nature, could have flourished so fervently that it reached my ears in London."

The Queen smirked and said, "Of course, my husband. What else could it be? You so frequently order your guards and your spies to track down impossible rumors in small provinces, claiming that you had once been there to sow your royal oats."

The Queen stepped out from behind the bar and came to our table. Something in her expression led me to believe that she was playing a game. Perhaps she liked to torture the King with his past infidelities, but I thought I detected some humor in her face. She couldn't be so cruel that she could feel true enjoyment from trapping the King as she had, but there it was; the curl of her lip; the twinkle in her eye; she was here to tease him and laugh about it later.

She studied my face, then glanced over to the King and then my father and said to me, "Stand straight, boy. Let me have a better look at you."

I did as she commanded and she circled around me as if examining a fine stallion. "This boy could be a prince. He has the stature and the carriage of a highborn, but his features clearly come from his father, Don Fernando, except for his eyes, which I assume take after his mother."

I nodded my head and said, "Yes. The Marchioness Luisa Esmerelda De La Roca."

She smiled at me, but there was a tint of condescension in her smile, as if I were merely a young boy overly proud of his mother.

She turned to Walter and studied his face. "Now this one has my husband's jawline, but I see none of the royal posture. Stand up, boy."

Walter stood as commanded, as I had just done previously.

May giggled, which caught the Queen's eye, and I swear I saw a quick wink exchanged between them.

"My God!" the Queen exclaimed. "This boy has the royal backside! The spine is a bit flimsy and there's too much beef on the tail."

"My dear!" the King interjected. "I know not who this boy is, but he certainly is not of my loin!"

"But look at him!" The Queen said excitedly. "He bears your features as if he were your own brother, or dare I say, your SON!"

May had to cover her mouth to keep from laughing out loud.

"Look at his father!" The King insisted. "Does he not also bear some weak resemblance to the royal family?"

The Queen walked over to Lord Chamberlain. Chamberlain bowed low at the waist and the Queen examined his back side and turned to look the King in the eye. She squinted, which to me looked more like theatrics than any visionary problem, then exclaimed, "Your grandfather was a randy little bastard when he was young, was he not?"

Chamberlain quickly snapped to attention. I thought he was going to defend the honor of his mother and grandmother, but he stopped short.

Perhaps he realized the advantage if they were to decide that HE was the royal bastard in the rumors.

"If I may," I said meekly, "I believe I can shed some light on those rumors that have brought you both here. In fact, I'm rather sure of it."

The Queen looked down her nose at me and said, "Continue."

"For starters, Lady Elizabeth and I grew up together here on the Leatherby estate. Even though I was only the gardener's son, or so we thought at the time, I was always treated with the greatest respect and was afforded an education alongside Elizabeth."

The Queen's posture told me that I was taking too long.

"We had always been great friends with Walter, the son of Lord Chamberlain, but as we grew older, we had to hide our friendship from both Lord Leatherby and Lord Chamberlain because of the silly feud between their families. Lady Elizabeth and Walter fell in love and were, in secret, betrothed, but the problem was how to get their fathers to allow such a union."

The King interrupted me, "You were going to tell us about these rumors of a royal bastard."

"I'm getting to that. In order to engineer a way for them to be together, I planted the seeds of several rumors in this very tavern."

"But first," Elizabeth interrupted, "my father discovered

the betrothal ring, so I told him that Hector here had proposed to me. I thought he would be furious that I would promise myself to a gardener's son, but he was not."

"No doubt," the Queen said disapprovingly, "he already knew that your friend was a Spanish Marquis."

"Wait," the King said, "what could you have hoped to accomplish by involving the royal blood in your little lie?"

"As it happens," I said, "Lord Leatherby had already suspected that Elizabeth might be Lord Chamberlain's daughter, and so naturally he could not allow such a union with Walter."

"Very sensible," the King said.

"That," I said, "was when Lord Leatherby had contracted a matchmaker to come find the perfect match for Elizabeth."

Walter added, "It's also when my father had intercepted the matchmaker to arrange an alternative bride for me so I would not marry Elizabeth, because he believed WE were brother and sister."

May was still seated at the table when she raised her hand to wave at everyone and meekly said, "That's me, the alternative bride."

"Who is this matchmaker?" the Queen demanded.

Giovanni stood and bowed. "I am Giovanni, the matchmaker."

"I've heard of you," the queen said with disdain. "Nothing good, I'm afraid."

"Oh stop it," the King said to her. "He arranged a wedding for your great niece and they have been very happy together."

She shot him a look that said she did not like being contradicted, even with the truth.

I coughed gently to regain the floor and said, "I started the rumor mostly to teach our parents a lesson. First, because they distrusted their wives' fidelity so much, but also because they seemed to place so much value on our breeding. At first, we thought Lord Leatherby to be the most open-minded and modern man in the world to allow his daughter to marry a lowly servant's boy, but then we learned of my title and came to believe that all any of them cared about was our titles. So I invented a rumor about a long-lost royal bastard. I didn't even say who. I let the gossipers make up their own minds who it might be. So, as you see, it is my fault entirely that your honor has been impugned."

"No, it wasn't," Walter said. "I was in on the conspiracy almost from the start."

Elizabeth and May both stood and said, "As was I."

The King chuckled at the absurdity of it all, but the Queen held her stoic stare as she seemed to drill her gaze into our souls. Then she turned to the King and said, "It is not their fault, the fault is yours! If you could have just kept it in your pants for all those years, none of this would have ever blown up like this."

All the mirth evaporated from the King's face as he shrunk under her stare, but then her gaze broke and she started to laugh. Apparently, this was the game she was playing all along.

Several of the King's personal guards turned to each other,

pretending to have conversations, but I could tell that they were just trying to stifle their own laughter.

The King regained his composure and said to the room, "The Queen has had her laughter at your king's expense." He pointed to the captain of his guards and said with a wink, "Wipe that smile off your face!"

The Queen curtsied and said, "Apologies, husband, but I could not resist."

The King mumbled some sort of acceptance of her apology.

"After all," she continued, "it was such a long time ago, and the King was so young and fertile."

The King stood a little straighter and said, "I like to think that I still am."

"Which?" she asked. "Young or fertile?"

"You go too far," he said, mildly irritated.

She curtsied again and continued, "That long ago, the King had to ensure that he had rightful heirs and the Queen had yet to prove that she wasn't barren."

"Quite right," he said strongly.

"But she wasn't barren, was she? You have three very fine young lads to carry on the royal line, yet you come running out here to learn if there is another?"

"It is my duty," the King said, "to make sure there won't be a challenger to the throne. I knew the rumors to be false, but still, a false bastard could create as much of a problem as a true bastard, so I came to squash the rumor and, if need be, to pay off the imposter."

The Queen scanned the room and asked, "So? Which of these young men is your imposter?"

No hands were raised.

"Good!" the Queen exclaimed as she clapped her hands. "Now that the unpleasantries have been settled…"

Sebastian opened his mouth as if to extend the argument, but the Queen cut him off, "It HAS been settled, and since you are no longer required here, you may go!"

"At once!" the King commanded, "My guards will stand watch with you outside. I wish to talk to Mateo before you leave."

"Always with the business!" the Queen said. "I wish to hear more of the scandal and intrigue going on here."

Mateo shrugged his shoulders towards the King. "I am in no particular hurry."

"Then it's settled!" the Queen exclaimed. "First, tell us of the feud that was mentioned before!"

"Yes!" the King said. "Was anyone killed?"

"No, your majesty," Leatherby said. "There were no deaths."

"At least," Chamberlain added, "none by killing. We both lost our wives. Lady Leatherby by childbirth, and my own from illness."

The room drew quiet for a moment before Leatherby added, "The feud was my fault. I have already told you that I was unfairly suspicious of Lady Leatherby with Lord Chamberlain, and we had been best friends. I felt betrayed."

"It was never true," Chamberlain said. "Lady Chamberlain

was already with child when Lady Leatherby came to stay with us while you were away in Spain. You were barely gone a fortnight when we discovered that Lady Leatherby was also with child at the same time. There was nothing irregular going on in Chamberlain hall, and with two expectant mothers, there was no rest either."

Leatherby hung his head low and said, "I am sorry, my friend. I never should have doubted you."

"The fault was mine," Chamberlain said. "When our boy was born and Lady Chamberlain insisted on naming him after you and appointing you as his God Father, I became suspicious of the two of you. I think my suspicious nature may have led to her illness."

"Nonsense," Leatherby said. "Having two pregnant women in the home would have been a strain on any of us. You can hardly hold yourself responsible for your thoughts under those circumstances."

"Is that it?" the King demanded. "You already said that nobody was killed, but you never went to blows over this?"

Leatherby shrugged. "We haven't really spoken for eight years, and we used to be very close."

"Enough!" the Queen barked. "I don't want to hear any more about this silly feud! You may be seated."

The King grumbled, "I'd hardly even call it a feud. More like a little spat. An itty bitty tiny little spat."

"That's not true and not fair," I said, stepping into the conversation. "Lives may not have been lost, but they have been altered in meaningful ways. Our friends George and Agnes have had to conceal their love and their marriage because of this feud. You do an injustice to their struggles when you call it an itty bitty spat. I'll agree that the basis for this feud is absolutely silly, and I've done what I can to show this to our parents, but this whole mess that brought you hear was spawned by this feud and the love between my friend Walter and the Lady Elizabeth."

Lord Chamberlain stood and said, "If he is not the rumored bastard of the King, then we may as well address my son with his true title, the Viscount Walter Chamberlain."

Walter's face swelled with pride, but I don't think it was from the title; the glow in his eyes told me that it was from his father's long overdue recognition of him.

The Queen clapped her hands and commanded, "Stand, Lord Walter. Your Queen summons you."

Walter stepped forward to my side.

The Queen took his hand in hers and said, "Congratulations. I take it that this honor has been due to you for some time."

"Too long," I muttered.

"And this," the Queen said as she pushed between us and took Elizabeth's hand, "must be the Lady Elizabeth. Your friend here has spoken highly of the love between the two of you."

The queen took Elizabeth's hand and pulled her forward between us, then placed her hand in Walter's.

Captain Sebastian let out a low moan and said, "Can we dispense with all this sensitivity before my men and I have to plug our ears with candle wax?"

"Why?" the Queen asked. "Does the Spanish army require equal time to discuss your feelings? Or is it just your turn to be overly dramatic?"

Mateo quipped, "Sebastian is probably suffering from his monthly courses."

The Queen failed to stifle her laugh, despite the vulgar nature of the joke, but Sebastian was not amused at all.

"This man," Sebastian said, referring to Fernando, "is a fugitive of Spain and I demand..."

The King cut him off, "You will demand nothing while you are in my presence."

The Queen smiled at his strength.

"As I understand it," the King continued, "Don Fernando and his family are only fugitives of the church and not the crown. Is that not so?"

Mateo nodded his head. "It is so."

"And," the King strutted around the room as he spoke, "you may have noticed that the Church of Rome has not been so kind when dealing with the Church of England. I fear that the church's influence upon the Spanish crown may lead to war. Already we can see Spain's navy grow. The inquisition is no friend to us, but I think that Don Fernando and Don Hector are. Where does this leave you, Captain Sebastian? Are you friend or foe? Should I lock you up or let you go?"

Mateo's grin lit up the room. "You should definitely let him go. He will give your message to the inquisition, as I will give it to King Philip. The King wants a single unified church for Spain, but in his heart, he does not want the war that seems inevitable with the inquisition. I fear that the church has grown more powerful behind the King's back and their influence upon the crown will grow. The church will march upon England and other protestant nations, but I will return home knowing only of the fairness I have witnessed here, and I will share my experiences with King Philip personally."

"When you do," my father said, "Please extend my best wishes to the King. I never intended to cause him any anguish when I fled Spain."

The Queen circled me, sizing me up like a hungry wolf. "How certain are we that this boy is noble? He certainly has a strong bearing, and he has come to the rescue of his friends like a nobleman, but is his blood truly of the Spanish nobility?"

"Without question," Mateo responded. "His father, Don Fernando, is The Most Excellent Marquis of Avila. The church has demanded many times that King Phillip strip him of his title, but the King has refused repeatedly."

"Such Loyalty," the Queen said. "It is not often seen in a monarch." She glanced over at the King and gave him a flirtatious wink.

Mateo continued, "The King would like to see his friend back in Avila, as would the people of Avila, but the inquisition would never allow it, and the King understands and approves of his exile."

"Why?" The Queen asked. "What is his crime? Why does the church want him so badly?"

Mateo sighed. "His only crime was being a protestant and not swearing fealty to the Church of Rome."

"Don Fernando," the Queen said sharply, "is this true? Was there nothing more?"

Fernando stood at attention and clicked his heels together. "It is absolutely true. I had already had some disagreements with how the church was treating my people of Avila when my good friend Lord Leatherby had introduced me to the new faith of England. I broke with the Catholic faith. That is not to say that I do not believe in God, just not the men governing the Catholic faith. They declared me a heretic and came for my blood."

The queen turned to her husband and said, "You should recognize his rank and invite him into the House of Lords."

Fernando bowed and said, "You do me great honor, but as King Philip has not stripped me of my title, I am still master of the people of Avila and cannot accept an English title."

"How about land?" the King asked. "Can you accept land? And an honorary position in English society?"

Fernando thought about it a moment, then bowed and said, "I could accept land, yes. Perhaps a position that is akin to an ambassadorship would be acceptable. If the church ever abandons the inquisition, my son may wish to return to Avila as their Marquis."

"Yes!" Mateo exclaimed. "King Philip is a staunch supporter of the inquisition, and it was his idea to cleanse Spain of heretics, but he has made a personal exception for Don Fernando. Did you know that they knew each other as children? They didn't grow up together, but they were both fishing together when Prince Philip fell from the dock and young Fernando dove into the water to pull him out. King Philip has never forgotten that and would welcome him as his ambassador to England."

One of the Spanish soldiers returned to the tavern with a large package wrapped in a leather blanket.

"What has taken you so long?" demanded Sebastian. "No, wait! I do not want to hear your excuses. Just bring it to Mateo."

"Is that it?" I asked, not meaning to speak aloud, but unable to curb my astonishment. "I have never seen a printed bible before, but if that is it, then it is truly enormous. How could any man actually bring something so large on his travels?"

"That is an excellent question," Mateo said. "No normal man would do so. A man would have to be extremely devout to carry such a burden. Such a man would never defile it by swearing to it if he intended on being untruthful."

There were general murmurs of agreement that circulated around the room.

Mateo took the package and carefully removed the leather wrapping. He opened it in several places to verify that it was what we all believed it to be, then held it out in front of Sebastian. "Place your hand on it and swear a solemn oath that you will not try to escape and will remain peaceful and will return to Spain."

Sebastian's cheeks darkened as he put his hand on the book and said, "I do so swear. On my honor and as a promise to God, I will peacefully allow these soldiers to escort my soldiers and me directly from here to the shores of England, where I will board a ship. From there, I will travel directly across the channel and back to Spain. I swear this under pain of eternal damnation should I break this oath, that during this journey, I will make no attempt to escape or thwart my delivery to Spain."

I could see a measure of surprise and satisfaction in the King's face, that Sebastian would swear such a thorough oath.

"And your men, too," Mateo added. "Swear that your men will behave."

"I also swear that my men will cause no harm on this journey and will peacefully accompany me back to Spain."

Sir Nicholas looked back and forth between us before asking, "Those were certainly inspiring words, but can we truly trust him?"

Mateo nodded his head. "He will not go back on his word

to God, and I will also be there to watch over him and remind him if he falters."

"It would seem," the King said, adopting a deep authoritative voice, "that we have both friends," he nodded his head towards Mateo, then he gestured with his thumb pointing at Sebastian and continued, "and enemies in Spain. England would like to maintain healthy ties with Spain, but she will not succumb to the whims of the Church of Rome. I fear that conflict between our great nations may soon be unavoidable. With that weighing over our heads, I cannot allow this kind of bickering among my own people." He turned so he could face both Lord Chamberlain and Lord Leatherby. "Your King demands that you end this silly feud at once."

In truth, I had already come to believe that the revelations of the past hours had resolved any conflicts between them, but as I read the King's face, I saw this as an opportunity for him to somehow take credit for ending the feud by royal decree. A sly smile from the Queen told me that she also noticed the very political move by the King, and I think she was impressed by it.

Both Lords fell to their knees and said, "Yes, Your Majesty."

I don't believe it was my intention to speak out so boldly at the time, but I blurted out, with a snicker, "Wow! If I would have known it would be that easy, I would have spread rumors of a royal bastard years ago." Immediately upon loosening my words in the air, I regretted speaking aloud.

The King looked at me sternly, and was about to admonish me, but the Queen interjected, "A bold political move, Don Hector. Are you quite sure you wish to retain your title in Spain? King Philip seems somewhat adamant about wanting the whole of Spain to follow the Church of Rome. The inquisition seems quite willing to take his wishes to the extreme, including the genocide of innocent people who wish to follow their own faith."

Sebastian's voice echoed in from the doorway, "It is imperative to cleanse Spain of all heretics."

The Queen raised her voice and shouted out, "Thank you, Captain Sebastian, for illustrating my point so thoroughly." She turned back to me, and with a glance towards my father said, "If war is to come, I doubt that King Philip would reserve your title for long."

"This is true," Mateo admitted. "King Philip owes Don Fernando a life, so he sent me here to spare him from Captain Sebastian, but as he empowers the church with control over his navy, it is inevitable that Avila will need a new Marquis, or maybe it will be annexed to one of the old kingdoms. Even he sees that this would happen."

"You see?" the Queen asked pleasantly. "The world is changing and you have a keen mind, and knowing some of the King's advisers as I do, I can say with some degree of certainty that the King could use a mind such as yours."

I tried to speak, but I felt as though I had no breath in my lungs.

The Queen gave me a motherly smile and said, "Relax. You do not need to answer us this instant."

I took a breath and replied, "It is all too much for me to comprehend. Two weeks ago, I was the lowly son of a gardener, and now I'm told that I am the son of a Marquis of Spain. I will consider what you have said."

"A wise answer," she said with a knowing smile, "and something the King's jackals would not have given."

The King leaned in close to his wife and said, "You go too far, my dear. You should not speak so of my advisors."

She smiled a treacherous smile at him and said, "I would not if they were not."

"Enough Work!" the Queen ranted. "I tire of hearing you men talking about your titles and your appointments. I want to hear more about the betrothals and the marriages tangled up in this place."

"Majesty," Giovanni said with a low bow. "It is early yet. The couples are only just meeting each other."

"Why must they meet?" the Queen asked. "The King and I met on our wedding day! Is matchmaking not your profession? Have you not matched these couples together?"

"Yes," Giovanni replied, "but I have found it best if they can meet before the wedding so they can see that they are a good match. So many children these days resent the marriages they are pushed into and wind up straying from their vows."

The Queen looked over her shoulder at the King and said, "Yes, I can see the truth in your words."

The King put on his most innocent face, but let the Queen have her tease.

"So tell me," the Queen said, returning her attention to Giovanni, "how much time do they need? Will one day suffice? If so, we can start planning the weddings now while they get to know each other."

Elizabeth grabbed Walter's hand and said, "We are ready now!"

Walter's face did not imply that he was ready yet.

May caught his expression and found it all quite amusing. "Yes! Let's have a wedding!"

Giovanni smiled at the Queen, but looked a bit constipated at the same time.

Again, May did not miss Giovanni's look of panic. She jumped up and wound her arm around mine. "When?!? When can we have a wedding?"

The Queen smiled and absorbed May's enthusiasm. "Right away! Or as long as it takes to prepare! I assume that one of these Lords will have a hall fit for a royal wedding, because that is what it will be."

"But," the King interrupted, "the groom is not my son! I thought we established that."

"Just look at him," the Queen said. "If he is not your son, then he is your brother, or perhaps your nephew. Besides, I am throwing this party, and I say that even if it is not a royal wedding, it will be as posh as if it were!"

Giovanni was furiously reviewing his notes when he blurted out, "No! This is all wrong."

"What was that?" the Queen asked. "Are you saying that your queen is wrong?"

Giovanni stood and said, "This match is wrong. Lady Elizabeth belongs with Don Hector. I'm sure of it."

The Queen pointed to me and asked, "This Don Hector? The same young man who practically put them together himself?"

"Don Hector is her intended."

Lord Leatherby shook his head and said, "Giovanni is confused. The betrothal between Elizabeth and Hector was my fault entirely. I had forbidden any match between Elizabeth and Walter, but they ignored my orders and he had even given her a betrothal ring, but she falsely told me it was from Hector."

"Is this true?" the Queen asked.

"It is," Elizabeth said, "but I only said that so my father would be shocked and embarrassed that I would promise myself to one of the servants!"

The Queen glanced over at Lord Leatherby and said, "But it didn't work, did it?"

"No," Elizabeth replied. "He knew all along that Hector was noble born."

"Did you hear that, Master Giovanni?" the Queen asked. "Were you simply confused because of the false betrothal?"

"No! Don Hector loves the Lady Elizabeth so much, he only wants what is best for her, but all of his life, he believed that he was only a lowly gardener's son, so what was best for her could never have been him."

The Queen poked her finger in Giovanni's chests. "You have three days to settle this and make them ready while I prepare for the celebration. That is a royal command."

Giovanni pursed his lips and bowed, accepting his orders, but I swear I read upon his lips a silent, "They aren't ready."

"Then it's settled!" the King bellowed. "We will have a wedding in three days between the Lady Elizabeth and young Don Hector!"

The Queen beamed with pride and asked, "Which of you fine lords will lend us the use of your hall?"

Lord Chamberlain started to raise his hand, but Walter quickly cut him off, "No, father! We cannot be part of this!"

Lord Leatherby, on the other hand, thought it was a wonderful idea and puffed out his chest as he said, "Leatherby House is at your disposal."

"No!" I blurted out. I wanted to pull my hair out, but that would serve no purpose. "It is too soon! You have not heard our case! Walter and Elizabeth are in love!"

"Love is such a fickle thing," the Queen said. "Look at Walter and Lady May, for example. They make a fine-looking couple, and even Master Giovanni has brought her here for him."

Giovanni bowed gratefully.

The Queen turned to the King and asked, "Should we knight Giovanni? Can we? He deserves a title for his service to the crown."

I couldn't believe my ears. What title could they present to a matchmaker? Shall he be Saint Giovanni? He may soon be, as I had an urge to kill him in the heat of the moment. "He is a matchmaker!" I declared. "A humble matchmaker! You cannot seriously be considering bestowing knighthood upon him. That would cheapen the heroic acts performed by your true knights, such as Sir Charles and Sir Nicholas! What has this man done on a par with them to earn such a title?"

Sir Charles blushed slightly, and I suddenly thought that I did not know exactly what had earned him his title.

I wasn't done speaking and paced the room before the royal pair, saying, "Marriage is a sacred vow! We cannot enter into this so lightly, and on the word of a man who sells his craft, which is basically selling daughters to rich noblemen."

The Queen smiled condescendingly and said, "The young can be so naïve at times. What does love have to do with marriage? That is a peasant concept. Nobles marry for advantage, which I'm quite sure Master Giovanni has fully considered." She blanched slightly and said, "Master Giovanni sounds juvenile. He must have a real title."

"I am not rich!" I said, believing that I had just found a loophole in their plans. "I am a humble pauper living by the grace and charity of Lord Leatherby."

"You forget," Lord Leatherby said, "that I have already awarded you with a monthly stipend."

"That is still charity," I shot back.

"If I may," Mateo said politely, "you still have a sizable fortune waiting for you in Avila."

"What good is that to me?" I argued. "The inquisition would never let it out of Spain."

"The boy is right," said Sebastian, who had apparently

been listening from outside the entrance.

"I wish to marry for love," I declared, "not for advantage!"

The Queen smiled as she shook her head from side to side. "You still do not see what the rest of us can plainly see. You do love the Lady Elizabeth. You will be marrying for love."

"But she does not love me! She loves Walter."

Something shifted in Elizabeth's stance. She looked at me like I was throwing stones into her plans to marry Walter.

The Queen just smiled. I was not winning my argument. I grabbed May and pulled her towards me. "I love Lady May! There! I said what I've been hiding this whole time. I love Lady May!"

I'm not sure who was more shocked, Lady May or Elizabeth, but neither of them looked ready to accept my declaration of love.

The Queen also wasn't convinced. "Do you really think you can wriggle out of this wedding by falsely declaring your love for this woman? You have convinced nobody present."

I released May and hung my head as I whispered, "Sorry," so only she could hear it.

"Wait!" Elizabeth cried out. "Why is everyone in such a rush to marry us off? Giovanni has it in his head that Hector and I should be together, but I love Walter!"

"Love?" the Queen asked. "Love is fleeting. When has a marriage based upon love ever worked?"

I cleared my throat, concerned that I was about to contradict the Queen. "My parents' marriage was based on love. Is that not so, Papa?"

"Yes!" my father said, a little too enthusiastically, as if he feared that my mother might be listening. "My love for Luisa will last forever."

The Queen frowned and said, "Never the less, Giovanni is well known and he thinks that Lady Elizabeth belongs with Don Hector."

"No!" Elizabeth cried out. "Giovanni was fooled by our fake betrothal!"

"I do not think so," the Queen said as she patted Giovanni on the shoulder. "He is a very meticulous man and even I can see the fondness between you two!"

"Of course!" Elizabeth exclaimed. "We are quite fond of each other. We have grown up together since childhood, but we are like brother and sister! Tell her Hector! Tell her how I am like your sister and you could never love me as a wife!"

I opened my mouth to speak, but I could not tell her what she wanted to hear.

"You see?" the Queen asked. "He cannot deny his feelings."

My words came to me even as I felt the circumstances tighten around my throat. "I am very fond of Elizabeth and I do love her as a sister. She is a wonderful woman and if it weren't for her being like my sister, I believe I could love her more."

Elizabeth cocked her head and gave me a glaring look that said, "You are not helping us!"

"There!" the Queen said triumphantly. "He admits his love for you. And he did ask for your hand, did he not?"

"No!" Elizabeth almost screamed as her emotions took over her temper. "Walter asked for my hand. He even gave me a ring! But I could not tell my father while the silly feud kept our families apart, so we concocted a fake betrothal in an attempt to show my father how wrong the feud was! Walter is the one I wanted to wed!"

The Queen came close to me and placed her hand on my cheek. "And you love her so deeply that you would let her marry another man just so she could have the happiness she desired?"

I felt trapped by the question and could not respond.

The Queen placed her hand on her heart and said, "I do not believe that I have ever heard a more romantic gesture than this."

She then took May's arm and pulled her away from my side. May stopped giggling over the situation and looked as if she suddenly found herself in the Queen's wrath. She slowly backed away from us until Walter took her in his arms to reassure her.

"Write up the invitations! Lady Elizabeth is to wed Don Hector in three days hence!"

"AAARRRRHHH!" Elizabeth screamed at full volume.

The Queen smiled patronizingly at Elizabeth and said, "In time, girl, you will see the truth in this."

I turned towards the Queen, still with my head hung low, and said, "My apologies, your Majesty. I have become so accustomed to telling lies in this matter that it has started to come naturally, but I promise you that it was all with the best of intentions.

"Walter and Elizabeth had grown so close that it was no surprise when Walter had given her a betrothal ring, but the stupid feud between the families meant that they could never have a normal wedding or a normal life. I did not want them to elope, which would mean abandoning their families and running away."

"You are a good friend," the Queen said.

"The best," Walter added.

"Lord Leatherby," I continued, "is a very modern and a very fair master. He has never before entertained the idea of trading his daughter to another noble for advantage, but we believed that there would be limits on exactly how fair-minded he would be. I was mostly just thinking aloud when I spoke of Elizabeth telling her father that she had promised herself to a servant boy. Before I even had time to think it through, she ran and told her father that it was I who had proposed to her. We fully expected him to object. I even feared that it might reflect badly on my family, but instead, he was thrilled. This was before we had learned of my title, and we were quite perplexed.

"With Lord Leatherby inexplicably in favor of our union, I needed to hatch some plans to change his mind. I needed him to see that Walter was a much better choice than I, so I began to spread rumors that put me in a rather poor light. Things snowballed from there. Elizabeth was seen in the market looking at baby cradles. She was only looking to purchase a gift for her friend, another victim of the feud, by the way, as her husband works for the Chamberlain estate. Unfortunately, when Elizabeth was seen looking at baby cradles, rumors of her being with child sprung forth and spread like summer flies."

"This news may have put me in a bad light, but it also hastened Lord Leatherby's plans to have his daughter wed. I needed to escalate my plans. I planted rumors that someone in the area was the son of the King. I didn't use names, but I thought I left enough clues for people to assume it was Walter. Perhaps then Lord Leatherby could see Walter as a better match than I was."

"That's when he sent for the matchmaker Giovanni to find her a more suitable mate. That was when I started to lose control of the events."

The Queen pointed to Giovanni and asked, "Is this true? Is this how you recall the events?"

Before he could respond, Lord Chamberlain interrupted, "I had heard news of Lord Leatherby sending for Master Giovanni, and I had my men intercept him and bring him to me. I proceeded to bribe him to find any match for the Lady Elizabeth other than my Walter. I didn't detain him long. I offered him money to be paid after the deed was done and sent him on his way."

"Why?" the Queen demanded. "For heaven's sake, why would you stand in the way of their happiness?"

"I believe I can answer that," I said. "It all goes back to the same rumors that had sparked the feud. Lord Chamberlain suspected that Walter was actually Lord Leatherby's son."

"Ah yes," the Queen admitted, "I do recall you saying that before."

"And," I continued, "Lord Leatherby believed that Elizabeth may have been Lord Chamberlain's daughter."

"Right," the Queen said. "And your father, as I recall, suspected that you might also be Lord Leatherby's son, so he disapproved of you and Elizabeth being wed."

"Yes," I said with a nod of my head. "This whole mess boils down to those stupid suspicions. So I hatched an additional plan to teach them a lesson."

The King joined in, "That is when you planted the rumors that I left a bastard behind here. Rumors that are totally unfounded."

"Yes dear," the Queen groaned, "we are all quite satisfied with your innocence."

The King looked puzzled and asked, "What did you hope to accomplish with that rumor? All of your parents already suspected you had different fathers. Why one more?"

"Not all of our parents," I replied. "The suspicions were only our fathers'."

"Of course," the Queen said drolly. "The women always know better."

"But still..." the King let the last syllable draw out and fade away.

"It was my hope," I said, "that they would cease lusting for noble matches and just allow their children to be happy."

"Is that what you believe?" the Queen asked.

"Which?" I asked. "That they want only to better their children's standing? What else could I believe when they brought in Giovanni? I need no more proof than the change in their attitude when it was revealed that my father is a Marquis, and I was heir to his title. As to allowing us to find our own love and be happy? Only a fool can't see true love when it's presented to them."

"Careful son," the Queen said, taking on a stern edge to her voice. "The King and I married out of duty."

"I mean no disrespect, but clearly you love each other. Your teasing banter bears testament to your love. It is most obvious."

The Queen blushed and asked, "You can see that?"

"Of course," I replied.

The Queen shook her head slowly and said, "Curious."

The Queen pointed to Giovanni again and asked, "Can you confirm this? Were you witness to these rumors and were you brought here to find a proper match for Lady Elizabeth?"

"Yes, your majesty." Giovanni pointed to some of his papers that were spread across the table. "I have taken copious notes of what I have learned here and I..."

The Queen didn't let him finish. "What about Lord Chamberlain's accusation?"

"It is true that Lord Chamberlain did intercept me on the road and he did have me taken to Chamberlain Hall."

The Queen shot a slant eyed glance over to Chamberlain and asked, "By force?"

"No!" Giovanni replied. "That is, his men never mistreated me, but my compliance was not optional."

"So he offered a reward for you to guarantee that Lady Elizabeth would not be betrothed to his son?"

"He offered a reward, but I'm not in the habit of falsifying my findings for money. I investigated young Walter and found a more suitable match for him. In this way, I would not compromise my integrity and at the same time, avoid Lord Chamberlain's wrath."

"And still get the reward?" the Queen asked with a sly smile.

"I could in good conscious accept a fee for matching young Walter, but it would not be a reward for exercising Lord Chamberlain's request. I stand by my findings. Lady May is a fine match for the Viscount Walter Chamberlain."

The Queen spun around the center of the room as if dancing and announced, "Now that the silly feud has been settled, we have a wedding to plan! Bring the happy couple forth!"

I glanced over at Elizabeth and saw that she was hesitant to volunteer herself. I couldn't tell if it was the confusion over who the groom would be or if it was just all the undue attention as all eyes fell upon her.

"No!" she cried. "This doesn't feel right."

The Queen pointed directly at Elizabeth and said, "Lady Elizabeth, your Queen summons you to come forth and plan your wedding!"

Elizabeth took a step backwards, but with a simple nod from the Queen, two guards retrieved her and brought before the monarch. Lord Leatherby started to raise a hand, as if to protest, but then thought better of it.

"And where is your intended?" the Queen asked.

The Queen's head turned towards me, but Elizabeth pointed to Walter and with a simple glance towards the guards, he rose from his chair and came forth, lest they assist him.

"Ahh," the Queen almost sang her words. "The happy couple."

A small amount of tittering and the shuffling of feet circulated around the room.

The Queen frowned. "Why don't you look very happy? You should look happy! Is this not what you wanted?"

"It is," Walter replied. "This is something that we have wanted since we were very young."

"So what is wrong? The feud is over. You are free to marry with your father's blessings."

Walter swallowed hard and took Elizabeth's hands into his own, but said nothing.

"Is that it?" the Queen asked. "You only wished to marry each other so you could defy your fathers? Now that the feud is lifted, you have no more drive to marry?"

"Please," I said, "I cannot believe that their love was based on defying their fathers. I have known both of them far too long for them to fool me. The three of us grew up together. It wasn't until we were nearly ten that the feud came about and they were already inseparable before that."

"Then why are they not happy?" the Queen demanded.

"Perhaps because it seems like you are forcing this upon them."

"Do you suggest that I am forcing them to have what they have always wanted? How cruel of me!"

"No, Your Majesty. It is what they have always wanted, but I think things may have changed. We are not as young as we once were, and our feelings may change over time. Lord Chamberlain engaged the services of Master Giovanni..."

The Queen threw her hands in the air. "Again with the *Master* Giovanni! I tell you again that he needs a better title."

The King bowed his head towards his wife and mouthed something compliant that nobody could hear.

"The Incomparable Giovanni," I said with a smile, "has come and given his best advice. He brought with him Lady May, who at first conspired with us to teach our fathers a lesson, but I believe that Lord Walter Chamberlain and Lady

May Cranston may have found something unique in each other."

Elizabeth looked sharply into Walter's face and quickly withdrew her hands from his. Walter looked pleadingly at me, then over at May, but could find no way to avoid hurting the woman he has loved since childhood.

Elizabeth turned sharply and darted towards the exit.

The Queen commanded, "Stop!"

Two burly guards moved in shoulder to shoulder, blocking the double wide door. Elizabeth quickly spun around and headed towards the back exit, but another guard was already blocking that door. There was no way for her to escape, so instead, she ran to a dim corner and collapsed, hiding her face in her hands and sobbing lightly.

Walter made a move to console her, but I shook my head and whispered, "Give her a moment. The day has been a whirlwind for her."

The Queen put her arm around me and softly said, "As it has been for you all."

The Queen released her light grip on my shoulders and

turned to face Walter. She said nothing, but stared sadly into his eyes.

"I know what you are thinking," he said. "You are thinking that this is my fault, and you are not wrong."

"Why didn't you tell her that you stopped loving her?"

"Who said I stopped loving her? We've been best friends forever. I will always love her."

"Is it true that you were promised to her?"

"Yes, Your Majesty."

"And you broke that promise for Lady May?"

May sucked in her breath, stung by the Queen's words.

"Yes, Your Majesty, I mean, I think so. I don't know, we just met." Walter pointed to Giovanni and said, "It was his fault. I mean, I think I have him to thank."

May shrank away from Walter for a step, but he grabbed her and pulled her close and said, "I mean, I'm quite sure I have Giovanni to thank. I'm sorry Elizabeth."

I patted him on the shoulder and said, "Don't be sorry. In truth, I think Elizabeth has been drifting away from you for some time now, though I know not where she would go."

"Do you not?" the Queen chided me. "You see so clearly everything else that has gone on around you, yet you don't know where Lady Elizabeth's heart has gone?"

I bowed low and said, "Perhaps I am too blinded by Her Majesty's brilliance to see everything."

"Oh, bollocks!" the Queen exclaimed. "If you'll excuse my parlance. Although, your words were spoken like a true politician, and may I add that you are certainly fool enough to hold a title."

Sebastian tried pushing into the room. "How can you talk about love and marriage when you have a heretic and his family hiding among you?"

The King motioned the guards to allow Sebastian just inside the room.

Sebastian composed himself before the King and said, "Souls are at stake here."

The King scoffed, "Whose souls? According to you and your Roman church, we are ALL heretics and infidels here. Your beliefs on this do not matter to us. We have seen through the churches politics to understand the truth that God has brought to us."

"But what of the people of Avila?" Sebastian asked. "Whole families who await that man's return." He pointed rudely at Fernando. "As long as he clings to his title, they will all be found guilty of heresy."

Mateo stood. His hand was on the pommel of his sword and it was clear from his expression that he had no love for Sebastian. His hatred for the man went far deeper than his duty to his king. "Only the church and the inquisition would threaten an entire people of heresy over one man. King Philip has already allowed for Don Fernando to leave

Spain rather than face the tribunal."

Sebastian wagged his finger at Mateo and said, "You come perilously close to heresy yourself when you speak ill of the church."

Mateo moved closer to Sebastian. I knew already how ripe the soldier was and saw Mateo wrinkle his nose when he was too near. "I speak only of the king's debt to Don Fernando. You would do well to honor the king's wishes."

Sebastian pointed to the heavens and said, "I serve a higher king."

Mateo balled up his fist as if to strike Sebastian until the King said, "Captain Mateo, you will have Captain Sebastian to yourself soon enough when you journey back to Spain. I would ask that you do not shed any blood just yet, not while he is under my protection."

"Let him shed my blood," Sebastian spat. "I do not need your protection."

The King laughed and said, "I believe you do."

Mateo turned and walked away, taking deep breaths with each step.

My father saw the rage in Mateo's eyes and said, "Sebastian, my old friend, I do not believe you have properly valued Mateo's animosity towards you. You should take care on your trip home."

"YOU!" Sebastian yelled, his rage now boiling over. "How dare you speak to me in this way?"

Sebastian lunged for my father, but I jumped in front of his path and will be forever grateful that he had already been disarmed as my face blocked the full blow of his fist that was aimed for my father. What followed was a blur as my eyes teared up and the room wobbled around me. Some of the details were filled in for me later, but I will relay it to you as it happened.

Elizabeth let out a blood-curdling scream and leapt onto Sebastian's back, pulling his hair and scratching his face. I've been told that the Queen stayed clear of the fray and found it all quite amusing, but I promise you, it was not so amusing to me.

My head started to clear just enough to see Sebastian swing his elbow in to Elizabeth's face, who was still on his back, but quickly fell off of him. This was all but moments; a blink of the eye before the guards took Sebastian by the arms and restrained him.

Then was Mateo's turn to waggle his finger in Sebastian's face. "You promised! You swore an oath on your bible. And now, you risk your immortal soul for what? Your temper?"

Sebastian's face was twisted with hate as he growled, "I swore that I would do nothing on our voyage back to Spain. I never said I would shirk my duty to bring the heretic back for trial."

I had seen and heard all of this, but my true attention was on Elizabeth, who lay crying on the floor beside me, with the side of her face in her hands. She rolled over, nearly on top of me, and I could see clearly her injuries. Our faces each sported swollen cheeks around the eyes; hers on her right and mine on my left. I could not fathom how any man could do this to a woman, or how he could still consider himself a man after doing so. She reached across and gently touched the side of my face. It hurt, and yet I did not mind her touch as it brought on a warmth that I thought might be a magical healing power.

I heard the clank of irons being placed on Sebastian's wrists and the scuffle as they dragged him back out of the tavern. But then I heard something quite unexpected.

The Queen clucked and cooed and asked me, "Now? Now, do you see where Lady Elizabeth's heart has gone?"

Elizabeth and I ignored her odd question. Our eyes remained locked together as my head tilted right and left, as if seeing a new wonder for the first time. My head spun now, not from the Captain's punch, but from a strange intoxicating glow radiating from her face. She winced slightly as she spread her lips in a smile, still staring deeply into my eyes. I raised my head slightly to meet her lips. If there was any further botheration from our wounds, neither of us showed it as our lips touched, parted, and touched again. Any residual discomfort from the captain's punch was but a memory now.

"Rise!" the Queen commanded. "Tell me what you have learned."

The Queen's voice was like a splash of cold water on my face, jarring me back to reality, but not enough to wipe away the tingle from our kiss. My feet felt a bit wobbly under me, but not so unsturdy that I couldn't help Elizabeth to her feet. Her legs must have been equally unsteady as she clung to my waist to keep upright.

"What have you learned?" the Queen repeated.

My voice was unusually light and airy as I replied, "Well, for one thing, I have learned not to step in front of a grown man's fist, I think."

The Queen pursed her lips and narrowed her eyes, saying,

"Do not trifle with me, boy. What have you learned?"

My head was still woozy, but not so blurred that I did not know what she was trying to get me to admit. "Begging your pardon, Your Majesties, but I think perhaps I should speak with Elizabeth in private before I declare my feelings to the world."

The Queen frowned and shook her head. "Why are men so fearless in the face of mortal enemies, but so timid in the face of love? Lady Elizabeth? Do you require a private audience with Don Hector before you declare yourself?"

Elizabeth never looked at the Queen; not even a brief glance. Her eyes remained locked with mine as she shook her head no.

Never in my life have I ever experienced such joy. My face may have still burned with pain, but my entire body was overcome with a wave of something I had never felt before. My skin rippled and the hackles on my neck stood on end. I spoke soft and low, so I thought only Elizabeth could hear, "I love you. I have always loved you, even when I was not worthy to do so."

Evidently, my message was not as private as I had thought as the Queen exclaimed, "Hallelujah! The blind man can see again!"

Chapter Eleven

I think Elizabeth and I would have never parted if it weren't for the sea of family and friends that came flooding in to shake our hands and hug us.

The Queen stood back and beheld the sight as if she were solely responsible for our coming together, but off to the side, Giovanni also held the same look.

I want to believe that things in this world tend to work out as they should, but the truth is that I would have had Elizabeth and Walter marry and somewhere deep in my heart, I would have regretted what might have been for the remainder of my life.

As the congratulations finally quieted down, I rejoined Elizabeth, who was standing with May and Walter.

Elizabeth looked forlornly at Walter and said, "I feel as though I have just broken an age long promise, and doing so must have struck you, as an arrow would, directly in the heart."

Walter hugged her as a friend would and said, "As do I, but we both know that no matter what was, or what we thought was our future, this is how it should be."

I was pretty sure from watching her countenance that Elizabeth's head swooned much the same as mine did.

"You and May?" she asked.

"I think so," Walter replied.

"But you barely know her."

"Perhaps," he said, "but it feels as though I've known her all my life."

"It's funny," May said, "how things work out sometimes. Isn't it?"

"Truly," I replied. "In all my scheming, I never once saw this coming. I have always loved Elizabeth, but as a friend. And as that friend, I always wanted what was best for her."

"You loved her?" May asked. "Yet you still championed Walter for her groom?"

I sighed heavily. "I was unworthy."

"You thought you were," Elizabeth corrected me.

Walter slapped me on the back and said, "I think maybe you always loved her, as you said, but you just wouldn't allow yourself to love her as anything more than just a friend."

I could only grunt and shrug my shoulders.

"You always were a bit different," Walter continued, "and never once behaved like any of the other servants."

The Queen had been listening in on our conversation and said, "It's breeding. Good breeding always comes out."

"That can't be," May said. "I don't believe in breeding, at least not with people. I've seen good peasant men who were nobler than other men with long lineages of so called good breeding."

The Queen didn't like being contradicted, so I added, "Perhaps it's something very akin to breeding, but not in the blood. I think a proper upbringing can produce the same results as good breeding."

"Yes," May said. "That makes much sense."

The Queen nodded her head, willing to accept the hypothesis.

Elizabeth pulled Walter aside and said, "I hope we shall remain friends."

Walter smiled broadly and told her, "I shall become what Hector has been all these years: your best friend and confidant. You must come to me with all your joys and complaints about life with the great Don Hector; especially the complaints."

He laughed and winked at me with the last of his remark, but Elizabeth glanced over to May and said, "Perhaps I'll save the girl talk for May, and in return she can tell me of all the annoying quirks of yours that I was spared by not marrying you."

Walter placed both fists over his heart and said, "Now that is the arrow to the heart that stings the most."

Elizabeth sighed and said, "Life will certainly be different around here."

May looked a bit left out and said, "I wish I could have known what life was like here before, so I could share in how improved it will be."

Walter took her in his arms and said, "It was dark and dreary here, until you came to shine your brilliance upon our lives."

"You're a poet?" May asked. "I LOVE poets."

"Wait a moment," Elizabeth said as she corralled me into her arms. "I don't think it was quite so dark and dreary as you describe. It was pretty good and now it will only get better."

"For us maybe," Walter replied, "but maybe not for poor Isabel."

I hadn't thought of Isabel in days, but he was right. I wonder if Giovanni could help her.

The Queen went to the King and spoke softly. I could not hear her words, but he had the look of a man who was sitting through the love scenes of a play, just waiting for the action where someone would die by the blade. He gestured around the room as he spoke with the Queen, then his face suddenly turned stern.

"Captain?" he barked.

Several men replied, including Mateo and Sebastian, but it was his own man that came to him and bowed his head.

"Captain," he repeated authoritatively, "bring me that Spanish captain for a word."

The poor man looked sheepishly towards Mateo and shrugged his shoulders.

"Not him," the King growled, "the scoundrel you are

holding outside."

The English captain motioned to a couple of men at the door and Sebastian was brought before the King.

The King circled Sebastian, sizing him up. "You must think yourself very clever; taking an oath upon your bible then breaking that oath claiming a technicality. I should have known you were not to be trusted simply by the size of that book that you haul around with you."

Sebastian was defeated and held his head low, but his lips sneered contemptibly at the King's words.

"Clearly," the King continued, "you are not a man to be trusted, and while I would like to have peaceful relations with Spain, I fear that I may not. If your church insists on waging war with England, be assured that we will take what steps are necessary to protect the sovereign rights of England. It is most unfortunate that the church has sent you as their emissary. I would much rather deal with Captain Mateo here. I trust him in ways I will never trust you. Don Fernando over there has shown himself to be an honorable man who I believe I can trust implicitly."

"And don't forget Don Hector," the Queen added, "who I am sure will find a place amongst your advisors at court."

"Exactly!" the King exclaimed as he wagged his finger in the air. "Mateo! Please thank King Philip for sending me these fine new subjects."

Mateo bowed officially to the King and said, "That leaves us with deciding Sebastian's fate. He swore on the bible that he would go peacefully back to Spain. If you command it, even though I am not one of your subjects, I will keep him bound during the trip."

"There is a dark part of me," the King said, "that would rather just execute him and be done with the matter, but no, I would like you to keep him bound until you reach the opposite shore, at which time you may rely on your own judgment as to whether you should release him or not. If he breaks his vow again, then I would ask that you please kill him and send me word."

"As you wish. I will send a correspondence to Don Fernando, outlining the entire trip when I return to court."

"You honor me," my father said, looking up from the notes he had been taking, "but perhaps you can address it to my son, for if what the Queen says is true, he will be at court more than I."

"I will send two letters then," Mateo decreed. "One for each of you. King Philip may wish to send you his own thoughts as well."

"Mateo?" my father said as he folded up the notes he had been writing, "If you would be so kind, I would like you to deliver this to King Philip for me."

"I would be happy to do so. What, if I may ask, does it contain? Should I guard it with my life?"

My father thought about it a moment, then replied, "I hate putting you in any more danger than you may already be facing, but perhaps it would be wise for you to guard it. I'm resigning my position as Marquis of Avila. I fear that my absence there may have put my people in danger from the inquisition. Please, if you would, beg King Philip to assign one of his men and not a puppet for the inquisition in my stead."

Mateo smiled broadly and said, "Don Fernando, please allow me to be the last to address you as the Most Excellent Marquis of Avila, and to let you know that King Philip had already anticipated that you might make such a selfless gesture. He has authorized me to inform you that you may retain your noble rank of Marquis even without having Avila to rule. He also suggested that some of your fortune may find its way to you. I will volunteer to deliver it myself personally, assuming it hasn't already been raided by the inquisition pirates."

Mateo and my father gripped hands, then pulled each other into a great bear hug.

My father's eyes appeared damp as he said, "I will miss you, my friend, but I look forward to seeing you again one day."

"As do I."

Mateo paused to bow before the King. "Your Majesty. I hope to see you again one day in a time of peace and prosperity."

The King gripped Mateo's arm, a gesture I later learned that he didn't ordinarily share with anyone. "Safe Journey's Mateo. I have ordered some of my knights to accompany you as far as our nation's shores."

"There is no need," Mateo said. "My men can handle these

inquisition hoodlums."

"In that, I believe you, but I wanted my knights to guarantee safe passage for you should you run into an English patrol that does not know what has transpired here tonight. I have no doubt that Sebastian would use such an opportunity to create trouble for you if that were to happen."

Mateo bowed again and said, "A very wise observation. I thank you for their company."

Giovanni was clearing his parchment, ink and quills from the table where my father had borrowed them to write his resignation.

"Master Giovanni," the King said, then turned to the Queen and said, "You are correct again. That really doesn't work as a title for him. Giovanni, come here."

Giovanni dropped his supplies on the table next to his satchel and came to the King.

"You arranged these couples as they are?"

"Yes, Your Majesty."

"Well done," the King said. "It would seem that you knew these couples better than they knew themselves."

Giovanni looked confused and simply nodded his head.

The King looked around the room and said, "Normally I would wait for a more appropriate moment, but I simply cannot let this go on any longer. Giovanni, please drop to one knee. I don't know if Giovanni is your true name, or if it is merely a name you chose for yourself, that sounded more appropriate for your craft, but I would like to make it official."

To my great surprise, and probably that of everyone else in the room, the King pulled his sword and tapped Giovanni on the shoulders as he said something in French that I did not understand at all, then he smiled to the crowd and said, "Inn keeper, put out some ale so we may all toast Sir Giovanni, for as long as he is on English soil, we shall recognize him as a knight of the realm."

Giovanni was clearly overcome with emotions, which left him a bit wobbly as he climbed back to his feet and was met by a crowd of soldiers congratulating him. I was frankly surprised that the other knights would accept him into their fraternity, but they must have seen something in the King's demeanor that expressed great respect for the matchmaker's craft.

While everyone was still congratulating Giovanni, I mean SIR Giovanni, an argument grew on the other side of the room.

"She's my daughter," Lord Leatherby growled, "of course the wedding will be held at Leatherby house!"

"But she's not the only one being married," Lord Chamberlain replied with equal vigor, "and Lady May is not from around here! What if her father wants to have them wed in their home?"

"What of it?"

"What of it?" Chamberlain spat back. "You heard the Queen yourself. She intends to plan both weddings, and that means we'll be holding them together and Leatherby House hasn't held a banquet in ages. At least Chamberlain Hall has been kept up."

"You need have no fears on that," Leatherby replied. "The banquet hall at Leatherby House has been kept in perfect order."

"But the staff at Chamberlain Hall is well practiced at holding balls and ceremonies."

"Is that so?" Leatherby asked incredulously. "Since when has Chamberlain Hall ever held a banquet? Why have I never received an invitation?"

"Really?" Chamberlain asked. "Are you actually asking me why I never invited you over to my home for a Yule Tide celebration?"

The two men stared at each other until Leatherby closed his eyes and uttered, "Oh."

"The season," Chamberlain continued, "has been celebrated at Chamberlain Hall ever since you stopped holding the banquet yourself."

Leatherby stared down at his feet and nodded his head. "Of course you couldn't tell me at first, because Lady Leatherby's death was still too fresh in my memory."

Chamberlain put a hand on Leatherby's shoulder and said, "She died on the eve of the great banquet. Nobody expected you to hold it the following night, and when you weren't preparing for it during the next year, I took over for you. Your grief was terrible, and I thought it would never end."

"It never did end," Leatherby said. "I was a fool, and I just turned my grief against you with that damned feud between us."

"The fault of the feud was not all yours, my friend. I played my part to perfection."

The Queen stepped in and asked, "Lords, if both houses were in perfect upkeep, whose would be the better banquet hall?"

Chamberlain was quick to respond, "Leatherby house."

"And," she continued, "is there an adequate chapel for the ceremony?"

Again Lord Chamberlain replied, "Leatherby house used to have a room that was completely enclosed in glass with some very beautiful plants grown there. If it is still there, I have always thought that it would be a wonderful place for a wedding."

"Well?" the Queen asked, "do you still have your glass room?"

Leatherby looked up, with a glint of life in his eyes. "Indeed I do, and it is still well preserved."

"I shall like to see this room," the Queen said. "Lord Chamberlain, since your staff is more recently practiced, could they assist with a banquet at Leatherby House?"

"Indeed, they could!"

I'm quite sure that I saw tears welling up in Lord Leatherby's eyes. "My staff would welcome Lord Chamberlain's staff."

"Excellent!" the Queen exclaimed. "We shall begin preparations immediately!"

Elizabeth's normally porcelain skin appeared even paler than normal and her eyes had glassed over from the whirlwind of emotions that had been running through us. I had no doubt that my own visage carried the same pallor and dazed expression.

I pulled her aside and asked, "Do you too feel like our lives have become a grand performance being played out before us?"

She looked back at me with eyes that were equally confused and lost. "How can you wax so poetically when our lives are being planned for us without even a nod to our approval?"

"Did I not just say that?"

Frustration and fear boiled up inside her. I thought she might scream, or worse, start hitting me, so I took her in my embrace and said, "It is okay. If you do not want this, just say the word and I will put a stop to it."

She opened her mouth to speak but said nothing and turned her back to me.

I took a step back and whispered, "I understand. We were just swept up in the heat of the moment. I will tell the Queen."

She turned sharply towards me and grabbed me by the collar. "What? What will you tell the Queen?"

"That this is not what you want. That in the end, I am still the gardener's son…"

"How can you be so clever and smart and yet at the same time be so dim-witted? We can't deny who we are or what we have. I just wish we weren't pawns in their game as they plan our wedding."

A massive wave of relief overtook me. I wrapped my arms around her again and said, "Then let us take over! It's our wedding."

"We can't," she said sadly. "It's the Queen, and look how our fathers are getting along again! Everything is going to change around here with them working together and we can't ruin that."

"Then let us demand one thing that they haven't thought of!"

"And what would that be? My favorite flower? You're the great schemer. What should we demand?"

I thought for a moment, and it came to me. "You said it yourself. Everything will change with Lord Leatherby and Lord Chamberlain getting along. We will use that peace to add something to our wedding." My smile told her that I already had an idea, but wasn't telling her.

"What?" she asked, but I was already heading towards the Queen.

"Your Majesty?"

"What is it Don Hector?"

"We would like to make a special request, well more of a demand, if you'll allow it, for our own wedding."

She chuckled and said, "Let me hear your demand and we will consider it."

I paused a moment as I considered how I would even say it to her.

As I was taking too long to answer her, she turned to Elizabeth and said, "Lady Leatherby, your intended seems reticent to share your new demand with me. Perhaps you can?"

Elizabeth's eyes were held extraordinarily wide as she shrugged her shoulders and pointed to me.

"We have some friends," I started, "who are already married, but one of them is from Chamberlain Hall and the other from Leatherby House. They are servants and are expecting their first child, but they have had to hide their marriage for fear of losing their positions due to the feud. I was hoping..."

"WE were hoping," Elizabeth said with a broad smile, indicating that she had caught on to my plan.

"We were hoping," I said, "that they could renew their vows along with us. It would be a wonderful celebration for their marriage, as well as a beautiful symbol of the two great houses renewing their friendship after all these years."

The Queen almost shed a tear as she said, "That is a very generous and beautiful sentiment. I would be happy to include your friends in the wedding. It is also very crafty of you to provide such a symbol for the peace between the Leatherby and Chamberlain families."

Elizabeth clapped her hands as she hopped up and down. "Their names are George and Agnes. George works for Lord Chamberlain."

The Queen delicately wiped a single tear before it spilled out from her eye and said, "It is so seldom that I see nobles with so much care for the peasants that work for them. It shall be done. Go tell them."

Elizabeth and I barely had time to appreciate our victory, getting to include George and Agnes in the celebration, when we heard a new ruckus grow between Lord Leatherby and Lord Chamberlain.

Elizabeth marched up to them and demanded, "What are you two fighting about now? Hasn't this community suffered enough from your bickering?"

The two lords stopped mid-sentence to share their blank, sheepish expressions with her.

"Enough!" she commanded. "I've heard enough; the people of Greenshire have heard enough; I dare say the King and the Queen have also heard enough!"

The Queen was nearby enough to hear her and clapped her hands.

Lord Leatherby's cheeks reddened some as he said, "We weren't fighting, as you say. We were just discussing where you would live. As your father, I felt it was my duty to grant you a plot of land from the Leatherby holdings."

"And I," Lord Chamberlain volunteered, "thought that Lord Leatherby has already been charitable enough to have given Hector's family refuge on the Leatherby estate, that I should find a parcel of our land for the two of you."

"Your points are well taken," I said to them, "and much appreciated, but I think that I can find a way to take care of my family."

"But I insist," Lord Leatherby said.

"WE insist," Lord Chamberlain corrected him.

"In that case," I said, "your lands border each other. All you need do is find two adjacent plots of land that we can call our own."

Lord Chamberlain closed his eyes and nodded his head. I could practically hear his thoughts that they should have thought of that first.

Lord Leatherby bowed to me and said, "It will be done."

The Queen clapped her hands and said, "Marvelous."

Lords Leatherby and Chamberlain wandered off chatting with each other, and based upon the animation of their arms, I presumed that they were discussing where along their borders they planned to stake out a plot of land for us.

I smiled sheepishly at the Queen, completely overwhelmed by the turn of events. I tried taking stock of everything that has transpired. Just being in the presence of the King and Queen would be enough to overwhelm anyone, but they were here as a result of my own deceptions. Then, all of a sudden, Elizabeth and I are to be married and as if that weren't enough, we would be given a plot of land, and if I knew Lord Leatherby, it would be a generous plot that Lord Chamberlain would be only too happy to match.

All of those feelings, spinning around in my head, paled to the revelation, or perhaps the realization, that I was hopelessly in love with Elizabeth. She was the young girl that I grew up with, but she was also the noble woman with whom I could not have a relationship until... I closed my eyes and sighed. I completely overlooked the revelation that my father was not just a refuge from Spain, but he was a nobleman in his own right, and therefore, so was I for all those years.

The Queen snapped me out of my reverie when she asked, "What are you thinking, Don Hector?"

I opened my eyes and found both the Queen and the King standing before me with genuine smiles on their faces. "I was merely recounting the whirlwind of events that has brought me to this moment. To be sure, I have never had occasion to speak with a monarch before, but then, only a few days ago, I thought myself to be a common servant."

The Queen's smile broadened even more. "I don't think a mere servant boy could have settled the dispute between Lord's Chamberlain and Leatherby so easily."

"That wasn't me," I said. "They were bound to settle the feud on their own, eventually."

"I was speaking of their dispute to give you land for your wedding. You handled that like Solomon himself."

"Oh that? Anyone could have done that."

"Could they?" she asked. "Solomon was a king. You handled that very much like a king."

I shook my head and said, "I'm no king."

She glanced over at the King and said, "Do you hear that? He's no king. Your job is safe, at least." She turned back to me and added, "You're no servant boy, either. I think you would make a grand ambassador."

I'm quite sure I blushed at that point. "You honor me, but given my father's resignation, I doubt that Spain would want me as their ambassador. Besides, with the tensions between Spain and basically the rest of the world, I doubt that such a position would actually be able to accomplish anything of importance."

"You misunderstand me," she said. "I think you would make a wonderful ambassador to represent England."

"Of England?" I asked. "Mere moments ago, I was an

infante of Spain. I was in line to be Marquis of Avila."

"And now?" she asked. "Do you still own any of those things?"

She was right. King Philip granted my father the right to bear the title of Marquis, but without him actually holding the office, could I inherit the title?

"You were born here," she said, "were you not?"

I nodded my head.

She looked over at the King again, who seemed to be mulling it over.

The King gave the Queen an affectionate wink, then walked over to my father. "Don Fernando, allow me to congratulate you on retaining your title as Marquis, but it is unfortunate that circumstances have forced you to relinquish your previous title."

I could practically see the thoughts churning in my father's head. Kings only make such statements as a prelude to something they want. It was clear, from my father's posture, that he did not know what that would be. "Thank you, your highness. Retaining the title is far more than I expected and more than I ever required."

"Your modest needs notwithstanding," the King said, "you do have the title and such a title needs to be recognized. Please allow me to be the first to welcome you to Britain as a British citizen, if that is what you wish."

The Queen leaned close to the King and whispered,

"Don't you think parliament would like to approve this first?"

King Charles whispered back, "I'm still king, am I not?"

My father bowed his head and when the whispering died down, he said, "You do me too much honor, but I have been quite content to live here in your country and I would relish the chance to be considered one of you."

The King smiled. I believe that he appreciated my father's way with words. "You must come to London, so I may introduce you to the House of Lords."

The Queen hadn't expected so much from her husband and tried to hide her gasp with her hand as my father bowed, low this time, at the waist.

"Furthermore," the King continued, "a man of your standing must have a home befitting his station, and I believe I know of just such a place. The grounds are a bit modest, but if you will grace me at court on occasion, I would want for your stories of King Philip and life in Spain. I fear we may all be in for some rough years ahead and I'm not above asking for advice from someone that knows how they think."

"Really," the Queen whispered. "Cromwell will not approve, especially with that property."

It was rare for me to ever see my father at a loss for words, but he stood there, unable to respond.

Lord Leatherby came to clap him on the back. "Well done Fernando. It is good to have friends in high places, and they don't come any higher than this."

"And when you are in London," the King continued, "as I expect you will be, we will always make a room available to you at Wimbledon House."

The Queen clucked and slowly shook her head. "You know perfectly well that Cromwell is really not going to like that. You're just baiting him now."

King Charles smiled slyly and admitted, "I know. I have a special spot on my arse where he can pucker up."

I ran to congratulate my father, which meant elbowing my way between Lords Leatherby and Chamberlain, plus a host of other locals who knew him well. When I reached him, he wrapped me in a bear hug and the man whom I had always known to be absolutely stoic shed tears like I had never seen.

"Son... son..."

I knew he was trying to say something, but the words were stuck in his emotions.

"I know Papa," I replied. It had been years since I called him papa, or had it just been days? The past week was a jumble of images in my mind, and even though I was to be married soon, I felt like his young child again and it felt appropriate. "You must let us come visit you when you and Mama get settled in."

"Your Mama! I must go tell her!"

"Anon!" the Queen said as she gently held my father's arm. "The King has something of great import to say."

I stepped back from my father so the King could speak to him directly, but instead of facing my father, King Charles came to me.

"Don Hector," the King started. "I would like to offer a

wedding gift to you and your bride. If Lord Leatherby and Lord Chamberlain can agree to this, I would like to purchase some additional land adjacent to the land they have already granted you and I would like to offer the skilled craftsmen required to build an estate that is grand enough to befit my newest Earl."

Quite beyond my control, my breathing stopped as I glanced over to the Queen to hear what she had to say on the matter, but she just smiled and nodded her head towards me.

"I know," the King said jovially, "I know. Cromwell will not like this. In fact, I imagine that all of Parliament will not like this, but they will like you in spite of themselves. I am sure of it. When they get to know you and your father, they will understand that you have truly made yourselves British citizens; especially you, Lord Hector..."

My mouth fell open, and I felt the weight of Elizabeth's arm, which had clung to mine through the entire presentation, tug on me to steady herself.

The King raised a glass of ale and toasted me, "To Lord Hector!"

And just like that, my name and my new rank reverberated around the room.

Chapter Twelve

The Queen released my father's arms and clapped for me. "Thank you for waiting," she said to him. "I believe you were going to go tell your wife of your good fortune."

"Indeed," my father said with a nod.

I grabbed Elizabeth's hand and said, "Come with us. You and I have much to tell my mother, too."

We followed my father out of the tavern. He had apparently walked here and when he started down the long trail back to the Leatherby estate, I called to him, "Father! Wait! I'm sure we can find a horse for you."

Sir Charles was waving goodbye to his comrades in the distance who were accompanying Mateo and the inquisition soldiers. He had apparently heard me yell to my father and asked, "Are you in need of a mount?"

"My father is. We are going now to tell my mother of our good fortunes."

"I was not there to hear it from the king, but I was told of your appointment. It is seldom that any of us ever hear of such great news, and to hear it directly from King Charles himself is a great honor. You can have my horse. I'll get it for you."

"Why are you not escorting the Spaniards with your friends?"

"My place is with the King. I serve him and sometimes do small errands for him."

"Like investigating rumors of long-lost sons in faraway hamlets who might challenge him for the throne?"

"More like investigate those same rumors for sons that he might wish to know better. If they would wish to challenge him for the throne, they will have to get in a very long line."

Sir Charles fetched his mount and handed the reins to my father.

"Father," I said, "I don't believe you were here yet when introductions were made. This is Sir Charles. He's one of the King's men, but he's been somewhat secretive about his true duties. He may be a spy, so you should probably watch what you say around him."

Sir Charles chuckled. "No wonder the King favors you. Very few people can deduce that from so few clues."

I bowed and said, "Thank you, sir. I bet fewer still live to share that tidbit of information."

He laughed and said, "Go now. I have some drinking to do."

Elizabeth took the lead since her horse knew the way the best. I was able to ride alongside my father.

"So, father, how do you plan to tell her?"

"Me?" he asked. "I think you and Elizabeth should tell her first. Your news is far bigger than mine."

"Bigger than keeping your title and gaining an estate?"

"You are her son and you are getting married. Your news is the bigger. It's even bigger than you being made an earl."

"I don't know about that. She may even have had suspicions about Elizabeth and me, but she'll NEVER have imagined me being made into a British Earl."

"That may be a bigger surprise to her, but trust me; the wedding news is the greater of the two. You should go ride with her so you can both greet your mother together."

Always the dutiful son, I pulled forward to ride alongside Elizabeth. Once we had passed the gates to the Leatherby estate, I turned my steed, taking the lead down the path towards our cottage.

"Are you anxious?" Elizabeth asked.

"Aren't you? You're the one who is marrying the gardener's son."

"I thought I was marrying the Marquis' son."

"That too, but my father has not yet officially resigned his gardener post."

"I've seen him work in the gardens," she said with a smile. "I don't believe he will ever quit gardening. It's his passion."

"It is. I've seen it too."

We turned the corner around one of the estate's oldest hedges and there it was; the cottage in which I grew up. I slid off my horse and helped Elizabeth down. She didn't really need the help, but her waist fit comfortably into my hands as I slid her down the length of my body.

My father coughed in a quiet, but obvious, way. There would be time for intimacy soon enough. I kept my arm around her waist as we walked the short cobblestone path to the door. I considered knocking, as it no longer felt like I truly lived there.

"Just open it," my father said, without hiding any of the amusement from his voice.

I pushed the door open and heard my mother in the kitchen. "If you're hoping for some dinner, you're too late. I'm washing up now."

"We're not here for a meal," I said. "We have some rather extraordinary news for you. If you could leave that for a moment and sit down, we have much to say."

I lead Elizabeth to the dining table and sat her down.

My mother put the towel down that she had been using and came to join us while my father was content to close the door and stand just inside of the doorway.

My mother gasped and pointed at us. "What has happened to your faces?"

I looked at Elizabeth, having completely forgotten about our blackened eyes, and said, "Oh these? It is nothing."

"It does not look like nothing!"

"Then it is something I will explain later," I said. "It is difficult to know where to start our story. Did you know that the King and Queen came to Greenshire? We just met them in the tavern. The Queen is remarkably sensitive, and she revealed some things about us that I think we always knew, but were in denial. She said that we..."

My mother jumped to her feet and held her hands to her mouth. "You're getting married!"

Elizabeth's jaw fell slack.

I smiled sheepishly and said, "Yes, mother, but I would appreciate it if you don't frighten my bride off with your witchcraft.”

“Don’t be silly. It doesn’t take witchcraft to see that you two belong together. It just takes a woman’s intuition. Something the Queen must have in abundance.”

“Well, you are correct, but there is more. Would you like to amaze us more with your woman’s intuition, or shall I tell you?”

“Sorry,” she said as she retook her seat. “Don’t let me take your fun from you. Go ahead.”

“Well, as you guessed, we are going to be married. Rather soon too, I believe. The Queen is arranging it. It will be a royal affair. Lord’s Leatherby and Chamberlain are giving us adjacent parcels of land so we might build our own estate.”

“Together?” she asked. “Both of them?”

I must admit that I thoroughly enjoyed the disbelief in her voice. “Yes, mother. I neglected to mention that they have settled their differences and ended the feud.”

“Ha!” my father laughed. “Your son had a very great hand in settling their feud. You should be proud of him.”

“I am,” she cried.

I know not how my mother could have seen through her tearful eyes, which darted repeatedly back and forth between Elizabeth and me.

“There’s more,” Elizabeth added. “The King will be purchasing additional adjacent land for our estate.”

“Why on Earth would the King do that?”

“Because,” my father said. “In the King’s own words, no less, their estate should be large enough to befit one of his newest Earls.”

My mother leapt from her seat again. “An Earl? Our son?

An Earl?"

"Yes dear. And I would expect their estate to have a stable with horses and carriages so they can come visit us."

My mother spoke in gasps as she tried regaining her breath. "If their new estate is bordering both the Chamberlain and Leatherby estate as you said, I doubt they should need a horse to come visit us, certainly not a carriage."

"There is more," my father said, "but the short version of the story is that we won't be living in this cottage any longer. The King has granted us an estate too."

My mother sat back down as my father fetched a drink of water for her. "Why on earth would he give us an estate? Are you to be an Earl, too?"

"No," my father chuckled, "I will still be a Marquis. King Philip has granted me the right to retain the title, even though I relinquished my claim to Avila."

"But," I added, "the king has asked father to come to London, from time to time, to give his advice."

"The king wants your advice?"

"I think his interest in me is purely as a defense against Spain, should the inquisition choose to attack England."

"And," Elizabeth added, "Hector is to be an ambassador for England."

"The queen," my father explained, "was rather impressed with Hector's keen mind and his ability to remain calm in the face of danger."

My mother shot out of her chair again and shouted, "Danger? What danger? How could you put our son in danger?"

"Calm yourself, mother. The danger was mostly my doing."

"Not really," Elizabeth said. "It was the Spanish soldiers that wanted to spill blood. I have never seen anyone behave so bravely as you did tonight. I am so proud of you."

"As am I," my father added.

"What Spanish soldiers?" my mother asked.

"It was inquisition soldiers," I explained, "and swords were drawn, but nobody was seriously injured."

"Is this where you explain your bruises?"

"It was nothing," I said. "A mere skirmish."

"Bah," my father retorted. "Your son leapt before me to take the blow that was aimed at me, then, seeing how Hector had fallen, Lady Elizabeth jumped onto the assailant's back. She was quite fierce, but paid for her actions with an elbow to the eye. "

My mother paused for a moment, glancing back and forth between the three of us. "Why did your son have to come to your rescue? Who was trying to hit you?"

"Oh," my father said quite innocently, "did I not mention him before? It was Sebastian."

My mother's eyes opened like saucers. "Not THAT Sebastian?"

"The very same."

"You knew him?" I asked, quite astonished. "He came with his soldiers to capture father, but with the help of the English soldiers, Captain Mateo and the king, of course, they were stopped and sent away."

"Mateo?" mother asked. "Little dog faced Mateo? Did he come with Sebastian?"

"I do not think he is the same Mateo who you are remembering," I replied. "This Mateo was not so dog faced. This

Mateo was one of King Philip's personal guards and was most certainly no friend of Captain Sebastian. He said that one day, when tensions between the nations relax, he would try to bring some of the family fortune to us on behalf of King Philip."

Father laughed and said, "Yes, it was Mateo Moya, but he has grown into a much more handsome man than you remember."

"And all this happened at the tavern just now? Why is it that I was not invited?"

"That is a much longer story," I said, "and given the danger there, it is better that you were not with us. I expect that tomorrow all the fun will be at Leatherby House as the Queen will no doubt commandeer everybody to get the hall ready for a wedding."

My mother was still swooning from all the news when Elizabeth took my hand and tugged me away from the table. "Come, we have more news to deliver."

"Do we?"

"By order of the Queen, we must prepare George and Agnes."

"It is dark already, and it is such a long way to George's home."

She pulled harder and said, "But it is not so far to Agnes's."

I got up and followed her to the door. "If you will excuse me, mother and father, it would seem that even Earls have masters that they must follow."

Father laughed and said, "You are not even married yet. You must learn to put your foot down!"

Mother hit him playfully and said, "This is a good omen. She already has him trained well. You should come share tea with me, Elizabeth. The next lesson is how to get them to do what you want, but think it was their own idea."

Elizabeth smiled, and I also laughed. While it was all said as a joke, a shiver ran down my spine as if it were not so fanciful after all.

The ride to the Agnes' father's farm was not long, but the darkness and the distant moon made judging our progress challenging until we were close enough to see the dim light through the window shutters of the farm home.

Elizabeth was beyond anxious and urged her horse forward. I was not so experienced on the horse to go any faster in the moonlight. When I arrived, she was already hugging Agnes and, to my great relief, George was there with her.

"Is it true?" George asked. "Is the Queen actually planning a wedding gala for us? I mean, it's not that I don't believe Lady Elizabeth, but this sounds more like one of your extravagant schemes than actual life."

"It is true," I said, "although technically, the Queen is planning the gala for Elizabeth and me plus Walter and his new intended."

"You and Lady Elizabeth?" Agnes asked. "You should have told us that first. We thought you would never see what everyone else saw so plainly."

"No," Elizabeth said, "I wanted to include you first! We talked the Queen into including you. Hector was quite insistent and said that if we were to be married in such a grand celebration, then our good friends George and Agnes must be included."

"I don't think that's what I said."

"It doesn't matter what you actually said with your words, that is what your heart said."

"When is this to happen?" George asked.

"Soon." I said. "I would expect a couple of days at most. The King and Queen will need to return to London."

"And from there," Elizabeth added, "they will send for their new Earl to come join them to advise the King."

George's mouth fell agape as he pointed at me and asked, "You? An Earl? I was just growing accustomed to Don Hector, but now it's to be Lord Hector?"

I shrugged my shoulders and smiled sheepishly. "I lost my title of infante when my father relinquished his claim to the Marquis of Avila. This is probably just an honorary title, so Lady Elizabeth will not be marrying the gardener's son after all."

Elizabeth frowned and hit my shoulder, something she was bound to repeat many times in the coming years. "The Queen was actually quite impressed with Hector's ability to solve conflicts and make sound judgments. She is a very sensible woman."

Elizabeth continued to share the rest of the tale while I sat back and toasted their futures with Agnes' father.

Queen Henrietta Maria wasn't an especially loud woman, but I marveled at how well her instructions were followed when she pointed at something and said what she wanted.

As promised, Lord Chamberlain's staff was well versed in preparing a hall for a gala celebration. While Lord Leatherby's staff knew the maintenance of every corner of the grand ballroom, Chamberlain's people understood the placement of flowers and decorations. It took very little interpretation when the Queen directed them to rearrange the handful of chairs that lined the more bare walls, or the placement of tables to display the lavish and ornate delicacies that would be served at the wedding.

Some consternation followed when they were ordered to move some of Leatherby's more prized busts of past Leatherbys, but a glance from the Queen quelled those moments rather easily.

The Queen spotted me standing back and admiring her handiwork. "Don Hector, I mean Lord Hector, good morning."

I bowed, as I thought an Earl should do, I must have done it wrong as it brought a small amount of mirth to her face. "Good morning Your Majesty. You certainly have things well in hand, and so early in the morning!"

She chuckled. "No doubt you thought that royals liked to

lounge around in bed until the late hours of the morning."

"One might think that," I replied.

"And one would not be wrong, but I love a ball, and weddings in particular. I actually started quite some time ago. It is you who is the sleepyhead."

"I saw that," I said. "I've already been to the kitchens and saw Lord Chamberlain's cooks showing Lord Leatherby's staff some unfamiliar techniques; at least I gathered they were learning something new. They may have just been politely listening to appease the somewhat formidable queen."

"Formidable?" she squeaked, feigning injurious insult. "Did you just call your queen formidable?"

"When the Queen speaks, people listen and when she commands, people do."

"Well then," she said, assuming the visage and voice of a haughty royal, "show me this glass room that I have heard so much about. I command you!"

I bowed low, my smile matching hers. "Your command is my wish."

She laughed a sweet chirping laugh. I must admit that humor was another trait that I had never afforded to royals. She took my arm, and I led her out of the ballroom.

As we made our way from the ballroom to the atrium, the Queen would crook her finger to signal staff members to follow us and I began telling her of the great glass room.

"Lady Elizabeth and I have enjoyed many hours of education in the atrium, where we had learned not only about the flora grown within, but our instructors had availed themselves of the generally pleasant atmosphere to teach all sorts of sciences. We often sat in a circle in the center where the light was most excellent, due to the flowers and trees being planted along the surrounding wall. The very center of the rotunda holds a marble bird bath. In the spring and summer, windows along the dome are opened to allow small birds access to the inside where some of them have even stayed and nested. Nests can be seen in some of the trees, but also higher up in the rafters and frames that hold the glass in place.

The queen gasped as we entered the atrium. "It's quite extraordinary. I must have the King build one of these for me. So much glass! Even the cathedrals with their colored glass windows must be jealous of this place."

She motioned for the army of servants that had trailed behind us to enter. She started with the birdbath, moving it off to the side so she could line up several rows of benches facing an altar that was placed nearly up against an apple tree.

More benches were carried in and lined up. Apparently, the King's and Queen's guards pitched in, gathering benches from around the grounds and setting them on the grass outside the main doors. I stood back while she pointed and benches were brought in and arranged in rows until there were still a few benches remaining outside, but no more room to place them.

I counted the benches and mentally calculated the number of guests they could accommodate, and there weren't enough. "Your Majesty, a word?"

"Lord Hector, it has just occurred to me that it might be

bad luck for the groom to see the hall before the wedding?"

"I believe that superstition pertains to seeing the bride."

"Ah," she said, "so it is. In that case, you may stay. What do you think? There are so many flowers here already, I hardly have to bring any bouquets in at all."

"I was looking at the benches..."

"I know what you are going to say. Will the invited lords be willing to sit on such plain benches? The King is not overly fond of nobles who think themselves too good to sit a common bench."

"It's not that, Majesty. The benches are already too close together, and still there is not enough room for all the guests."

I watched the Queen count the benches then asked, "How many do you expect?"

"In addition to Your Majesties, there will be, of course, the local nobles, assorted gentry and probably most of the staff and families that live and work on both the Leatherby and Chamberlain properties."

The Queen shook her head slowly. "We can't fit that many in here."

"No," I said. "Not on these benches at least, but if we have only a few benches, family and royals could sit on the benches with the other lords and gentry standing behind them and the staff and locals standing in the back."

"I do not like separating the classes in such an obvious manner, from front to back."

"What if we sit the family on blankets in the front, then a row of benches for the royals and lords, and everyone else standing behind them?"

I watched her visualize it with her mind's eye. "Will they be able to see in the back?"

"They might, if we dare arrange them by height, instead of rank."

The Queen started to laugh. It was just a giggle at first, but slowly grew to a more boisterous laugh.

"I'm sorry," I said, "but I thought you just told me that the King would not favor such class distinctions, yet you laugh so boldly at the idea."

She laughed even harder and said, "You are quite brash to tell me so."

"My apologies."

"No! Do not apologize. You are wholly correct, except that is not why I laugh. I was imagining General Cromwell, who imagines himself quite tall, when in reality he is of average stature. I don't imagine that you actually know Oliver, but I think you will, as my husband's ambassador. To slate his vanity, I would instruct him to stand in the back with the other tall men, knowing that his pride would not allow him to argue and he would see nothing."

I barely held back a smirk.

"It is okay if you find it amusing. If you are bold enough to tell the Queen that she should not be so elitist, then you should feel free to laugh at General Oliver Cromwell, the big windbag."

The days leading up to the actual ceremony were a mixture

of good and not so good emotions. I suspect that every bride dreams of and anticipates the day of her wedding. She may even plan out who she would invite and while she was making those plans, the groom might be planning where they would live and how they would make their livelihood.

None of those would matter for this ceremony. This was the Queen's show, which in itself would be a curse and a blessing. None of the three brides, whether rich or poor, whether noble or peasant, would have dreamed any event as extravagant as what the Queen was putting together for us. And the fathers of the brides could only sit back and enjoy the generosity of the Queen and King as they accepted all costs for the extravaganza. On the other hand, the couples could not invite everyone that they would have wanted to the wedding. Couriers take time and the Monarchs had already enjoyed more than their share of our small burgh.

The grand moment had arrived, and I was ushered just inside the door to the atrium where everything was set-up as the Queen and I had discussed. My mother was on a blanket in the center, just a few paces from the altar. Lord Chamberlain was on the left, and George's father and Agnes's mother were on the right. Agnes's mother clearly showed an unprecedented level of pride that her daughter was included in such a grand wedding, but George's father looked apprehensive that he should be so close to the royals and seated in front of them.

The King and Queen sat in their most splendid regalia, in the center of the front row of benches with a few assorted noblemen to their right and left.

There was only one row of benches, behind which stood

an assortment of people, including family members and staff. Agnes's family, in particular, were generally of shorter stature, and found themselves in front of numerous lesser nobles and gentry. The crowd continued all the way to the back of the rotunda. I wondered if the Queen had really invited Sir Oliver Cromwell to the wedding. If so, I had no doubt that it was just so she could place him in the back, as she had said.

Sir Charles joined me on my right. I had never before been prone to nervousness, but at that moment, my legs did not wish to honor my commands. Sir Charles gently took my arm and led me to the altar where I stood before a bishop whom I had never met. George and Walter had already been arrayed in front of their families. At the back of the atrium, the double doors were opened and knights entered to part the sea of onlookers that stood behind the King and Queen.

Agnes was the first to enter, escorted by her father. Lady May Cranston was then escorted in by my father, wearing another very royal looking suit that I had never before seen.

All three brides wore the most dazzling dresses I could have ever imagined. Each had a different color that, as I saw them, matched the colors of the blankets upon which our families sat.

Agnes's dress was a strong green that draped from her shoulders to the ground and buttoned at the neck.

May's gown, on the other hand, was a luxurious blue with a scandalous neckline that dove from her neck and exposed the center of her bosom nearly to her belly. It was breathtaking. As they neared the altar, I saw the subtle undulations in the fabric as they walked. What a clever use of velvet and satin to create such a heavenly mirage.

When Agnes and May were settled in at the altar, Elizabeth was led in by Lord Leatherby. Her gown was the most royal red I had ever seen. Only the Queen could have arranged such a deep red. Like the others, it seemed to have a life of its own; as the folds rippled around her as she walked. Like May's gown, there was a plunging tease of a neckline, but it was paneled with a sheer red cloth. She joined me at the altar and I was unsure whether my knees would keep me upright.

I'm told that the bishop tried several times to get my attention, but my eyes were locked on Elizabeth's. Walter eventually tapped me on the shoulder, breaking me from my trance, and when I turned to see what he wanted, I saw the bishop's smiling face staring down at me.

"What a joyous occasion to have three young couples wishing to be bound in matrimony such as these."

Agnes giggled slightly, and the bishop joined her with a smile and added, "I understand that you two were already married in secret, but wish now to make your bond public."

Agnes giggled again as she rubbed her belly and said, "We three."

The bishop proved to be a most jovial man, as he did not mind being either interrupted or corrected. He simply nodded his head and said, "This is even a more momentous occasion as we publicly welcome your child into your family."

The ceremony was kept brief at my suggestion. Some weddings, especially extravagant royal weddings, can go on and on, but the majority of our guests were standing, and I thought it best if we kept the proceedings short and moved on to the ballroom.

Unlike the atrium where I had advised the Queen regarding the placement of the benches and the guests, I had not ventured into the ballroom to offer an opinion, and in fact, except for my brief visit on the first day when the Queen was making arrangements, I hadn't been there in many years, not since Elizabeth and I were young enough to play hide and seek throughout the manor.

I was utterly unprepared for the splendor exhibited across the reception area. Flowers from my father's gardens surrounded the hall in wall mounted vases that were hung between the many glass doors that opened out into the garden. Tables upon tables were laden with the most intoxicating delicacies that I had ever feasted my eyes upon.

I had been to the holiday celebrations at Chamberlain hall and recognized many of the dishes that were on display now, but others that were laid out before me now were another notch above our usual feast. Servants stood ready at every table to assist the various celebrants with their plates. Mrs. Brindle had already apprised me that the staff was given the choice to volunteer to serve the event or attend as guests. Apparently, the Queen herself shared French recipes with the staff, and even though she was not the most popular person to parliament, a surprising number of staff members availed themselves of her hospitality and were rewarded with wonderful lunches which the Queen herself attended right alongside them.

Elizabeth and I were lined up at the entrance with the other couples where guests could come in and congratulate us down the line, one by one. The out-of-town lords and gentry who were at the head of the line skipped past George and Agnes and before I was able to excuse them from this humiliation, the Queen stepped in and guided the guests to George, introducing them personally. Once started, the others fell in to the pattern and congratulated George and Agnes and wished them good fortune.

Being so near to the door, I heard the ruckus created when the Queen went out to prevent the nobles from pushing in front of the other guests. She mixed the locals in with the nobles in a way that afforded George and Agnes much more sincere wishes for their futures than the halfhearted best wishes from the unknown nobles.

After everyone had been introduced and allowed to roam the buffet tables, the Queen came to us and said, "You did splendidly." She indicated all three couples and continued, "All of you. You are released now to find something to eat, assuming, that is, that these buzzards have left any scraps behind."

"Thank God," Elizabeth said, "I'm famished."

"Me too," Walter said.

"I'll join you in a moment," George told us. "I think I need to get Agnes off her feet."

"While you do that," the Queen volunteered, "I'll fix a plate of food for her. Being with child is a wondrous and miraculous burden that I do remember well. Never let it be said that I could not feel for another woman's burden."

Elizabeth and I wandered over to the table nearest the fireplace, where Lords Leatherby and Chamberlain were having an animated conversation.

"You two aren't arguing again," Elizabeth said, "are you? If you are, I'll be forced to sick Lord Hector on you, as he has recently become one of the King's favorite ambassadors of peace."

Leatherby laughed. "We were just discussing how we would divide the holidays and festivals between our great houses."

"Really?" Elizabeth asked skeptically.

"It's true," Chamberlain said. "This event is a splendid example of how a feast should be; it only served to remind us of how wonderful this ballroom can be."

"And how fabulous it is," Leatherby added, "when our houses work together to prepare it."

"It is quite spectacular," I agreed, "but if you'll excuse us, we're rather hungry."

Elizabeth kissed her father on the cheek and daintily waved goodbye to them as we headed to the nearest table, that still appeared to hold any food.

Our first night as husband and wife was spent in Elizabeth's room within Leatherby House. I call it a room, but it was more of an apartment and rivaled my parents' cottage in size.

We were alone for the first time and it could not have been more awkward. It's not that I had never imagined what it would be like to bed Elizabeth. I had always loved her, but it was unthinkable to do so as one of the servants. I smiled awkwardly, and she returned an equally uneasy grin.

The silence between us grew chilly. "Nice weather tonight." I closed my eyes and cringed. *Nice weather tonight? Is that the best you can come up with?*

"Yes, it was," she replied. "The moon was so big and bright." She turned her back so I couldn't see her face.

"I don't believe I have ever seen your father so cheerful." Again, I grimaced at my inane words.

She turned to face me. Tears had begun to gather in her eyes. "Have we made a mistake?"

I was stunned by the question.

"I mean," she explained, "why does this feel so strange? If we were really in love, wouldn't this be much easier?"

I took her in my arms and held her to me. Even when we were just friends, I could always hold her to comfort her. "I think the fault is mine. I have always loved you, Elizabeth, but as a friend and a confidant. It was only a brief few days ago that I admitted to myself that I love you in that way. I think that even the Queen knew that I loved you before I did. You ask if this is a mistake. It is not. I have ruined our wedding night by turning back into the gardener's son that you have known all your life."

She pushed me away and said, "Pish posh. You cannot take all the blame when it is I who stands here without the feminine wiles to lure my husband into bed." As soon as the words had escaped her lips, she covered her face in her hands. "I can't believe I just said that."

I smiled broadly. "Well, you did. If it is you who are to be the aggressor tonight, then be the vixen and take me by the hand so you may lead me to a night of blissful anticipation."

She took my hand in hers and flashed a seductive visage. "Anticipation? Is that what you wish tonight? I was looking for fulfillment."

Again she tried to hide her face, but I refused to release one of her hands, forcing her to choose whether she would hide her mouth or her eyes. She hid her mouth momentarily, then pulled her hand away and lit up the room with her smile. I pushed her backwards against the bedpost and said, "I do love you. I always have and I always will."

"Always?" she asked coyly.

"Always," I reassured her, "and forever."

"Not like this," she said in a seductive voice that was not her own, or at least was not one that I had ever heard before. I had never heard her sound so randy, anyway. She continued, "We will both have duties to perform, but I think we may have all of this night to ourselves before our duty calls upon us."

This time, she did not try to hide her face and instead, pulled me close to her so our lips could meet. At first, it was she who kissed me. It was a gentle touching of the lips, allowing me to taste her rouge. A great heat rose in my face and throbbed to the beat of my heart, which now pounded in my head, but I wasn't lost in her embrace yet. I breathed deeply of her aromatic oils and returned her kiss, firmer and longer than hers.

She fell against my body as if her legs could no longer support her weight. I wrapped my left arm around the small of her back while reaching up with my other to untie the neck of her cloak. It was just a wrap and fell to the floor, exposing her shoulders, which begged for the touch of my lips.

She pushed back slightly, still held in my arms, and slid my cloak from my shoulders. She wrapped her arms around me so I could let her go enough to allow my cloak to join her wrap on the floor.

Her dress had a torturous convolution of laces over her bodice, but once I found the tie and pulled on it, they loosened some and the dress fell to her hips.

She gripped the collar of my blouse, which was held closed by three bone buttons. She pulled hard, but only the top button let loose. I reached down and ripped the remainder of the buttons free and tossed the torn garment off my shoulders so it would slide down my arms to the floor.

I wasn't the hairy bear that my father was, but she found the small patch of coils down the center of my chest all the same and explored them with her fingers. She dipped her head and found my nipples with her lips; first one and then the other. A ravenous moan escaped her lips as she looked up and gripped the hair at the back of my neck, pulling me forward for a fierce mashing of lips.

My veins were on fire and she was still armor clad in bodice and petticoat. I silently cursed whoever had invented lace ties as I struggled to find the knot that held the bodice tight. My hands shook violently and my fingers felt far too brutal for the task at hand. Elizabeth took my hands and raised them to her lips to kiss them, then lowered them to her bosom, where they rested and felt the full weight of her breasts while she undid the bodice and pushed it, with the dress, to the floor.

She lifted her feet out of the pile of clothing and stepped backwards, pulling me by the grip I had on her breasts. She fell onto the bed, with me atop her. We kissed again as she brought her foot up and pushed at the waistband of my trousers. This time it was my turn to help as I undid the tie of my belt and let her push them down.

I could go on, but I feel I have gone too far already. Suffice to say that the rest of the night was filled with multiple encounters of bliss, but not any that are fit for my memoirs.

I awoke, after far too little sleep, to the clanging of metal and the shouting of men as King Charles wasted little time the following morning by ordering his men to prepare for a return to London. I could not allow the royals to leave without seeing them off and leapt out of bed, hastening to throw on some breeches and boots, barely tucking my night shirt into the belt.

"Where are you off to so early?" Elizabeth asked. "Have you a suspicious wife at home that I don't know about?"

"They're leaving! The King and Queen are preparing to depart already!"

Elizabeth rushed out of bed and started pulling a brush through her hair.

"I shall do what I can to delay them," I said. Outside her door was one of the new maids. "Where's Isabel?"

"We know not, m'lord. Nobody has seen her this morn."

"Lady Leatherby needs some help getting ready to address the Queen. I guess it is up to you now to help her."

The maid curtsied and said, "Right away, m'lord."

I may have overreacted, for as soon as I sprinted out into the courtyard, neither the King nor the Queen appeared interested in leaving without saying goodbye.

The Queen scowled as she scrutinized my appearance, examining me from top to bottom. "Lord Castillo, or is it de la Roca? I never have understood the formalities of the Spanish names."

I didn't believe her for a second. She was born royal and raised royal. She probably knew the Spanish customs better than I did.

Her face grew stern. "Is this how you choose to ready yourself to address your queen? You look like you slept the night in the tavern. No! You look like you have not slept at all, with your tousled hair and your unshaven face!" A strange contortion overtook her face as her great anger morphed into a smile, followed by a nod of approval. "You have the look of a man who has slept hardly a wink."

"In truth, Your Majesty..."

Elizabeth burst through the doors into the courtyard. "Don't you dare say another word!"

The Queen doubled over in laughter. "Well done, Lady de la Roca."

Elizabeth skidded to a stop, not recognizing the name.

"It is important," the Queen advised, "to learn when and

how to muzzle your husband!"

The King joined us and slapped the Queen playfully on the butt, saying, "unless, of course, you are married to the King of England, anointed by God to rule over England and Scotland."

"Of course, my dear," she said with a sly wink aimed at Elizabeth. "That is what I meant to say."

King Charles came over and gripped my arm in the warrior's way. "I expect to see you at court soon." He glanced over at Elizabeth and added, "But not too soon. Even with the army of engineers I will be sending, it will still be a while before your new home is ready. We have an apartment at the palace that you can use in the meantime."

I bowed low at the waist, "That is very generous, Your Majesty, but I must confess some trepidation over being so easily spied upon by Her Majesty."

The King chuckled and said, "You will do well in court. I look forward to seeing you soon. I've already said my goodbyes to Lords Leatherby and Chamberlain, so we'll be off now." He signaled the captain of his guards and climbed into the royal carriage.

Returning to Leatherby house would have been all about getting some breakfast had it not been for Lord Leatherby displaying the same insidious grin on his face that the Queen had just shown us mere moments ago.

"Oh Daddy, wipe that ridiculous look off your face."

"I can't help it," he said. "It is not often that a father can see his daughter find so much happiness while at the same time marrying so well."

She frowned as she walked past him towards the kitchen.

"Where are you going?"

"We're hungry."

"Then have Isabel fetch you something to eat."

"I'm a married woman now, and even though we don't have a home at present, I think it's time I learn my way around a kitchen so I may take care of my husband, should the need ever arise."

"What need would you ever have to fix your own meals?"

She shrugged and said, "I wonder if Hector's mother was ever asked that same question before they came here. You know she is a very fine cook, and she keeps a very fine home."

"It was all a subterfuge to hide their true identities. You know this."

"So? If we ever must hide our noble identities, I hope that I can prove to be half the homemaker that the Marchioness De la Roca was."

Lord Leatherby looked at me for support, but as he did it, I could see the resignation in his eyes. He knew I would back Elizabeth in this debate.

"Fine," he said with a private wink to me that she couldn't see, "then go fix us some ham and soft eggs."

"Hmmmph," she said, "I think I shall start as a beginner. Your gruel will be ready when it's ready, and you shall like it no matter what it resembles."

I couldn't hold back my laughter any longer. "Actually, I thought I might go to town to see if I could find Isabel."

"Why?" Lord Leatherby asked. "Did you send her to town for something? I've been looking for her since the wedding. I wanted to give her contract to you as a wedding gift."

I grimaced. "She may not want to be in Lady Leatherbys..."

"Lady de la Roca!" Elizabeth corrected me.

I smiled and nodded my head towards her. "I stand corrected. Isabel may not wish to remain as Lady de la Roca's personal maid."

"Oh?" Leatherby asked. "Does she hold some ill will towards you?"

"Quite the opposite," I said. "She had always been quite fond of me and had pursued me somewhat aggressively."

"But she's a maid!" Leatherby exclaimed.

"And I was but a lowly gardener's son. She may be nursing some hurt feelings and I would like to smooth things over with her. I believe she was an excellent housemaid, while she was in your employ, and she may wish to have your referral."

"She shall have it!" Elizabeth shouted, "Although I shall miss her terribly."

"How was the new girl?" I asked. "The one who helped you this morning, in Isabel's stead?"

"She was adequate," Elizabeth replied. "Eager even. She is young yet, but I think she will do well with some training."

"Then you shall have her," Leatherby said.

I nodded my head to acknowledge his generosity. "We appreciate your gift, but we have little use for a housemaid when we haven't a house yet."

Leatherby's face brightened significantly. "You shall have your home soon enough. King Charles had thrown in with Lord Chamberlain and I to see it happen and the King comes with considerable resources and the best craftsmen available. I don't believe you could possibly realize the great impression you made on the King and Queen."

"Maybe," I said, "but I think much of that impression was on my father and the insight he brings to bear should conflicts arise with Spain."

"No," he replied. "Although he certainly saw significant value in your father's knowledge, you impressed the King on your own."

"I think I impressed the Queen."

"That you did, but the King sat back and quietly watched. When the Queen said that good breeding will always show, the King heard, and he is a staunch believer that the royals and nobles were put on this earth by the hand of God. Your nobility has always shown through to the world, even though you thought yourself a gardener's son. It was you, more than anything else, that impressed him."

I paused a moment and processed what he had said. I don't believe that we were placed here by God to rule above the commoners any more than I believe that it is our breeding and not our education that gives us our advantage, but who am I to disagree with the King?

"Speaking of the King," Leatherby continued, "I under-stand that he has arranged an apartment for you."

"He did," I replied, "for times when I'm in London."

"I suggest you take him up on his offer, at least until your estate is built up."

"I was hoping to stay on and work with the engineers on the design of our new home."

Leatherby squinted as he nodded his head. "I think there

is nothing that you cannot do. You have an extraordinary mind, young Hector."

Elizabeth puffed out her cheeks and put on a deep voice, sounding much like one of the more disgruntled guests at our wedding. "That's Lord Hector to you. Do not presume to be one of us, just because you stand in front of us. It is our superiority that places us behind you, after all."

We all laughed and Lord Leatherby continued, "Even should you stay to see to the estate's construction, Elizabeth could stay in London, so you could use a house maid after all."

"Father? Are you saying that I am not welcome to stay here?"

"No! That is not at all what I mean." He frowned and crossed his arms. "You are both welcome to stay here. Perhaps I am the one who should go to London and accept the King's gratitude. Perhaps then I wouldn't put my foot in my mouth so readily."

Elizabeth laughed and shook her head. "Life here shall never be boring."

I stood to leave. "And on that note, I think I shall go to town to face Isabel. I am certain that it will also be a conversation that shall not be boring."

Giovanni was checking the harness on his horse when I entered Greenshire.

"Sir Giovanni!" I shouted while still a short distance away.

He appeared uncomfortable to hear the title used out loud. It was an embarrassment that I knew well, but I was glad to use it all the same. "I hope you are not leaving so soon."

"My job here is done. In fact, I think I have done more than I had set out to accomplish."

"You are a remarkable man," I said, "and you have done a splendid service for this small burgh, but I don't think you are quite done here yet."

"How so? I've seen to it that both Lady Elizabeth and her previously intended have found their proper mates. I don't see what more I could do here."

"Life is not always about love and marriage. There are many other relationships that need to be groomed and cared for."

He looked at me quizzically, which was understandable, as my statement was more than just a bit vague.

"I'm speaking of the childhood relationship that you had with my father. Whether it was good or bad, you know each other and I think you should talk and part friends."

"But we are friends," he said. "We spoke in the tavern."

"I think you parted as acquaintances, not friends. If you were friends, you would not turn down a meal with my parents. My mother is a marvelous cook, you know."

He smiled and nodded his head. "I recall. You may not know this, but I knew your mother before your father ever did. Not romantically, of course, but I grew up with your mother and father as friends. Plus, being a matchmaker allowed me to come to know many of the unmarried women of the court. She was already a fine woman, even when she was quite young."

"Then you'll come? I'll bring Elizabeth and you can toast our success, which is really your success, one more time before you leave us."

"I was right to suspect that you were after my job," he said with a chuckle. "I can be grateful that your new title of Earl and being an ambassador for the King will leave me some work to do."

"No doubt," I said, "and when I do appear in London, there will be many unwed women who will learn of how you matched me with Lady Elizabeth."

I saw him mentally salivate over the increased business he might get. "That is all well and good, but it is their fathers that need to know of me."

"And they shall! I promise your good works will be known throughout London!"

A silence fell between us.

"You must come to dinner! Please tell me you will come."

"How can I refuse? I would not wish to risk such a great referral. I will be there."

His words said that he was aloof and only appeasing me for the promise of continued income, but something in his voice and his eyes told me that there was a part of him that would appreciate an opportunity to properly close things with my father, or perhaps he merely coveted an opportunity to sample my mother's cooking again.

"Come early," I said as we parted, "before sunset."

He nodded his assent, and I turned for my next appointment.

As I left Giovanni at the livery and continued on towards the tavern, I saw Walter leaning against the haberdashery.

"That was pretty smooth," he said, "but what's your game? Why do you care if they renew their friendship?"

"My mother and father were exiled here, hiding out from the inquisition, but now their location is known, and more than that, they have been expatriated into British society. I don't know if father can ever return to Spain, and he may want to talk to someone, now and again, who is able to travel freely between the two nations."

"What about Mateo? I thought he would be returning with news from King Philip."

"That depends on many things. If there is to be war, will Mateo be lost in it? Worse, if the inquisition chooses to challenge King Philip for control of Spain, either of them could be lost. I wish the best for Mateo, and I hope we can see him again."

Walter nodded. "Especially if he returns with some of your father's wealth, as he promised."

"I don't think it was a promise, but he did say he would try. So, how was your first morning as a married man? Did you have to endure the uncomfortable gawking of your father looking at you as if he knew what you had been doing all night?"

"You too? I'm glad to know we were not alone in that fine torture."

I laughed and said, "You don't know the half of it! I heard the sounds of the royals leaving and barely threw enough clothes on to see them off, only to have the Queen absolutely blast me for my disheveled appearance. She can be quite vicious when she wants to be, emphasis on the *wants*, because she was just teasing and burst out laughing over the whole thing."

"Wow, I guess I really dodged an arrow there."

"You did. Please allow me to invite May and you to dinner tonight."

"You mean with you and Giovanni? I've been to your house. Your table is not that big."

"Have you not heard? I'm an Earl now. I merely need to snap my fingers and tables will be brought down for the event."

"So," Walter said, "it's not just an intimate dinner for your father and Giovanni to renew their friendship?"

"Not exactly, but it will be a dinner highlighting the couples Sir Giovanni has brought together. Please tell me you will come."

Walter shrugged his shoulders and said, "How can I refuse? I am sure you are playing some game here and May and I will both want to see what it is. May I come with you when you tell your mother she will be preparing a meal for, what is it now, seven people? I'm sure she will love you for it."

I chuckled and snapped my fingers. "Again, I can easily get help for her."

"I can't wait."

"Excellent. If you could, can I ask you to stop at the manor and walk Elizabeth to the cottage? Depending on how things go, I may be too busy to get her."

"Of course, the more the merrier."

Walter wasn't wrong when he suggested it was such a huge imposition I was making upon my mother, but I'm sure she would be more than happy to have a more private celebration for our wedding. That, however, was neither my current concern nor the true purpose of the dinner. I was still intent on locating Isabel and soothing what I was sure would be some tender hurt feelings.

I didn't really want to think that she would have spent the entire night in the tavern, but she wasn't at either the wedding or the banquet yesterday, and nobody had seen her at the manor, so it was the first place I planned to look.

Nelly was sweeping the floor when I entered and said, "It's a little early for you, isn't it?"

I scanned the room, expecting to see Isabel passed out drunk on one of the tables. "I was looking for Isabel. I thought maybe I should have a talk with her."

"Ahhh, yeah, that's something that would bring you here so early. She's upstairs in my room. She was hitting it pretty hard yesterday. I had to cut her off and take her to my room to sleep it off and that wasn't even sunset yet."

I clasped her on the shoulder and said, "You are truly a

good person, Nelly. One of the best. Can I see her?"

Nelly shrugged. "I don't know if she will want to see you, being that you're the reason she's in such a state, but knowing how you could sweet talk a charging Pict into having a pint with you, I see no reason you shouldn't try. Be gentle, or maybe be careful, or at least don't let her break nothin' in my room."

"Thanks Nelly."

She pointed to the back stairs and said, "Top of the stairs at the end of the corridor. The first two doors are just storage."

I had never taken the stairs to Nelly's room before and found their narrowness a bit offputting. They squeaked as I climbed them and I found myself admiring Nelly's bravery for using them day in and day out. Or maybe it was I that was scared to confront Isabel that made the stairs feel more daunting than they truly were.

Three knocks on the door brought a response from Isabel. "Come on in. I'm decent."

I opened the door and went in. She was sitting on the bed with her head in her hands, never even looking up to see who had come to see her. "Are you okay?"

Her head snapped up, and she nearly shrieked, "What are you doing here?"

"I came to see if you were alright and I wanted to do something to make amends."

"You want to make amends? So you know what you did to me was wrong, then?"

"No, Isabel, I did nothing wrong. As much as you had always wanted something between us, there never was."

Her voice dropped low. "Then why have you come to see

me if you don't care for me? Please tell me it's not to gloat."

"I care about you. I always have, but it was never that way between us."

"It was for me."

"Would you really want a one-way relationship? Can you imagine what your life would be like if you were married to someone who didn't love you like that? Your life would be filled with endless infidelity. Is that really what you want?"

She hung her head and shook it. "No, but I always thought we were going to see the world. You were never destined to stay in this place. Everybody could see that. You were always too smart or too good. We should have known you were noble born from how you talked."

"I'm who I am because of how I was raised, not because I'm noble born."

"Well, your mother and father are both nobles, so if it's not because you are noble born, and it's because you were noble raised, then it works out to be the same."

"So you see that anybody can be noble in their hearts regardless of how they were born?"

"You mean like you used to say that nobles weren't really any better than the rest of us, except that some of us get a bit resentful, so we acts less noble?"

"Exactly," I said.

"Well, you're noble now. The shoe is on the other foot, ain't it? I'll bet that's all changed for you now."

I sighed. "You know better than that. I'm still the same person that I always was."

"Because you was always noble like."

"Isabel, I want to make it up to you. I want to give you that chance to see the world. I'm having a small private dinner tonight at the cottage. I would like you to come. My mother will be preparing something very special."

"Dinner? You think a dinner can make up for what you've done to me?"

"What have I done to you? I found happiness for me. Now I want to find happiness for you."

"I love your mother's cooking, but I don't think that is going to make my life so happy."

"I've also invited the matchmaker. We are going to find you a proper match."

She looked up with doe eyes, still not believing what I was saying.

"Isabel, I know you saw me as a means to see the world, but did you really truly love me, or did you just want to feel that way so I would take you with me? Are you sad now because you have lost me or because you have lost the future that you had always dreamed of?"

She shrugged, but I could see that she understood what I had just said, even if she wasn't quite ready to believe it.

"Let me help you see the world. Come to dinner tonight and I will work with the matchmaker to find you your great love."

In truth, I wasn't sure which would have been the hardest part; facing Isabel, or informing my mother that I required her to prepare a meal for several guests. The revelations of the last few days had restored her noble status and here I was, asking her to slave in the kitchen to feed my friends.

I knocked on the cottage door, but it felt awkward since I had lived there just yesterday. My mother opened the door, which was an unexpected relief to me. I had not prepared a speech for the chance that my father had answered the door.

She smiled broadly and hugged me, but her head bobbed around left and right. "Where's your bride? Is she not with you?"

"No, it is just me. I wanted to ask a favor of you."

"Of course, son. Anything."

"It's kind of a big favor," I said. "I wish to invite a few friends here for dinner."

"Here?" she asked. "Not at the manor?"

"I wanted us to have a more private celebration. I've already invited Walter and Lady May."

"Already? Before I agreed?"

"I was sure that you would help me once I told you who else I invited. I've invited the matchmaker Giovanni. I feel like he and father still have some things to say so they may part as friends. I think it would be good for father to have a friend from Spain."

She smiled and nodded her head. "I think the Queen was right about you, but I also wonder if you have another scheme hidden within this event."

"Who? Me?"

She laughed and asked, "Is that all? You haven't invited Lord Leatherby or Lord Chamberlain?"

"No. I feel like they would insist on hosting such a meal and I wanted father and Sir Giovanni to have a less formal opportunity to talk."

"A wise decision," she said.

"I've also invited Isabel."

"Is that wise? Didn't she..."

"Yes mother. She had always dreamt of me taking her away from here to see the world. I never encouraged her and tried numerous times to have her let go of such a fantasy, but still, I feel as though I have let her down. With Giovanni's help, I believe we can find her the right man to take her away from here."

"I will do this for you, son. It sounds like a noble cause, but our cottage is so small."

"The cottage is large enough, but the table won't support so many people. I will have additional tables brought down. I will also have one of the cook's assistants sent down to help you."

"It seems you have thought of everything."

I hugged her. "Thank you. With your help, it will be a very successful evening."

"You mean your true scheme will succeed?"

I smiled and shrugged.

My mother took the initiative of going to Lord Leatherby's kitchen and choosing her own assistant for the meal. She also raided the larder for those spices that she didn't have in her garden and some special cuts of meat. Nobody questioned whether Lord Leatherby would object, but everybody agreed that he didn't need to know, lest his feelings be hurt for not having an invitation. I planned to tell him later, once I knew the success of my plan.

Arranging the additional tables was pretty much the extent of my help in the preparations for the meal. I tried seeing how mother was doing; the aroma was intoxicating, but every time I entered the kitchen, she shushed me away.

As the hour approached, I became increasingly concerned that my father wasn't going to show. I hadn't bothered to invite him; it was his home after all; I just assumed he would be there. I couldn't imagine where he was or what he was doing. I just hoped he hadn't fallen into his old habit of tending the grounds. His arriving for dinner covered in dirt might dampen my plans.

Instead, however, he arrived with Sir Giovanni. They were laughing and talking. My plans were already out of my control, but that's just the way it is when dealing with other people. I would simply have to improvise.

"Well, if it isn't Lord Hector de la Roca," my father said when they were near enough. "Imagine my surprise when I learned that my old childhood friend here, Sir Giovanni, was invited to dinner at my own table and I wasn't invited?"

"You weren't here," I said. "I've been fretting all afternoon over where you were so I could invite you."

"Have you? Well, I'm here now, so invite me."

"It would seem that you have already learned of my plans from Sir Giovanni, but I invite you all the same. I felt like there may have been some unfinished things between you and I hoped you could settle them before he left."

"Well, as you can see," my father said, "we have already

settled what was between us, so there should be no further need of this celebratory meal you have planned."

"Oh, but there is," I said. "Mother has been preparing a very fine feast for us, and I would not want to be the one who tells her that her efforts were for nothing now, if I were you."

I thought myself rather clever to place the risk on him rather than myself, but I think he had already figured out my ploy.

Walter arrived on time with both May and Elizabeth, leaving only Isabel. I couldn't be completely sure that she would actually show. She's had all day to change her mind and choose not to face me again.

"What's wrong?" Elizabeth asked when she saw me peering out the door. "Are you expecting more guests?"

"Just one. I invited Isabel."

"Isabel? Do you really think that's such a good idea?"

"Yes. She's still my friend and I don't like seeing her hurt this way."

Elizabeth wrapped her hands around my neck and whispered, "You have a tremendously kind heart, but I have no intention of sharing you with her."

"She's not coming for me."

"Well, May is not sharing Walter, so that only leaves Giovanni."

"Who better," I said, "to find her a perfect match than

Giovanni?"

"Don't look now," Elizabeth said, "but here she comes."

I did look, of course. My plan was taking shape. I left the cottage, but remained in the yard and said, "Isabel! I was afraid you wouldn't show."

"I almost didn't." She turned to Elizabeth and curtsied. "Lady Elizabeth. Are you okay with my being here?"

Elizabeth hugged her and said, "Of course it's okay for you to be here! How long have we known each other?"

"But under the circumstances..."

"Nonsense," Elizabeth said. "Hector has already told me his plans. You are most welcome."

Walter and May had already found their seats at the enlarged table. My father was directing Giovanni to a seat next to him, but I interrupted him and said, "Sir Giovanni, would you sit here, please? Isabel, you can sit here next to Sir Giovanni. Do you two know each other? This is Isabel. She's a world traveler like yourself."

"What?" Isabel asked. "I haven't been anywhere yet."

"Then," I said, "You're a world traveler who hasn't been anywhere yet, but Sir Giovanni here has been many places and I'm sure he must have many fascinating stories that he can share."

"Indeed," Giovanni said, "have you ever been to Portugal?"

"I've never been anywhere."

"Portugal has some of the most beautiful sunsets I have ever seen."

"I would love to see that one day."

"And the people," Giovanni continued, "they tend to be

some of the friendliest and most trusting that I have ever known, especially in the smaller villages."

"Isabel is quite a people person," I said. "She has a way to meet new people and just learn everything about them. People just tend to trust her. Isn't that right, Elizabeth?"

"Oh, yes." Elizabeth looked at me curiously, unsure why I was leading the conversation like this.

"Some people," I continued, "think that Nelly at the tavern knows all the secrets of the people of Greenshire, but she only knows about the tavern patrons. Isabel here knows ALL the details of everyone. She has a knack for getting people to open up to her. That is something that you two must have in common."

"It is true," Giovanni said, "that I must get the people's confidence when I enter a new territory. It's a rather large part of my business."

"I have seen that about you," I said. "You managed to learn quite a bit about Walter and myself in a very short amount of time. The Queen was quite impressed."

"Not just the Queen," Elizabeth added, "but the King too. Enough so to honor him with knighthood."

"That's right," I said while thumping the table, "yet I wonder if Isabel here could give you a run for your money. I bet she would make a fine matchmaker. What do you think, Elizabeth?"

Walter and May had been watching the conversation curiously up to this point, but May chose to join in with a robust endorsement. "Absolutely! With her skills, she could certainly do well in your line of business."

"What is this?" Giovanni asked. "Did you invite me to

dinner to patch up my relationship with your father, or am I really her for you to warn me that someone new will be stealing business from me?"

"What?" Isabel asked. "I did not come here to steal business from you! I thought we were going to retain your services."

"That is good," Giovanni said. "You probably don't have the constitution required to do what I do."

"Oh no? You think I cannot bring people together? Who do you think introduced Agnes and George? Look how well they are doing! And they have a baby coming too!"

Giovanni tssked. "One match does not mean you have the skills. Besides, I was referring to the business of studying people's tendencies to know just what kind of mate would be their perfect match, not to mention negotiating proper compensation for your work. I bet you didn't collect a penny for George and Agnes."

"They are my friends. I didn't need money from them."

Giovanni chuckled. "It's easy to arrange friends together. You already know them."

"Nonsense," Isabel said. "Being close to them makes it even more imperative to make the right match, or you risk losing their friendship."

I could see that Giovanni wanted to argue, but he surprised me and conceded, "You're right. The risk is high."

"Sir Giovanni," I said, "have you ever found a town that wouldn't open up to you? Does your charm always win over everybody?"

Giovanni frowned. "I must confess that I have found some towns that were more close lipped and difficult to crack."

"Have you ever considered having help? A protégé, perhaps?"

"Who? Her?"

I put on my most confident looking smile and asked, "Why not?"

"What makes you think she could do well where I couldn't?"

"She's much prettier than you are, for one thing. Some people would certainly respond to that."

I knew little of the politics that surrounded King Charles and Queen Maria at the time of my wedding, but in later years I had come to learn that the Queen's choice to treat commoners fairly may have been a carefully crafted political ploy to distance her from her husband's belief that a King was anointed by God to rule over his people. Even in the days when they had come to Greenshire, the writing was on the wall. I grew to know both monarchs and believed that her heart was torn between the two. She felt deeply entitled to her royal lifestyle, but I also believed that on those occasions when she allowed herself the opportunity to free herself from the strictest of the royal behaviors, she truly enjoyed her time spent with the commoners.

For myself, the transition to nobility was made easier by my parents' upbringing, but I also held a deeply rooted belief that all people were worthy. It was something that made me popular with parliament and even though King Charles did not share my ideals, he still liked me and appreciated that I could converse with both the House of Lords and the House of Commons, and even settle differences between them.

My title of Earl was initially received with a great deal of suspect. It wasn't until I had actually begun advising the King and later when I had advised some of the lords that I was finally accepted as one of them, but there were still those who saw me as someone who might rock the boat and destroy their way of life. My friendship with King Charles kept them at bay for the most part, as he also valued maintaining the royal lifestyle, but my acceptance from the House of Commons protected me when King Charles met his untimely end at the conclusion of the civil war.

Elizabeth was immediately accepted into the ranks of the nobility, which was mostly a life of endless balls and receptions, to which I gladly accompanied her. She became a favorite confidant of Queen Henrietta, who walked the tight line between the royal life and the more modern view of the power of the people.

Life hadn't really changed that much, but it was clear that it had evolved and would continue to evolve.

To my great regret, we never did see Mateo again, or the wealth that had been my father's, but we had already established a good life in England and weren't wanting for funds. My father continued to maintain his own gardens; a hobby which remained one of his great pleasures.

Elizabeth and I have made a habit of having meals with my parents and Lord Leatherby at least once a month, where I am able to share with them the latest schemes I have hatched to shape the future of our world, and of course, their grand babies.

Jonni Jordyn was born in Oakland, California in 1957. She started writing at an early age, writing music, poetry, short stories, radio, film, and stage scripts. She didn't start writing novels until later in life, after she retired from playing music, and found herself travelling away from home for extended periods.

She currently lives in Denver, Colorado.

www.ingramcontent.com/pod-product-compliance
Lightning Source LLC
Chambersburg PA
CBHW031203310726
48969CB00001B/202